The Pretend Daughters

Mary Clancy

POOLBEG

Published 2023 by Poolbeg Press Ltd.
123 Grange Hill, Baldoyle,
Dublin 13, Ireland
Email: poolbeg@poolbeg.com

The moral right of the author has been asserted.
A catalogue record for this book is available from the British Library.

ISBN 978-1-78199 -502-0

www.poolbeg.com

About the Author

Mary Clancy was born and raised in Tipperary town. She lived for many good years in Cahir before moving to Kill in County Kildare where she currently lives with her husband Michael, her sons Michael and Fionn, and their beloved canine pal Lady Coco.

After graduating from Trinity College, Dublin, Mary worked for many years as a social worker, taking up writing in her spare time. This is her third novel (published by Poolbeg Press).

Acknowledgements

Thank you so much, Paula Campbell and the team at Poolbeg Press, for helping me get to this point. Paula, you have set me on the path and I will be forever grateful.

Thank you, Gaye Shortland, my editor from whom I have learned so much. Gaye, thank you for your keen eye, your patience and professionalism. Your encouragement has spurred me on.

To my loyal women friends who have read the completed manuscript in its rawness. And I mean raw. Rosemary Cooke, Marcella Cotter, Mel O'Donovan and Dearbhaile Shine – thank you all so much.

To my husband Michael Dargan for being there by my side on life's journey. X

To my wonderful sons, Michael and Fionn, for their continued encouragement and support. For putting up with my constant pestering, pressing them to listen to another page as they pass my desk. "Just a page."

To my dear consistent friends who have had to listen to my ramblings. I am without doubt my own harshest critic.

Thank you, readers, for taking the time out to read my books. I am truly grateful.

For Michael and Fionn

"All we have is who we are."

Chapter 1

EUNICE CLARKE

The Phone Call

1960

The phone rang just as Eunice Clarke was passing the hall table. She was going to let it ring out then changed her mind. It might be her husband Malcolm calling from Dublin. She picked up the receiver, clearing her throat.

"Yes? This is Eunice speaking."

Silence.

"Malcolm?"

Silence.

"Hello? Hello?"

She was just about to hang up when she heard a voice – raspy and difficult to make out.

"Eunice Clarke. That baby you brought home from St. Mary's Hospital, that youngest one, she's not yours at all, you know. And you've no-one to blame but yourself."

Click. The line went dead.

Eunice dropped heavily onto the chair beside her and let the handset fall to the floor.

Who in God's name had decided to call the house after all these years to say that Ramona was not hers? Why now?

Her heart was pounding in her chest, she couldn't think straight.

When she tried to stand up she felt dizzy and flopped back down on the chair. She sat where she was, unable to move. Nauseous. A slow mournful wail rose from her throat.

Malcolm had taken a few days off from the boot factory across the yard. At seventy-two, retirement was not yet an option he was willing to consider. He insisted that he would remain at the helm until his health dictated otherwise.

He had left earlier that morning to visit the tannery in Wicklow, before continuing on to Dublin to meet with the leather suppliers. He would be having dinner at the Shelbourne Hotel on St. Stephen's Green.

"One of the perks of being a factory owner," he told her. "I might give Arthur a call to join me, if he can see fit to take time out to catch up with his old man."

The sarcasm in Malcolm's voice had not gone over her head. He would be staying with his sister out in Howth. Or so he said. It wasn't like the old days when his absence used to cause her great distress, causing her imagination to go into overdrive.

Eunice wasn't at ease being on her own in the big old house but, after the shock of the phone call, she felt relieved to be alone.

Alone, on any given night, she flicked the light switch off in the hall on her way up to bed, looking to the right, looking to the left, then up the stairs in front of her. No sound or movement, just a creepy feeling around her, causing her to sharpen her pace –

knowing that once she got to the landing she would be fine.

She had suggested they get an outdoor dog, but Malcolm said best not. She would be twice as frightened if she heard a dog barking in the yard at three or four in the morning.

The two boys had long since left home. The younger one, Dermot, had chosen the academic route – Regius Professor of History in a London university – and he seldom came home anymore. It bothered Eunice at times, but not so much that she let it get in on her, or let it fester.

Arthur, their eldest boy, was married to Lucy from England. They lived in Dublin, out in Skerries. At least Lucy made some concerted effort to stay in touch. Malcolm said if Lucy were a bird she would most likely be a vulture – hovering over the factory – biding her time. Eunice took no notice. She liked Lucy.

Ramona, their youngest child, was in boarding school up the country.

Ramona. The source of her torment. The child about whom her husband wouldn't hear a cross word spoken, constantly rebuking her for scolding her.

"Leave her alone, can't you?" or "Why are you always at her?"

The child that Eunice had distanced herself from.

She had sensed from the early days that Ramona had the measure of her father – setting her and Malcolm up against each other to get her own way. The daughter who had been given everything she had asked for since the day she had uttered her first word: *Dada.*

Dada – who had insisted on driving his only daughter to school regardless of what he had on at the factory. "They can surely wait for ten minutes, can't they?"

Malcolm would collect Ramona of an afternoon, with her propped up like a porcelain doll in the front seat, raised up on a deep leather cushion that Will Murphy had made for her at the factory. Until the day came when she defied her father by refusing to sit on it anymore. She threw it out the car window in a tantrum.

They removed her from the local primary school and sent her to boarding school before she turned eleven – as was the Clarke tradition. Malcolm had been reluctant to let her go, but it was nudged along by Eunice once she acknowledged to herself that she was losing control. Taking it out on the child. One too many times she had aimed the wooden spoon at Ramona's bare legs. *Slap!* And again – *slap!*

It was the force of her own anger that bothered her most.

Ramona would run away from her, red-faced and hurt, finding her voice only when she was far enough away to avoid another belt. Humiliated. Shouting back through the tears that she hated her mother. Crying, calling out for Gretta the housekeeper at the top of her voice – lifting her dress – searching. Eager to point out the vivid red marks on the backs of her legs – availing of Gretta's comforting embrace. That which her mother knew she was lacking in offering.

The mother who was there – but not there.

The mother who doubted the child's right to a place in the Clarke household.

And afterwards there would be guilt, until the next time when Malcolm was out of sight and Eunice's frustration caused her to lash out again.

Gretta hummed her way around the house unobtrusively. Aware. It was she who snatched the wooden spoon from Eunice's hand that last time, causing Eunice to retreat. Gretta had lunged forward, pulling the child out of the way, guiding her to stand behind her, before grabbing Eunice by the wrist, shaking the spoon out of her hand, disabling her. Boldly giving her boss's wife a warning glance from behind her winged-top glasses, her head turned ever so slightly. Daring.

Never in a million years would Eunice have thought it possible that Gretta had it in her to challenge her. Yet she had, and in that moment Eunice recoiled and learned her lesson.

She had fully expected to get a lash from Gretta when she retrieved the wooden spoon from the floor. The housekeeper held it firmly against her left shoulder, her fist tightened around the handle, her knuckles white, ready to strike with a backhanded slap. The steely look in her eyes frightened Eunice, causing her to gasp and step back further, triggering a snapshot from her childhood, a memory of her father coming towards her, snapping his folded belt.

But it never came. Gretta threw the spoon across the room with such force it cracked in two on impact with the stone sink. Defiantly, the housekeeper stood her ground, Ramona cowering behind her.

Eunice was shaken, but she could not let the likes of Gretta Stokes dictate to her in her own home. It would be enough to have to listen to Malcolm later.

Regaining control, she inhaled deeply through her nose before stepping forward, thrusting her face inches from Gretta's.

"I am the mother here and you are the housemaid, Gretta. And don't you ever forget it. *Bed, Ramona. Now.*"

Unfazed, Gretta didn't move – she placed her right arm back across Ramona to secure her. She eyed Eunice who looked away. Weakened. Dreading the crippling tension to come once Ramona complained to Malcolm later in the day. The time had come for Ramona to be sent away.

Chapter 2

EUNICE

Family Life

Taking a few moments to compose herself, Eunice raised herself slowly off the seat, leaving the handset where it lay on the floor. She headed straight for the hot press in the kitchen, knowing instinctively where to put her hand to find the bottle of vodka, tucked in between the towels on the left-hand side, near the wall. Tepid, just the way she liked it. It would take more than one drink to settle her nerves after the shock of the phone call. She had tried to curtail herself of late. Today was no such day.

There was no fear anyone would be calling over from the factory to catch the boss's wife having a daytime drink at the kitchen table. As long as Malcolm's car was gone from the yard, Eunice was safe. She had nothing to do with the running of the factory, apart from her name being added to the company directorship a number of years before. On paper.

Ramona had returned to school after the Christmas break. So

the only person coming and going to the house would be Gretta, who knew enough not to pass comment on Eunice's drinking.

Eunice trusted few. She didn't know how to trust herself and she certainly hadn't trusted Malcolm over the years. The one person she felt she could half-trust was Gretta, who had witnessed enough drama in the Clarke household to give her plenty to gossip about – if she were that way inclined. Golden Gretta, who apart from her attempts to protect Ramona from being clattered by her mother, didn't involve herself in the more delicate situations in the household.

Ever loyal to the family, Gretta offered more than was expected of her. It had been Malcolm's idea to relieve her of her cleaning duties at the factory to help in the house after Arthur was born. The time had never been right for her to return.

Low-sized Gretta, whose thin red hair was pinned so close to her head there was little chance of an unruly rib of hair landing in the pot. She wore a plain blue housecoat these days, thick skin-coloured stockings and brown laced shoes. Her wing-top glasses were at odds with the rest of her, the rim-colour changing with each new pair. Malcolm said the glasses were her one redeeming feature.

It had never been a consideration for Eunice to regard Gretta as a friend. They came from different stations in life and as such friendship was not on the cards.

There were times when she felt irritated by the housekeeper's constant humming, but she wouldn't dare open her mouth about it. Not now. No matter how annoying the humming became, she had learned to put up with it. Leaving Gretta to get on with her work – and up on her bike to cycle the four miles home to her mother at six o'clock sharp.

Gretta was now a constant in the Clarke household. Mothering had not come easy to Eunice. She had never considered herself to be maternal, but she had given the best of what she had to offer to her boys. At thirty-seven, she had considered her childbearing days to be over but Malcolm had been beyond excited when she announced that she was expecting again. He hugged her and said it was a bonus to know that at fifty-seven he wasn't firing blanks. Malcolm could be crude.

Having been there for the boys in their early years, the housekeeper doted on Ramona, who responded with her wide smiles, raising her arms to be lifted out of her wooden playpen. Gretta more often than not obliged, while Eunice busied herself or looked away. Lacking.

Ramona's bond with Gretta unsettled Eunice more than she liked to consider. Hearing their laughter as Gretta chased the child about the house had its impact on her. It felt outside of her. There were times when she wanted no more than to drop her guard and join in the fun. Without consequence. To run recklessly around the house. To lose herself. Then she would feel stupid.

Eunice had become more keenly aware of Gretta's attachment to Ramona since the wooden-spoon incident. Although it had never been mentioned again, there was an unspoken understanding between the women.

Eunice felt that she had given everything to her marriage over the years. Arthur had been a smiling contented child. Dermot when he arrived had been quite the opposite, sickly for the first year, keeping nothing down. Screaming all day, demanding attention at all hours. Deprived of sleep, she knew then it was too much for her. She was anxious. Jumpy. The burden of motherhood overwhelmed her.

Her mother in Sligo said she had enough to be doing caring for her father – that she was available by phone as she had been for Arthur. Or had Eunice forgotten that? It was Gretta who had calmly reassured her. Who cajoled her gently without being intrusive. It would all work out, she said. And it did.

Malcolm had taken to spending his evenings at the golf club. It was around that time she first realised that he was no longer as attentive towards her as he had been.

She accused him of being unfaithful on occasion. He laughed in her face, telling her that she was beginning to sound more like her old man with each passing day. Paranoid and unstable. Suggesting that she could do a lot worse than have a drink to calm her nerves. Eunice refrained from then on in engaging in any meaningful conversation about her father. Careful not to provide Malcolm with enough ammunition to fire at her, often weeks after an event.

When she asked her mother in Sligo for advice regarding her suspicions, she was told to rise above it – affairs were commonplace in France and elsewhere, she said.

"Hold your head up and get on with it, dear – don't make it about yourself," she said. "Because it's not about you. Men all over the world have affairs and it doesn't affect their home lives. Nor should it."

Malcolm liked a chase. Hadn't he chased her? Men like Malcolm needn't take no for an answer as long as there were women waiting around in the wings. Women who would be charmed that the likes of Malcolm Clarke fancied them. The big shot Clarke. The handsome owner of the boot factory, with the slicked-back hair and the expensive tailor-made suits. The man who would make them feel special for five minutes, once he got what he was after and they didn't go blabbing all over the town.

Eunice had the measure of her husband because he lived in his head and in his pants. She smelt women on his clothes. Searched his pockets. He denied it, of course, making out yet again that she was paranoid.

She had threatened to leave him more than once – she changed her mind when she thought about it. Where would she go? Women of her standing didn't leave their husbands without good reason. And who would welcome her into their home without a penny to her name, dragging young children behind her? Going home to Sligo was out of the question.

She had wanted no more in the beginning than to make friends in Ballygore, to get to know people. The town was much smaller than where she had come from, but big enough to have a picture house and a dancehall. Malcolm said there were five thousand people living in Ballygore. Eunice would have liked to have gone to see a film with a pal. Have a laugh even. Until she realised she didn't have the way about her to spontaneously engage with people. She couldn't see the humour. She felt flat.

She had been over-eager in her efforts to socialise. She didn't feel comfortable stopping in the street to have a few words, so she held her head up in the air and walked on. She had nothing in common with them and nothing changed.

She found the men whose company Malcolm favoured in the golf club to be full of their own importance. The way they eyed her up and down. Loud aggressive types. Their wives all smiles. Smiles without substance. Tinny laughter. The ones she did like, those who seemed to enjoy her company, Malcolm dismissed as being too cute for their own good.

She loved and hated her husband all at the same time. The way he had courted her, proclaimed his love for her. She had been convinced that her life would change. That she would change. All she ever wanted from life was to be loved. To be wanted. But she was still Eunice.

Malcolm seemed to be having second thoughts the year before Ramona was due to leave for boarding school. Dismayed that he was actually considering sending her to the local secondary school, Eunice refused to indulge him. Surely he wasn't about to break tradition and renege on the very plan that he himself had been insistent on. Was he? Where would Ramona end up then? In the finishing room at the factory getting the boots ready for retail? Or sitting back to back with Alice Coyne over in the office? Is that what he had in mind for his daughter?

Once Ramona settled in at boarding school, which no doubt she would, Eunice assured Malcolm that she'd be fine. Hadn't they been through it ten years before with the boys? And look how well they had turned out – both independent, in great jobs. Why should Ramona be treated any differently to her brothers before her? It had been easier than Eunice had imagined when the time came.

Clarke children boarded and that was the way it always was, and the way it would always be. Boys educated by the Jesuits in County Kildare. girls educated by the nuns in County Louth. They would be home at the end of each term break, Easter, summer, and end of year. And any hangers-on in Ballygore would be weeded out in the meantime – having drifted back to their own sort. They wouldn't be hanging around for months on end, waiting for the young Clarkes to appear back in town.

Both boys had cried unashamedly when their time came to leave

11

home for boarding school. Malcolm had tut-tutted. He said they were soft. The Jesuits would toughen them, make men out of them. No harm to be sending them away from the two women who were making fools out of them.

Eunice had cried once she was sure the car bearing Dermot away with his brother for the first time had left the yard – mustn't let them see her upset. She had returned to the kitchen where she poured herself a Baby Power of whiskey into a mug – while Gretta hummed away and got on with her jobs, doting on eight-month-old Ramona.

Everything had changed after that. Each time the boys landed home Eunice could see that they had become more independent. They offered their hand tentatively to their father. No spontaneous hug for her at the door. Measured. Character-building, Malcolm had called it. Careful not to overdo the drink when the boys were home, Eunice got on with her life.

When the time came for Ramona to leave, the child kissed them all goodbye at the door and off she went in the car with Malcolm. Smiling.

Gretta removed her glasses, sniffling loudly into her hanky. Eunice felt an odd sense of relief.

Chapter 3

FRAN GAFFNEY

1965

Fran Gaffney lived with her parents in a small terraced house off the main street in Ballygore – a five-minute walk from Malcolm Clarke's boot factory. Most houses in the street had a family member working at the factory and, if not, they knew someone who did. In Fran's case, it was her uncle, Will Murphy.

Every morning at ten to eight, men from the road walked or pushed their bikes down the street towards the factory – and back in the evening just after half past five. Fran's mother Brigid said she could set her clock by the factory men, apart from payday when it wasn't out of the ordinary for some of the bikes to wobble their way up the road, steered by owners who had stepped off the trail to sup a few mediums of stout in one of the local public houses. And a chaser. Their women waiting for their wages, standing at their own front doors, chatting, craning their necks, waiting on those who might have forgotten that they had homes to go to.

An only child, Fran started school open-eyed and eager. From her very first day she did her best to join in. She wasn't bothered that she walked with a slight limp. She raised her left heel and got on with it. And when she was taunted and called Tippy-Toes Gaffney by an older girl in the school yard and the name stuck, she pretended it didn't matter. But it did matter. She felt hurt. Unwanted. She wanted more than anything to be one of the girls who gathered in a circle together to grin and laugh and have fun. To be included. But they shunned her, turned their backs and whispered. Girls as sweet as pie with ringlets in their hair. Girls who chose to isolate those unwanted at random.

So she became a follower, running around after them, doing her best to keep up, listening in on conversations, much to the annoyance of those who huddled together in the yard. Pest. Anywhere girls grouped together, Fran butted in.

She had no great interest in hanging around with the decent girls. Or the quiet girls. Or any other girls. She wanted to be part of the in-crowd and the more they shunned and ignored her and rolled their eyes to heaven, the more she wanted to belong. Snooty Ramona Clarke from the boot factory punched her in the stomach and told her to get lost.

And the worse Fran was treated, the more eager she was to impress.

Until Delia Blake, who came from the same road as herself, called her aside when they were in second class and told her to cop the feck on. That she was sick and tired of watching her going around with her head bent, feeling sorry for herself, because she would never be one of the in-crowd. She told Fran that she was far too good for the likes of that shower.

Fran was shocked. She couldn't believe that Delia Blake was

having a go at her. But, when she thought about it, she realised that there was some truth in what Delia was saying. She had been blind and stupid.

She had never taken any notice of Delia Blake before then, only to pass her out on the way home from school and she dragging her schoolbag along the ground with a big sour puss on her, her long straggly hair tied in a crooked plait, with a frayed ribbon hanging loose at the end. Always on her own and now Fran knew why. Because Delia didn't fit in either. One sock up and one sock down. Defiant. She wasn't one of the popular girls, but she didn't feel the need to run after the crowd, like she accused Fran of doing.

Delia said curses like *flying fuck* and *stupid bitch* and the like. She said whatever came into her head most times. She used the word *stupid* quite a lot. She said a lot worse when the mood took her, but Fran took no notice, because it wasn't as if Delia was cursing at people – she was just expressing herself. And Fran would burst out laughing when she started because she herself wasn't allowed to use bad language.

Delia and Fran would wait for each other after school. Delia said she had witnessed Fran being treated like shite on their shoes. That she was chasing around the school after young ones who didn't want anything to do with her. "Populars", Delia had called them, saying she didn't know if it was a proper word or not, but it sounded about right. She said the bitches didn't deserve a proper name so that's all they were getting. A made-up one. And if it wasn't a made-up name, they were getting it anyway. She said it was time for Fran to call a halt to all the bullshit before they started secondary school. Unless, of course, Fran was in the business of saving souls for Our Saviour on the cross. If that was her intention she could continue what she was at and she would deserve every damn thing they put her through. "Bleeding martyr!"

Delia stood up for Fran. She told the bullies to fuck off for themselves and leave Fran alone, or she'd bate the living shite out of them. And they did leave her alone. Because they knew what would happen if they didn't. Delia said that Ramona Clarke would never know how lucky she was that she'd be fecked off to boarding school after primary, because she was heading for an awful bating if she stayed.

When Fran asked Delia to be her best friend, her mother did all in her power to dissuade her from calling to the door. She said Delia looked like a hooded monk with the too-big duffle coat on her in the middle of summer, and not a sign of a coat on her in the winter.

Fran didn't need to be told that Delia and herself were firm friends. She felt it. They saw each other every day. They talked about being there for each other in secondary school.

Delia was the kind of girl Fran's mother classed as 'undesirable'. Her mother said that Delia must have some kind of a want in her. That she couldn't be right in the head. Fran's mother would stick her chest out and fold her arms across her chest when she opened the door to Delia. To block her. And when Delia copped on and refused to call to the house ever again, Fran was cross with her mother. Delia said that she couldn't give a flying fuck, that she only went places where she felt wanted. And Fran's mother didn't make her feel wanted.

Fran invited Delia down to her house for a slice of cake on her birthday, four days before Saint Patrick's Day, when they were twelve, and she said she'd come. Just the once.

She ate the cake and turned her nose up at the butter cream inside.

"I wouldn't be too gone on that filling now. 'Tis a bit thick. Are you sure 'tis alright to eat, Mrs. Gaffney?"

"Of course it's alright! You cheeky ungrateful . . ."

"Ungrateful what, Mrs. Gaffney? *Bitch*, is it? Is that what you're trying to say?"

Fran giggled.

"Frances Gaffney!" Her mother was fuming but Delia was only getting started.

Fran did her best to compose herself as Delia carried on goading her mother.

"And, yeah, her name? Isn't that a fella's name? Would you not have called her Patricia, seeing as she was born so close to Paddy's day and all. I've a cousin in Wicklow called Francis and he was called Fran too. And he's a lad. What's all that about then?"

And her mother couldn't handle the cheek. She wagged her finger and pointed to the door. "Get out!"

Delia was holding on to the back of the chair. Laughing.

"*Get out!*" her mother shouted.

After that Delia said she was definitely never calling back to the house again. She said she was going to call her Franny from now on, more of a girl's name. And no-one else was allowed to call her Franny. Only Delia.

Then, after a long time, Delia decided she wanted to even things out and told Fran she wasn't allowed to call up to her house. To swear on her mother's life that she wouldn't darken the door. *Ever.* Then she changed her mind and said that was far too easy, she could swear on her own life instead. It was worth more. And that made perfect sense to Fran, given the way her mother had treated Delia, and she wasn't put out in the least. She swore on her life and the girls met each other at the corner shop from then on. Delia always seemed to have plenty of money to spend and she wasn't shy about spending it on Fran. She wasn't afraid to tell people where to go, when they were annoying her. She was big where Fran was small. And that was most places.

She told Fran she liked the idea of looking like a raven, since she'd learned about them in class. Extremely loud but highly intelligent. And bigger than crows. They could fly away whenever it suited them, and that's what she liked most about birds. She said she already had the big part sorted, and the dark rim on her pale-blue eyes, so she might as well go the whole hog and dye her hair.

Delia dyed her stringy hair in the kitchen sink at home when she was fourteen. Black. Then she took her grandfather's tailor's scissors and cut it. Crooked. She said her mother cried like a baby when she saw the cut of it – Gary, her stepfather, offered her the money to go to the hairdresser's to straighten it out, but Delia told Franny that she would in her hole waste the money on her hair. She took the money and bought a packet of fags out of it. She said she was sick of having mousey hair. And she was tired of her mother finding fault with her.

"Now all I have to do is learn how to fly, over the rooftops and on to Dubai!"

Fran thought there was no one like Delia.

Then, out of the blue, Delia disappeared when they were both fifteen, leaving Fran imagining all sorts. The one friend she had counted on had left her high and dry and fecked off to England. Or somewhere.

One day Fran was left standing at the corner shop feeling like a fool, waiting for her, and when she didn't turn up she thought at first that Delia was sick. She wasn't going to call up to Blakes' door looking for her, because it had been so long since she had been up there, it would feel weird. Besides, they had a pact and it certainly wasn't up to her to break it.

She had no answer to give the girls in school when they asked where Delia had gone. They said she must have some idea. Surely? Except she didn't have one miserable clue where Delia had got to, so she decided to pretend that she didn't care. Except that she did care and she cared an awful lot.

Delia had been at school one day and gone the next, and there had been no explanation offered and nobody on the road seemed to enquire any further, other than wonder how Delia Blake could have vanished into thin air.

Fran was told by her mother, who said she heard them talking in the shop, that Delia had been sent over to live with relations in England, because she wasn't doing a tap in school, and she wouldn't amount to much anyway.

People on the road got on with their lives, and no one asked questions that they knew they weren't supposed to be asking, in case Delia had got herself "into trouble". And if she had, then that was another story.

And her mother said, "Poor Margie, and she after rearing that brazen bitch of a young one. She's chalk and cheese to that poor woman wherever they got her."

Fran wanted to go straight up and pound on Blakes' door, to find out what they had done with Delia. Poor Delia. But each time she plucked up the courage to go, she lost her nerve and knew that she'd never darken their door.

19

No longer interested in being part of the Populars now that she was on her own, Fran began to rely more on herself. Because they were all grown up by then anyway. And were dropping out of school like flies. Some of the Populars had been sent away to boarding school, splitting up the groups, exposing those who were no longer living in their own precious bubbles, believing they were above everyone else, because they weren't. Those who had no choice but accept what they were left with. Or maybe they were still living in their own precious bubbles, but had become experts at hiding it. Everyone seemed to be getting along just fine. And she with them.

But Fran held it in her all the same.

Chapter 4

EUNICE

1917

The Past

Eunice was born in Sligo a year after the Great War had ended. Her father, Lionel, served as an officer with the British military during the war. He was sent home from the front line having suffered a nervous breakdown. War-torn, he suffered from severe bouts of depression, spending days on end seated in his armchair. Staring. Or locked in his room, roaring and shouting, tormented with haunting memories of what he had witnessed in the trenches. Shell-shocked. Life for the family was dictated by her father's chronic psychological trauma.

Eunice arrived nine months after his return home. In her mind she had been deprived of the normal childhood that her older siblings had experienced. They at least had the benefit of a decent loving father for some of their lives. Eunice had no such recall. The atmosphere in the house felt tense; there was little gaiety. Her mother scolded her constantly for her lack of compassion and insisted that it had been harder on her older siblings, who'd had to adjust to a new way of life.

Home for Eunice was a cold place. Her father suffered from paranoia and was easily agitated. They tried their best not to irritate him, but nothing was ever good enough. There was no way of pre-empting his form. No way of knowing what mood he would take on any given day. He had good days and bad days. More bad days than good. No laughter. Their mother, in her attempts to keep her husband calm, became a tormentor of sorts, forbidding her children from raising their voices in the house. And no skitting either. They could scream and roar as much as they liked, she said, as long as they were far enough down the fields and out of earshot. They mustn't upset Father. Eunice screamed and roared at every opportunity. And upset Father.

When he was in top form her father ruled with a firm hand. The principles of loyalty and discipline were drummed into his children's heads – no room for disobedience. The belt would be flashed. Honour, order and compliance. Eunice became terrified of the belt. *Snap!* Punishment.

And during the darker days, he sat in the armchair, barely moving. And on those days her mother rested.

Eunice would take off through the meadow behind the house on a fine summer day, running until she was far enough away for the house to be hidden behind the trees. Only then would she twirl and spin and make herself so dizzy that she'd fall to the ground in a stupor.

Sometimes she'd run straight to the base of Ben Bulben without stopping, the stems of the tall summer flowers flaying against her legs as she raced towards her favourite spot. The pollen would pop in the air as she disturbed the flower-heads, airborne dusty particles floating in the sunshine. She would flop onto the grass, her ears homing in on the buzzing sounds around her.

She felt free and light during these times. Free from the weight of her father's instability, and her mother's exhausting attempts to corral her children into submission.

Eunice would lie on her back, allowing the magnitude of her surroundings to envelop her. Having voiced her woes to her beloved mountain, she would return home. Skipping. Caught up in her own world, she would hold her breath and ease the latch on the back door, having left her troubles behind her with the mountain.

In the darker days of winter, when it was too wet or too cold to go out, she would retreat to her room and press her face against the cold window. She would whisper her troubles through the window pane. Unburdening.

Eunice learned how to cope by detaching herself.

She had no empathy for her father's condition. No sympathy for the man who had tormented her childhood. A dogmatic tyrant, who in her mind lacked consideration for anyone outside of himself. And no empathy for a mother who refused to consider a university education for her daughter when the time came. She could work locally and pay for her keep.

Eunice got a part-time job in the office of the local school.

Eunice despised her father for the misery he inflicted – bad enough that the family were largely left to their own devices in a community which scorned former members of the British army, She had grown so intolerant of him that she mostly ignored him. But at least they had his military pension.

Eunice had been more than eager to marry when the time came. Being the last of the family to leave home, at nineteen she would gaze out of her bedroom window begging for a way out. Waiting for a sign that she felt was a long time coming.

Meeting Malcolm at a dance in Galway had been the most exciting time for her – even if he was twenty years older than her. With his dark hair slicked back at the sides and the most intense blue eyes she had ever seen, twenty-year-old Eunice was flattered to think that this distinguished man had taken an interest in her. Two dimples just under his cheekbones gave him a boyish appearance. And when he kissed her that first night she felt a warmth flow through her body that she had never experienced before.

Her cousin Valerie had tried to warn her about Malcolm, insisting that he was a charmer. A raconteur, entertaining whoever would care to listen to his outlandish tales. On the circuit for years, she said. And a dab hand at it. She said he had tried it on with her at a race dance in Tubbercurry just weeks before.

Eunice had dismissed the notion, believing her cousin to be jealous. In any case, she didn't mind if he'd been with every single woman on the west coast of Ireland – he had eyes only for her that night and she wasn't about to let him slip through her hands that easily.

From that first night, whatever he wanted from her he got, including her virginity on the third date. Eunice had been eager to please. He booked the two of them into a hotel halfway between Ballygore and Galway, where no one batted an eyelid at the well-dressed couple approaching the reception desk. She passed no remark when she saw the cheeky desk manager wink at Malcolm. Knowing. Mr. and Mrs. Malcolm Clarke.

Malcolm ordered a drink to be brought to the room.

It was her first time. Malcolm apparently assumed it was, saying that he'd be gentle with her. He said he had integrity and it wasn't as if he hadn't given serious consideration to a future together.

Taking him at his word, she didn't need to show reserve. She knew what integrity meant – hadn't it been drilled into her as a child? And Malcolm had given his word, hadn't he? And it was all over before she knew it. Hurt a bit and he hadn't been as gentle as she thought he might have been, but she held her tongue. He handed her a string of pearls in a pale-blue box the very next day, and told her he was smitten.

She didn't believe she was anything special to look at, even though people remarked that she was slender and straight and had beautiful eyes – green eyes that could be mistaken for brown, depending on the light. Her skin was pale and unblemished. Malcolm told her that very first evening that she had a look of a certain movie star about her. That she was a striking girl. He said he couldn't remember the movie star's name, but it would come to him in time. She felt like a star when she was with him – it didn't matter to her if he was lying.

The engagement came three months later. He drove to Sligo to ask her father for her hand in marriage. Eunice had begged him not to bother – it wasn't as if she respected anything her father had to say. Malcolm decided to go over her head and ask him anyway. He never divulged the details of how her father had reacted, only saying, "Jesus, that was tough going."

Giving up her job in the school had been a relief. Eunice had never been happy there.

They married in a small chapel in Sligo, with forty-five guests in attendance. They spent their honeymoon in Dublin.

She had bought him a plain wedding band in Weirs' jeweller's on Grafton Street in Dublin when she had seen them advertised during a previous daytrip. He had refused to consider a wedding ring at first, joking that all she wanted was to stake her claim on him. Like a patch of land. The latest new-fangled notion invented by women to keep their husbands in check, branding them like prize bulls – lining the pockets of the jewellers.

"And why shouldn't a man wear a wedding band when he expects his wife to wear one?" she asked.

Malcolm responded, "Fair point."

He agreed in the end and accepted the ring at the altar, until someone slagged him in the golf club a couple of weeks later and he used every excuse in the book not to wear it. He said the more he looked at the ring, the more it reminded him of something one might see in a plumber's tool-bag. It was beyond him why she didn't choose a man's dress ring with a stone in it. Like the one his father used to wear. Wherever that ended up.

"Eunice, the bloody thing is getting caught up in everything. It'll take my finger clean off one of these days over at the factory."

"Well, Malcolm, I suppose I could say the same about mine, but I won't."

Later, he said that rings were for sissies and he didn't know why he had agreed to wear the damn thing in the first place. It wasn't as if he was fighting a war on the front line and needed a constant reminder that he had a wife at home waiting for him. So he removed the ring from his finger and put it in the velvet box at the top of the wardrobe, along with the gold coin he had given her on their wedding day, and the wilted white rose he had worn in his lapel. He never put the ring back on again.

Malcolm worked just across the yard at the factory, but some days Eunice mightn't see him from morning till night. He could take off out the gate in the car without saying a word and not be seen again until the small hours. Sometimes he rang to say he'd be late home and more times he didn't. And Eunice felt lonely and ignored.

And when he'd roll into bed beside her on a cold winter night and his body like a block of ice, moving closer to her, shivering with the cold, longing to take her warmth, she would smell the whiskey on his breath and move her body away and let him fill her space. And on nights when she was in a good place and he cajoled her into his arms, nuzzling her neck, she would turn and face him.

He told her it was her duty to keep him happy. What she had signed up for. That she'd drive him away if she wasn't careful. Was that what she wanted? Was it? And Eunice didn't have an answer for him. But she supposed not.

So she gave in most times and resented him at other times. She had never been over-keen. If she never had it again it wouldn't have bothered her and when she blurted it out and told him that she'd rather he didn't persist so much, he said he felt hurt.

She was Malcolm Clarke's wife. If people thought she had airs and graces, well, so be it – she had no control over what anyone thought of her. She dressed in the very best clothes that Malcolm's money could buy. And he was good to her. As long as she towed the line. He bought her expensive gifts on her birthday in September and again at Christmas. He bought her Hermès scarves, saying that each was spun from the cocoons of two-hundred and fifty Mulberry moths. He bought her a Cadbury's milk-chocolate egg at Easter. His cheque book was left in the drawer in the marble hall-stand, so all she had to do was ask him to sign a cheque. A blank cheque. He never questioned her spending, or commented on the fact that her wardrobe was bulging with clothes. And, in the meantime, Eunice existed.

She often felt that the factory workers were talking about her behind her back. She knew what they thought. That she was a miserable woman, worse for putting up with it. That Malcolm Clarke chased skirt, that she knew well what he was up to, unless she was going around all these years with her eyes closed.

But she never spoke a word against Malcolm outside of her own head. She had her pride.

Chapter 5

FRAN

Green Lollipops

Fran had been born with one leg slightly shorter than the other. It had been her uncle Will Murphy who had pointed it out when he noticed she was raising her heel slightly when she walked. He said the plastic sandals Brigid had on the lass gave no support. Her mother had refused to accept that her daughter was in any way compromised. Her father did as he usually did – shrugged his shoulders and agreed with his wife.

When Fran started school, her mother pushed her up and down the hill in the go-car. Much quicker than trying to drag her the whole way there and back, she said. "Small children don't have the bounce in their legs to be marching up that steep hill on a cold winter's morning." So the pushchair was kept under the stairs and in constant use, and everything was put on hold.

Except that her Uncle Will wouldn't let it go. He said he knew what he was talking about "having spent all them years making boots at the factory". Feet were his thing, he said. And in the end his sister agreed. She'd make the appointment for Fran to see the specialist in Dublin, if only to shut him up. The appointment was made through the doctor in Ballygore. Will told her that she had done the right thing by the lass.

Brigid took a very excited Fran to Dublin on the train to see the specialist, who confirmed what Will had been saying all along. After the X-ray, Fran was measured, standing on various wooden blocks. Then she was measured lying down and standing up again. They aligned her hips and measured as they went. And measured her again and wrote down the precise measurements, and measured the block of wood they had put to one side and wrote it all down, while Brigid stayed where she was, in the corner, answering questions. *Yes, doctor. No, doctor.* And they wrote those answers down too.

They gave Fran a flat red lollipop wrapped in plastic from a jar full of lollies, and Brigid wondered would they offer her one, because her mouth was dry and she was dying for a smoke. So she reached across the nurse and put her hand in the jar and took a green one out and said she'd take it for the child for the journey home.

Then the head man looked out over his round metal glasses, and told her that she would be hearing from him. He said that if his suspicions were correct the child had a mild structural discrepancy. Very mild. She would need to be fitted for special shoes. He said that the discrepancy in Frances' left leg was just a fraction over what they would consider normal. Her foot was a full size bigger as well, which wasn't unusual in itself. They'd know more by the next appointment.

"Thank you, Doctor. Say thanks to the doctor, Frances."

And off they headed for the train, sucking their lollipops.

When the follow-up appointment arrived in the post, Brigid read it before folding it again and putting it in the drawer upstairs on the landing where they kept the important stuff. She mentioned to her husband Dan that the hospital wanted to see them for another check-up.

Dan said he might take the day off work and go with them on the train. Make a day of it up in the big smoke. They could go to the Zoo if 'twas a fine day, and have a bit of grub in that nice hotel on the quays. It wasn't much of a walk from the station, he said. Brigid said they'd arrange it all nearer the time. That it wasn't for ages yet.

The day of the appointment came and went without a word being mentioned about it. Whether Brigid had conveniently forgotten or not, she never said. The letter remained where it was, in the drawer of the pine dresser upstairs on the landing.

A week after the date of the missed appointment, Will happened to enquire when they were off to Dublin. Dan announced that he was taking the day off to go with them, saying it must be any day now. Asking Brigid for the date. Brigid went quiet and tried to change the subject.

Will asked to see the letter from the hospital, "just out of curiosity". Brigid told him to stop delving in their affairs and mind his own bloody business. Then she stomped up the stairs and brought the letter down anyway and handed it to him. Once Will had read the letter and checked the date, he scolded his sister for not following up with the appointment the week before.

Dan stood up, knocking the chair over. He told Will to take it easy, to calm down, that he'd forgotten all about it himself. Will had raised his voice. He called Brigid selfish and asked what she was at, ignoring the lass's appointment. He asked her what she was thinking keeping those cheap plastic sandals on Fran, that they would destroy the child's feet.

Brigid feigned tears before admitting that 'twas easier to ignore it all, seeing as the specialist at the clinic had said it was only very mild. That she felt awful bad for refusing to see what was as plain as the nose on her face. Then she got defensive.

"Will, are you the expert in orthopaedics all of a sudden? You're below in that bloody factory making auld working boots your whole life. So we missed the last appointment – so what? 'Tisn't as if we're moving out of town. There'll be plenty of other appointments until she's fully grown, and anyway it's just a *fraction* over it being an issue."

Brigid walked over towards the sink and beckoned Will to follow.

Lowering her voice in case Fran would hear them from the other room, she said: "All they'll do up there is bloody X-ray her and measure her feet for a mould and send us off to that special shoe place on Grafton Street. Can't you do the same below in the factory and make her a last for a nice decent pair? I remember you made them shoes for Aunty Biddy years ago."

Will was losing patience. "Biddy's complaint was completely different. She had the hammer toes. The orthopaedic people in Dublin know what they're doing. They wouldn't be recommending that the lass be fitted for special shoes if they didn't think she needed them."

A heavy, brown envelope dropped through the letterbox the very next week, offering a new appointment. A shoe catalogue was enclosed. There was a note attached, instructing Brigid to tick the box beside the footwear she wanted to order, in time for the appointment. If they weren't ordered soon they could be waiting for months on end and Fran would have to be measured all over again.

Brigid was annoyed with Will, claiming she knew damn well that he had contacted the hospital over her head. She had gone to the post office and had rung them herself to offer an excuse, only to be told that a Mr. Murphy had already been on to request a new appointment. Making a spectacle of her. The boots in the catalogue were rotten, she told him. "Pure rotten. Boots. Shoes or boots – I don't know what to call them." Adults and children's styles all the same. Black or brown. And plain. With two wide heavy straps across the front.

Brigid had pestered Will to have a go at making Fran a pair of shoes in time for the coming Christmas. He said he'd been thinking about having a go, but no way would he have them ready in time for Christmas. He had a lot on at the factory, but he'd work away on them on the side, in conjunction with the people in Dublin. He wouldn't have anything to do with it otherwise.

Brigid was just about to tell him where to go for himself, when Fran walked into the kitchen.

"Mammy, is Uncle Will going to make me my shoes? Red ones?"

"Of course he is, loveen!" Emphasising her words, she added, "*Aren't you, Will?*", throwing her brother a warning look.

Will let out a long sigh. "I'll have a go so, but I'll have to attend the appointment with you in the meantime, so I can work away with them. I'm a shoemaker, not a bloody surgeon."

Will attended the next appointment with Brigid and Fran. And the one after that. Dan said he'd hold the fort at home – there was no need for them all to go traipsing the whole way up to Dublin.

Will handed his niece a brown cardboard box with the factory logo on the lid for her seventh birthday the following March. When Fran saw what was inside she screamed with delight. A pair of shiny red shoes with a strap across the front, not unlike the ones she had seen in the shop window. The sole on the left one was a little thicker than the other one and, when she tried them on, her mother's jaw dropped.

Once she composed herself, Brigid started crying, her left hand holding her chest. She told Will he was a pure genius. He beamed with pride.

"Oh Jesus, Will, look at our own *creatúr* and she walking straight! I can hardly credit it." And then she started laughing. "Go on, Fran, walk the length of the room for us again, peteen! Go on! Oh Jesus, wait till your father sees you!"

Fran obliged, delighted with her new shoes.

"Now walk back towards me again."

Fran walked around the room with barely a trace of the limp that her mother had chosen to deny.

Chapter 6

UNCLE WILL MURPHY

Fran's Uncle Will had been offered an apprenticeship at the boot factory in Ballygore when he was sixteen years old. He had left home during the Emergency years to look for work, staying outside the town with a bachelor uncle. The war was raging in Europe and work had been hard to come by at home in Galway.

He had been going from shop to shop in Ballygore, yard to yard, working his way through the town, when out of the corner of his eye he spotted a ten-bob note shiver its way to the ground. It had fallen from the breast pocket of a suited gent, as he retrieved his handkerchief to blow his nose, before taking off in his car. Will's instinct was to stand on it, to conceal it, to quickly pick it up once the coast was clear. Except there were people standing around gawking at the car and he wondered had he been seen and changed his mind.

"*Mister! Mister!*"

People on the street watched the scrawny young lad with the spiky hair call after the moving car. One of them told him that the owner of the car was Malcolm Clarke, the owner of the boot factory just up the street. Will had thought he recognised the man but feigned ignorance. He ran after the car and straight into the yard.

Malcolm had been more than impressed with the honesty of the young lad who had arrived in the factory yard waving a twenty-pound note. Will was panting, explaining that he had seen the money fall from the man's pocket minutes before, when he was out looking for work.

Malcolm told Will to call back to see him the following week if he was interested in a start at the factory, that decent, honest young fellows were few and far between.

Will took Malcolm at his word, calling back to the factory the very next week. He wondered afterwards what he might have done if he had copped it was a twenty-pound note, not a ten-bob one. He'd never seen one, and he wasn't about to start examining it in front of everyone. It was the colour of the note that had fooled him. Walking back the road to his uncle's place, he skipped and jumped, feeling very fortunate to have secured a job in Ballygore. He would spent his time learning the trade.

Will got used to the heady smell of oil, rubber and glue that permeated the factory. He spent the first six months as general dogsbody under the watchful eye of Malcolm, as word of Hitler's invasion of Poland captured the headlines. The factory had since day one manufactured agricultural boots. Will, eager to learn from the skilled dedicated craftsmen, had proved himself to be a bright and willing apprentice, working his way up from stores where he checked and ticketed the batch rolls of tanned hide. Fearful that he would be left go, Will did whatever was asked of him – however menial the task, it was better than the alternative. When the British and Irish Government introduced travel controls, regulating travel across the Irish Sea during the war years, Will realised just how fortunate he had been to secure an apprenticeship in his own country under Malcolm Clarke.

Malcolm had elevated the reputation of the factory, a fact that was never openly acknowledged by those who begrudged him for refusing to allow his workers join the union. Malcolm believed that the union would undermine everything that he had worked so hard to achieve. He believed himself to be a fair boss who looked after his workers. Any mention of a union was prohibited inside the factory gate. If Malcolm got wind that one of his workers had attended one of Larkin's trade-union meetings in the town square, with a view to disrupting their co-workers, they ran the risk of being sacked on the spot.

As the war progressed in Europe, the queues at the docks mounted, thousands of Irish people leaving Ireland to work in England under the newly regulated group labour recruitment scheme. Will stuck to his plan to remain on in Ballygore and finish his apprenticeship, even though orders in the factory were at their lowest on record, when productivity was down to a minimum and shoe factories were closing all over the country.

Malcolm always seemed to have a plan, keeping the factory open on a skeleton staff, selling directly to retailers as the war raged in Europe. Factory workers such as Will, who remained loyal to Malcolm, took a cut in their wages during the worst years of the Emergency in order to keep the place running. By 1943, thousands of young soldiers were leaving the Irish army to join the British forces fighting the war against Germany. Will felt that he had made the right decision in remaining loyal to Malcolm, who had forged ahead in tough times to keep the factory going.

The war had impacted on imports and exports, even though Ireland had remained neutral. Malcolm managed to secure a regular order for safety boots for the construction industry. He had enough contacts built over the years to be assured of a regular supply of raw materials.

Will kept his head down. He remained steadfast in his eagerness to learn everything he could from Malcolm whom he had grown to admire. He became skilled at separating the prime quality hides from the lower-grade ones which had made their way past the factory door – those that would never make it past the clicking room. Hides that may have been damaged from barbed wire or scarred from one disease or another, were analysed by Will to see if they would make the grade. Those that were deemed too weak or damaged were dispatched to hand-stitchers who worked from home to produce by-products including various-sized leather work-aprons, and porous cloths for cleaning glass. No wastage. Carpenters, stonemasons, blacksmiths and more, all required leather aprons.

Malcom secured orders from England and Europe and as far as the USA. He sent out miniature handmade samples, designed by Will. The samples for America were individually stamped with a logo: *ÉIRE*. Ten workers were hired to work from home, including Will's sister Brigid, whom he brought down from Galway to be trained as a hand-stitcher.

Chapter 7

EUNICE

Pictures in Her Head

1960

Eunice Clarke was constantly plagued by the same recurring dream – when her eyes would shoot open in the dead of night, the picture of what she dreaded most in the world exposing itself. Accusing her.

A memory of stroking her baby's head, twiddling her finger around the cutest corkscrew curl growing out from the baby's hairline. A rebel curl. The rest of the hair was wispy apart from that one single curl. Obstinate, growing in the opposite direction.

"Look, baby," she whispered, feeling her own hairline for its defiant strand of hair, "you and I have the same cow's lick."

There were mornings when she would lie in her bed, maudlin and full of regret for what might have been.

The pictures had remained in her head. Snapshots of tiny fingers and toes. Fair skin. A smell so familiar.

The pink name-tag on Ramona's paper anklet had read *Clarke*. She had checked it herself just before Malcolm had arrived that day.

Hadn't she? Or had she convinced herself? Had she been wrong all along? Maybe they had brought the wrong baby to her that first day. *No.*

How did she know?

Because a mother knows. And there had been the corkscrew curl.

If it had all been some terrible mistake, then no-one else would have known. But someone did know. The caller at the other end of the phone knew.

Or had years of ruminating thoughts messed with her brain, leaving her imagining all sorts? Was she confusing one thing with another, and didn't know the difference anymore between what was real and what was imaginary?

Choosing to get caught up in Malcolm's excitement that first time he held Ramona in his arms. And he using the softest words that Eunice knew could only come from a loving father's heart. A father's love that she herself had never felt.

Then before she knew it, it was too late, and a week had passed and she dismissed her doubt and, by the time she arrived home with Malcolm's darling child with the olive skin and the dark wiry hair, on that cold January morning, there was no going back.

The boys eyed the new addition to the family cautiously, while their father doted on the new arrival.

There was no solace for Eunice, who couldn't cry out or disclose her fears – if only to seek assurance that she was wrong.

She couldn't go to the confession box to whisper her woes to the priest through the sliding screen. Because, for no other reason, it was not in her to do so. Neither could she allow herself to bond with Ramona, because her conscience would not allow her and the doubt was always there. Lurking. So she accepted her penance.

40

But something inside of her pressed on. She played the dutiful wife and mother and let them to get on with it. And over the years the drink helped her to get through the worst of times. Times when she would find her mind straying.

Wondering if she was right and wondering if she was wrong.

Unscrewing the cap of the vodka bottle, she flicked it towards the floor after downing a few gulps. She felt her throat burn but it took no more than a minute or two for her to feel calm. Holding the bottle under her arm, she got up and reached for a mug in the press above the sink.

The crisis in her head had eased. But Malcolm must not find out about the phone call. He was so attached to Ramona, it would kill him. Another drink.

But someone had known about it all this time, so she hadn't imagined it – there had to be some truth in it. But how could anyone prove it?

Taking a deep breath she topped up the mug. Switching the wireless on for company, she moved to the armchair by the oil stove.

Had the call come a week earlier, Ramona could well have been at home. Eunice had been annoyed with Malcolm. He had opened a bank account for Ramona's fourteenth birthday without saying as much. He had produced the bank book just as they were about to leave the house. Ramona had screamed with excitement, hugging Malcolm once she had checked the lodgement on the first page. Eunice had smiled and offered no comment. She had breathed a sigh of relief as she watched Ramona run across the yard towards the car – she was heading back to boarding school after the Christmas break.

It was raining heavily. Eunice stood at the door.

"Get back in out of the rain, Mother!" Ramona ordered, the rain dribbling down her face, blinding her eyes. Squinting. "And don't forget to tell Gretta I won't be seeing her in April! I'm off to Kerry with the hockey team for the Easter break – write it down or you'll forget! I'll ring you at the usual time next week!"

Malcolm had already started the engine – he was leaning across Ramona, reaching for the window handle, telling her to bring her bloody head back in or they'd both be drenched. He scolded his daughter for roaring like a fishwife across the yard, and off they went. Laughing.

Ramona wouldn't be home again until the summer break, plenty of time to ease the tension that had been evident in the house over the Christmas. At least Ramona had never been a clingy child. For that Eunice was grateful.

Chapter 8

EUNICE

Intrusion

It was two days before Eunice's head was clear enough to re-engage with the memory of the phone call. Had she imagined it all? Had her mind become so confused that she was losing her grip on reality?

She'd had an unsettled night's sleep that first night, tossing and turning in the bed, her thoughts racing, slipping backwards and forwards. The pictures creeping in. She had to allow the thoughts in, to revive the memory of that day fourteen years ago. Whether she liked it or not, she had to face the truth.

She had held her baby for a few minutes the Sunday she was born, and the morning after that again when that awful girl brought the baby to her. Hadn't she?

She had remembered that and not much more, until Matron was stirring her, tapping her wrist, calling her name, telling her that she had passed out in the bed while feeding the baby. Fainted. The doctor was taking her pulse. He needed to check her blood. Nurse Dawson was at the foot of her bed holding the chart.

Matron was flustered. "We could have had a right disaster on our hands had you rolled over on her. Best keep the baby down in the nursery for the time being. No harm done. She was only to latch on for three minutes or so." She turned to the doctor. "Day two post-partum. Our own formula and a drop of boiled water will do her no harm at all for a day or two until the mother's well enough to feed her. She's on the formula as it is for the night feed in the nursery."

Eunice woke up in tears having spent the night on the settee. She was shivering, her plaid skirt damp where the contents of the mug had emptied onto her lap. Her face felt sticky from crying. Tears without sound. Her white broderie anglaise blouse was stained. Breadcrumbs sat on her chest. A second bottle had been opened – it lay on the floor alongside a half-empty bottle of Malcolm's best malt whiskey. Her head was pounding and she didn't remember eating sandwiches or making tea but she must have done, because the Aynsley teapot was on its side, the lid in two pieces where it had hit the parquet floor.

Tea leaves had spilt onto Malcolm's precious rug, the deep rusty-coloured stain visible in parts along the white fringing. Her head was pounding, her stomach felt raw. She hated that rug and Malcolm knew it. The expensive hand-knotted rug that had been brought by his uncle all the way from the Middle East – the rug that Ramona loved to spin on with Gretta, ever since she was a toddler. Spinning round and round incessantly, singing, laughing, until the child became dizzy. Gretta's arms would encircle Ramona, to stop her from falling. And they would tumble down. Together.

Malcolm's rug. A hundred and fifty knots per inch. Hand-knotted. Not hand-tufted. Worthy of a place in their high-ceilinged living room. Eunice was of the mind that Malcolm had kept it there all those years just to annoy her.

There had been an invasion of moths in the house some years before. Male moths, which Malcolm insisted were smaller but tougher than the females. They'd had an awful job trying to get rid of them. Embarrassing when guests arrived and the place was speckled with the flying pests that moved into the mahogany wardrobe in their bedroom. Partial to wool, the moths settled for Malcolm's finest sweaters, leaving miniature holes that wouldn't be noticed until the sweaters were worn, and not even then at times. The smell of camphor around the house was sickening. Then more moths arrived to replace the ones they'd squashed into the wallpaper with slippers and folded newspapers, leaving brown powdery marks for Gretta to remove.

Until Malcolm lifted the corner of his precious rug one evening, to educate one of their dinner guests on the merits of a hand-knotted Persian rug. And there they were. White papery sacs hidden in between the red-and-white pile. And when they looked closer, they seemed to be many more. Far too many to count. Their guest, the local bank manager, began to laugh, which really annoyed Malcolm, while Eunice discreetly topped up her glass from the decanter on the sideboard. When the bank manager jokingly suggested to Malcolm that he open the front door and let the rug take flight back to where it had come from, Malcolm wasn't impressed.

Eunice remembered it clearly, because it was that very night he accused her of being a cold fish when he had tried and failed after one too many whiskies.

45

"You're cold, Eunice. You're as stiff as a bloody mannequin!"

But she knew what he really wanted to say. He wanted to tell her that she was frigid.

The boys from the factory were sent over to the house the following morning to roll up the rug and take it to an empty outhouse to be fumigated. Back it landed two weeks later, smelling of vinegar, minus the moths.

Malcolm accused Gretta of being away with the fairies for not copping the state of the rug. And he after wining and dining the bank manager.

Gretta, being Gretta, took it in her stride and carried on with the housework. Humming.

Eunice detested the rug even more after that, but Malcolm insisted on it staying put. There were unexplained spills over the years and each time, to Eunice's annoyance, Gretta would be down on her knees scrubbing, leaving the rug as good as new.

So the contents of a random pot of strong tea would do it no harm at all.

Looking around her, the living room was in a state. Newspapers were strewn around the floor. What was left of a half-pound of ham was on the rug beside the teapot, an empty brown-paper bag which had been twisted ever so tightly sat on the walnut coffee table.

Eunice raised her chest slightly, brushing the crumbs off her front, down towards the floor. No memory of the day before and her head pounding. She must have blacked out.

Her mouth was dry and the banging in her head grew worse when she moved. She needed a drink but she felt sick. She retched over the stone sink. The taste in her mouth turned her stomach. She drank water straight from the tap, swishing it around. It helped.

Stumbling past the kitchen window, she stepped back slightly when she heard crunching on the gravel outside. The workers were in the yard.

Confused, she looked upward at the January sky, a clean curtain of white clouds to one side, the other side blue without a speck of white. Her eyes watered. The blue-grey slate rooftops of the houses nearby were touched by a dusting of frost. The view from her bedroom window at home in Sligo flashed before her. She missed her mountain.

Were they coming or going? Must be coming. What time was it? She looked back at the carriage clock on the pine dresser. Squinting. What day was it? Friday, because the factory bins were put outside on a Friday and the usual stray cats were sniffing around. The bins hadn't been emptied.

Malcolm was due home from Dublin later that day.

Eunice then noticed Gretta setting her bike against the side-wall outside. Gretta waved through the window. She'd fix things up and sort out the mess in the living room.

She heard the key turn in the front door. Gretta's voice.

"It's only me, missus! I'll be with you as soon as I get myself organised here."

"Gretta the Great," Eunice muttered patronisingly under her breath.

Golden Gretta, who would no doubt take it in her stride when she encountered the mess. She never passed comment on the vodka bottles tucked in between the towels in the airing cupboard when she came across them. Unless they were empty. And off with her out the gate, with the empty bottle concealed in the carrier basket of her bicycle. No mention and Eunice didn't ask.

Gretta would get on with her morning's work. What if Gretta

were to stop her silly humming just long enough to see that she was troubled, Eunice wondered. That she might benefit from her support?

Reminding herself that there was no point in dwelling on what she couldn't change, Eunice decided to go upstairs and have a soak in the bath, take a Valium, maybe two, and come back down in her dressing gown to pick at the cold plate that Gretta would no doubt have left out for her, covered with a clean tea towel. Once Gretta had finished upstairs, Eunice would retreat back to the bedroom to sleep it off in time for Malcolm's return. And no drink until the next time.

Chapter 9

EUNICE

The Private Wing

1946

Eunice hadn't been well after the birth of her daughter. Matron had put a sign on the door: "**No visitors**." She had said no more to Eunice about her fainting episode.

Baby Clarke would be brought up to be fed once Eunice had recovered her strength. Not having breastfed her two boys, Eunice hadn't intended to breastfeed this time either, but Matron convinced her to give it a go. And she had, until she had passed out.

Matron held the view that the disinclination to breastfeed had played a significant role in the increase of often fatal gastroenteritis in infants. The baby would benefit going forward, having ingested the best of her mother's colostrum. Mother Nature. Eunice reluctantly agreed only after being reminded by Matron how ill her last child Dermot had been, ten years previously – plagued with reoccurring stomach infections in his first year. They'd nearly lost him.

"Eunice, if it works, it works, there's no harm in trying."

Malcolm was told by Matron in no uncertain terms not to dream of arriving at St. Mary's unannounced. He was to call beforehand. To check.

He hadn't been too pleased, according to Matron, who said that she was taken aback by the arrogant tone on him. He had been away on business for the past three days and here he was. Dictating. Malcolm could have that effect on people. He made it quite clear that he'd be visiting his wife and baby girl at two o'clock sharp on the following day. His time was precious, he said. January was a busy month – the factory didn't run itself, and it wasn't as if this was their firstborn.

Matron brought the baby up from the nursery an hour before he was due to arrive.

"I'm rushed off my feet downstairs, so no time for *ooh*ing and *ahh*ing" she told Eunice, half in jest. "Plenty of time for all that later."

Matron began fussing around the bed. Tidying. Fixing a pillow under the baby, settling her in the crook of Eunice's arm – guiding the searching mouth to Eunice's swollen breast. "Let her feed away now, Eunice, and put her on the other breast after seven minutes or so – you'll know yourself when it's time."

Matron stood back to check that the decorative coverlet she had folded over the end of the bed was even. Edge to edge. The lightweight cotton matched the fabric on the room divider and the floral curtains which had all been chosen by her good self. Matron took great pride in the private wing on the top floor of St. Mary's, which housed patients such as Malcolm Clarke's wife, who were in a position to pay for their confinement. The rooms had recently been refurbished under her guidance. The shared bathroom down the corridor housed a gleaming copper bath in the centre of the room. It had been in St. Mary's for over fifty years, to be used only by the private patients. The walls had been papered in an aquamarine print, off-setting the warm tones of the copper tub. The busy public wards housed on the ground floor housed no such luxury. Ten beds to a ward with a shared cast-iron bath across the hallway.

"Enjoy your visit, Eunice. We still have a shortage of staff on the wards downstairs. I'll run up again to keep a check on you. *Hmm … her skin … she looks a little jaundiced. I might get the doctor to have a peep at her when I get a chance.*" Matron rushed out the door, talking back to Eunice. "She latched on straight away, can you credit it? The colostrum will stand to her."

And she was gone – leaving Eunice to feed the baby before Malcolm arrived.

It wasn't until she eased back the blanket to change the baby's nappy that she sensed something wasn't right. Something odd. Or was she imagining it?

Once the doubt crept in, it planted itself there. Was this the same baby she had given birth to four days previously? Was this her baby at all?

Malcolm would be vexed to hear her voicing such uncertainty. He would insist that she was imagining things. He would scold her for her inability to recognise her own child.

Of course this was their baby girl. The anklet, when she checked had read *Baby Clarke. 7lbs 12ozs. DOB 13/01/1946.*

She had just began to question her own doubt when she thought she heard Malcolm's voice, laughing and joking with whoever he had met on his way up the stairs. Maybe not him. Sitting up in bed, she reached to her right to pull the bell cord, to call a nurse. She wanted to alert Matron to her doubt – to ask was she imagining things – to seek reassurance. Before Malcolm arrived. Then she remembered the staff shortage in the public wards below. She hesitated. Footsteps were coming closer. She checked her watch, looked up, and there he was.

Carrying a large flat box of chocolates with a wide lavender ribbon tied in a bow. His presence stole the moment.

"Here you are!"

Winded from climbing the stairs, his face looked puffy from one too many whiskeys knocked back to wet the baby's head. Wearing his charcoal-wool overcoat over his suit, he looked handsome as he held onto the brass bar at the end of the bed to catch his breath. Leaving the box of chocolates down on the bed, he removed his coat and folded it inside out, before placing it across the bed on top of Matron's floral coverlet.

Distracted, Eunice put her right hand up to check her straight blonde hair which she had pinned back earlier, her attention in that moment given to her appearance. Drawing her bed jacket in around her chest, she smiled at her husband.

The baby slept soundly as Malcolm came towards them. He put his index finger to his lips, gently moving the baby blanket back with his other hand to take a peek at his daughter.

It all happened so quickly after that. Far too quickly for her to react. To explain that she had doubts. The baby stirred, raising her chubby hand, wrapping it tightly around Malcolm's little finger. And she knew by the look on his face. He was besotted.

Overcome with emotion, the tears welled up in her eyes. Tears had always come easily to Eunice, and more so during recent months.

She was just about to speak up when something inside of her silenced her. She wanted to alert him without causing a scene. Then it was too late for her to open her mouth and tell him that she felt something wasn't right, because he claimed the baby immediately, lifting her gently from her arms, kissing her on the top of her head, telling Eunice what a marvel she was, exclaiming that the baby had the very head of a Clarke.

"Look at the full head of hair on her, and as wiry as my own!"

He looked proudly at Eunice before turning his attention back to the baby.

"You're your father's daughter, missy. And the plump cheeks on you, and your mother here after doing all the hard work and she didn't even get a look in."

He looked straight into Eunice's eyes. And in that very moment she felt valued.

Holding the infant in his arms, Malcolm had an air of giddiness about him as he waltzed around the bed, bonding with his baby girl. Singing a tune. She hadn't seen him this happy in years. She didn't remember him being anywhere near as moved when their sons Dermot and Arthur were born ten and twelve years before.

When Malcolm marvelled at the baby's olive skin, Eunice thought it best not to mention what Matron had said about the jaundice.

He handed the baby back to her, sitting at the side of the bed with a watery look in his eyes that told her he couldn't be happier. He spoke ever so softly.

"Eunice, you've made me the happiest man in the world – giving me this little miss. You know . . . 'tis about time my family became my number one. You don't believe me – just wait and see."

Everything she had needed to hear, as outside of Christmas Day and Easter Sunday the factory had taken precedence over his family. But here he was, all smiles and full of promises. Malcolm the family man.

He said he heard a song on the wireless that very morning and 'twas stuck in his head ever since. "About Ramona . . . meeting near a water fall."

Eunice smiled back at him.

"You like it, Eunice? Ramona? The name?"

She nodded.

"Yes? Ramona it is then," he said, beaming.

She wanted to say, why don't we think about it? She would have liked to have said, "We've plenty of time to pick a name." She should have brought her fears to his attention. To tell him that he may have claimed the wrong child. But nothing came out.

"Ramona it is then, Malcolm."

He put his arm around her, around them both, saying that he couldn't wait to take them home to the boys, where they belonged. That he might even take a day or two off, to help out, if he was needed. He said he must be going soft in his old age, but he felt like parading Ramona around the factory.

Eunice was so blindsided by his display of emotion that she dismissed her own doubt and fooled herself into believing that everything was fine. She was just being silly. Hormones.

He would have blamed her had her fears been realised. He certainly wouldn't have taken it in his stride if her breasts had been suckled by another man's child.

There would have been no repeat of his grand display of affection, once the mistake had been rectified. And no guarantee that he would ever connect with his own child … if that were the case.

Malcolm would never acknowledge that he had been wrong. He would have accused her of conning him. He wouldn't have cared who heard him shouting at the top of his voice in one of Matron's private rooms in St. Mary's. He would have grabbed his overcoat and taken off out the door, having reduced her to tears. Heaven knows where he would have ended up.

But Eunice would have cared. She cared enough to keep her fears to herself and carry on, because she didn't want anything or anyone take this precious time away from her.

A week later there was no going back. In Malcolm's eyes there was no child like Ramona.

They were home, and the future in the Clarke household looked promising.

Chapter 10

SADIE PRATT

1946

Sadie Pratt started work in St. Mary's in Ballygore when she was sixteen years old. She applied for the job after her grandmother had died, leaving her alone in the small cottage to fend for herself. She was told by the matron on the day that she had nothing suitable for her.

Less than a month later the matron knocked on her door up the lane on Spring Street. Her repeated hammering on the door startled Sadie. Peeping out through the net curtain, she got such a shock when she saw who it was that she went with her instinct and ducked down behind the armchair in the front room. Then, when she saw the thin face press closer to the window, she felt exposed and went straight out to open the door but stood there, blocking the woman from coming in.

The matron was flustered. She held a brown-paper parcel under her arm, tied with cord. She said she had been trying to find the house for ages. That she wouldn't have known a house existed up such a narrow laneway. She eyed Sadie cautiously then, craning her neck to look in behind her. Sadie pulled the door further out to stop her from seeing any more. The house was in a bit of a mess – she had no intention of allowing anyone in over the threshold.

The matron said she was stuck. That the young one she had hired upped and left her high and dry. The job would be varied, she said. Sadie could start straight away the very next morning. She'd see her at the back door of the basement at eight o'clock sharp, once she'd cleaned herself up. Because hygiene was of the utmost importance, she said, looking Sadie up and down. They'd take it from there.

Sadie couldn't thank her enough and timidly said she'd be there. She told the matron of her plan to apply for nursing in England once she had saved enough money to get herself there, that she'd do whatever she had to do in the meantime to gain experience. She thought to mention that she would need a reference when the time came.

The matron coughed and stifled a laugh. "Time enough to talk about all that, Sadie – we'd better not run before we can walk."

The matron rolled her eyes now and then when she spoke. Closed her eyes. Opened her eyes. Long winks. No patience. Sadie knew she was talking too much, but she wasn't quite sure what else to be doing, because the matron made her feel awkward. Then she handed Sadie the parcel and told her it might be a bit big on her. A uniform. She told her to be sure to have a good scrub before she put it on, because she couldn't stress enough the importance of being clean and tidy at all times at St. Mary's. Sadie took no umbrage at her words, figuring that she probably said the same thing to everyone, seeing as she was the one in charge.

Once she closed the door after the visit, Sadie covered her mouth with one hand and danced around the darkened room. She was beside herself.

Sadie stood five foot in her stocking-feet. Her grandmother said she was dainty. A clever pupil who had soaked up all that she could learn on the days that she had attended school. The nuns had been kind at first, praising her for her ability in arithmetic, encouraging her to keep up with the reading and writing. That she might have a future. But Sadie had seen the look in their eyes. Pity.

Handing her a bar of soap and a nit-comb had been the greatest mistake the lay teacher could have made. Telling Sadie that cleanliness was next to godliness and no child would want to sit beside her if she didn't wash herself. That she was "crawling". Showing her how to use the nit-comb to draw out the lice. Telling her to shake DDT in the bed. That she had flea bites all over her and her neck was black with the dirt and that wasn't good for anyone.

Twelve-year-old Sadie gave up on school after that. She didn't need to tell the teacher that they had only the one bed at home. That she went to the pump for a bucket of water to pour down the toilet in the yard, because it hadn't worked for as long as she could remember. That she washed herself in the basin with whatever water was left over. That she didn't care about the fleas, or anything else that might bite her – she climbed into bed beside her granny every night, snuggling close to her, to share the heat of her body. The fleas were the least of her troubles, she was well able for them and they hiding in the blanket, waiting to be picked out, and when she caught them she would squeeze them between her thumbnails until they popped, leaving their flattened bodies behind. She had more to be worrying about.

Sadie Pratt didn't have the loving parents that everyone else seemed to have. She didn't need the good shoes, or the warm coat, or the clean and tidy ways of some. She didn't have the clean braided hair smelling of carbolic soap, or the thick stockings that might slip down into her good shoes on a bitter cold day. The cup of hot milk before she went to bed or the warm supper eaten at the wooden table with a newspaper full of warm floury spuds left in the centre. Or the father who would defend her good name in any conversation. Or the mother who'd say, "Yes, love", and "No, love". A mother who was supposed to be loving and nurturing. No. Sadie Pratt had her grandmother who coughed up thick, dirty, green phlegm and that was all she knew.

Her gran stayed in bed most days. Coughing it up. She said she wasn't up to much anymore and it was just as well that she had Sadie to help out. Sadie collected her pension and brought her a mug of tea and a slice of cold bread every morning. She walked out the road to the farmer's house and knocked at the door and asked for a helping hand and gratefully accepted whatever she was given. And if it was a lump of salty pork too fatty for their own pot, or a bunch of carrots for soup, they ate well that day and the next. One meal a day and maybe an egg if they had it and that was good enough. Sadie made goody with milk and bread torn up and soaked in it. And a knob of butter when she could get it. What more did they need?

Her gran wore a knitted shawl around her shoulders. The same dark, old shawl that she never took off her shoulders day or night. She didn't put in or out with people very much but she loved Sadie and Sadie loved her and that was enough.

The morning before Sadie's sixteenth birthday, she opened her eyes and knew immediately something was wrong. Her grandmother who would lean over every morning bar none, asking for the chamber pot, lay flat on her back beside Sadie, her small brown eyes glazed. Sadie jumped up and out of the bed and straight out the door down to the basement door of St. Mary's hospital without stopping, because she didn't know where else to go, and there was no point in knocking at doors on her street, because her gran had never warmed to her neighbours. She told the women in the kitchen that her grandmother was dead above in the bed and they brought her in and gave her a mug of soup to warm her up. And, by the time they let her go home, the men were taking her gran away and she wondered would they let her have the two pennies they had placed on top of her gran's eyes.

They asked her was she alright, but forgot to ask how she would survive without her grandmother's old age pension.

Sadie would manage in the same way she had always managed. They wouldn't throw her out of the house because it was on a long lease and her grandmother had lived there so long the rent was low – as long as she found the money she'd be fine.

It was a small funeral. No sign of her mother arriving home to bury her own mother. People shaking her hand, saying they were related. Then leaving. No word from her mother. Nothing.

After that she hung around the town during the day, starving, mostly down by the hospital, mooching around until the women in the kitchen brought her in. Feeling sorry for her. Handing her a few slices of bread or a lump of hard cheese which she ate immediately, because she was always hungry. Once she got into the habit of being handed the food at the back door she knew to return, knowing that she would always get something to eat. After a while she wasn't let into the warm kitchen as much as she had been and didn't understand why, but she didn't mind. She collected odd bits of coal that had fallen off the lorry in the coal yard because she was small enough to fit in the gap in the barbed wire and she didn't mind the dark. A bundle of sticks along the road was easy to carry under her arm. Sadie had known no other life.

Sadie soon realised that the job she had hoped for at St. Mary's was a far cry from the reality of what Matron expected of her. She started out in the basement, sorting out the dirty washing before it was sent to the laundry. She scrubbed the floor of the mortuary and anything else that needed scrubbing. At least it was warm. Matron had joked that anything else that needed to be washed down would probably fall on her to do.

Sadie never once complained. She worked relentlessly towards her goal. Keeping her head down, she didn't partake in idle gossip with the women or get involved in any conversations that might tarnish her good name. Aware of the sniggering behind her back, she gave it no consideration. Laughter was for the idle.

She did everything that was asked of her, confident that one day she would get to work upstairs on the wards, gaining experience alongside the nurses and the doctors. In the meantime, she would continue to turn up every morning at eight o'clock, entering the basement through the small green side door down the steps at the back of the hospital. A means to an end.

Sadie could hear her grandmother's voice urging her on – telling her to keep her head down – to keep on going. To carry on what she was doing with pride, that she would indeed be rewarded. That she was a caring girl who had minded her grandmother against the odds. She had knocked on doors, holding her hand out, when many more wouldn't. Sadie felt that one day in the future her reward would come – when she would wear her nurse's badge on her crisp white uniform with honour. And when that day came, she would rise up the ranks so quickly she'd be running the wards in no time. Maybe even here in the hospital in Ballygore. *Sister Pratt.*

In the meantime, she would do whatever was expected of her. Keep her opinions to herself. Even when she knew she was in the right and she was being scolded, Sadie knew not to contradict Matron, though sometimes she found it hard not to explode when she was dismissed by her with the flick of a hand.

After six months working in the basement, Sadie still wasn't allowed up the back stairs to the wards. Matron scolded her at every turn. "Take that hair out of your face, Sadie Pratt, and for God's sake give it a wash. It's thick with grease."

One year into the job, Matron assigned Sadie to help out in the kitchen for a day or two. She had shown her eagerness from the beginning. In her own mind they couldn't do without her. She'd be on the wards helping the nurses out in no time.

When the women working in the kitchen complained to Matron about her poor hygiene, Sadie was furious. She lost her temper, shouting at the Matron that she didn't carry a bastard disease, that she washed herself every other bloody day, and they were still complaining about her.

She was called to the office. Matron told her to watch her mouth. How dare she feel familiar enough with her to speak in such a manner? And in front of the kitchen staff! Matron was furious. She said that Sadie smelled bad and there was no other way of putting it at that stage. They had tried to go easy on her, given her background, but nothing had changed and she stank to high heaven and that was the reason she wasn't allowed anywhere near the wards or indeed the kitchen from then on unless she managed her hygiene. Bacteria, given the chance to grow, smell. She'd better mend her ways or she'd be out the door. "And clip back that bloody hair!" St. Mary's was no place for her if she didn't commit to presenting herself properly. Final warning.

Sadie tried her best from then on in. She washed her hair and herself, and sniffed and smelt herself and Matron acknowledged the improvement in her.

By the time she was eighteen, she was confident that she would soon be in a position to move forward with her plan. She had done everything that was asked of her and gone out of her way to impress Matron who seemed to have little to say to her of late. Sadie didn't get upset at Matron's lack of encouragement. She took it as a sign that her work was satisfactory enough not to warrant correction.

Then her life had been turned upside down the day Matron told her that she couldn't give her a reference, that she didn't think she was a suitable candidate to pursue a nursing career. That she'd be lying to herself and to Guy's Hospital in London, or indeed any other hospital if she were to recommend Sadie as a suitable candidate. When Sadie said she was willing to train as a nurse's aide in England and work her way up, Matron shook her head, saying that in her opinion Sadie was not cut out for any type of caring profession. Best suited to the maintenance end of things, she had added. She said she was sorry to have to be the one to tell her that she had notions far above her station. Above her capabilities. That she could stay where she was and continue with her work. There would be days here and there where she would be called upon to help out. There was nothing for her beyond that.

Sadie believed that she was being tricked. Matron's opinion wasn't fact. Of course she was a suitable candidate for nurse training in England. Matron just wanted her to stay put in St. Mary's given that she was such a diligent worker. She would show Matron.

Chapter 11

FRAN

The Good Job

1963

When her Leaving Cert results came out, Fran couldn't have been happier. She had passed everything. She had no intention of staying on in Ballygore – it wasn't the same since Delia left.

When she heard her mother telling the next-door neighbour that her Fran wanted no more than to get a nice office job in the boot factory, Fran was horrified. She knew what was expected of her, but she wanted more for herself. She wanted to get the blazes out of Ballygore, to become independent and live a little. Since Delia had left, Fran hadn't met anyone she could call her best friend. She dreamt of the day she would leave Ballygore to start a new life. She loved her parents, but the time had come to leave the nest. She'd had enough cosseting to last her a lifetime.

She decided to apply for the National Civil Service exam. She would most likely be offered a job in Dublin or in Cork, in a government department, as a Clerical Assistant. Until she was married at any rate. Then she would have to give it up because that was the law. Several of the girls from school had left the town to take up positions in the Civil Service in Dublin, arriving back for the weekends on the bus, with their fancy weekend cases.

Fran wanted the same for herself. She needed her birth cert for the application but when she asked her mother, Brigid said she'd look for it when she had time. That she had one somewhere. When she asked her a second time and reminded her a few days later, Brigid sounded stressed and told her not to be tormenting her, that she'd apply for one for her if she couldn't find it. So Fran decided to have a look for it herself in the dresser at the top of the stairs. She rooted through the drawer, tossing loose letters and bills aside, taking out random envelopes, opening them. Photographs. Bills and receipts and not a sign of a birth certificate.

Then, bending down, she looked in towards the back of the drawer – and saw the tip of something sticking up from behind it. She put her hand in blindly and felt around. "*Aha!*" She could feel the tip of the object. She pulled it out.

It was an envelope. Opening it, she found two certificates – her parents' marriage cert and a birth cert.

She read the details on the birth cert. Frances Mary Murphy was born in St. Mary's, Ballygore, on the 13th January 1946.

Who was Frances Mary Murphy?

She read the mother's name: *Brigid Murphy. Spinster.*

Fran's eyes opened wide.

There was just a line drawn across from where it said "**Father's Name**".

She read it again. This certificate couldn't be hers. She had been born in St. Mary's Hospital, but in March of the same year. She'd ask her mother about it later. She read it again. And again. And then it dawned on her. She didn't have to read it anymore. No wonder her mother had fobbed her off when she told her she needed her birth cert for the application. She had been born before her parents got married.

She called down the stairs when she heard her mother opening the front door.

"Hello, Mammy! I'm up here, poking around for my birth cert for the Civil Service. I think I found it. Your wedding cert is here as well!" She was laughing inside.

No answer. Brigid appeared beside Fran on the landing one minute later, her face as white as Fran had ever seen it.

"See what the birth cert says – that Brigid Mary Murphy, Spinster, married Daniel Gaffney, Labourer, in St. John's Church in Limerick on the 8th of March 1946!"

Her mother snapped the certificate out of her hand. "Fran, why couldn't you just leave it be?" Brigid's mouth quivered.

Fran had expected a reaction but not this. She sniggered nervously. What was her mother so upset about? To find out her parents had her before they were married was no big deal – though to find out that she was two months older than she believed herself to be was a different matter entirely. She snapped the paper back. Her mother's face had turned a bright red. Fran waved the cert out of her mother's reach, a quizzical look on her face. She wasn't about to let her mother get away with this one.

"Frances Mary Murphy, date of birth 13th of January 1946? But, sure, my birthday is on the 13th of March, *Maaammy?"* Stretching the word. "What's going on? And where's Daddy's name, come to think of it? Cos it's not here under 'Father'. So am I a Murphy then?

Says it here. Not a Gaffney. I was born before you got married, right?"

Her mother reached out and caught her by the sleeve, doing her best to grab the papers out of her hand, but Fran was too quick for her. She pulled her arm back, waving the certificates above her head. Sniggering nervously, keeping an eye on her mother's face at the same time.

Brigid looked as if she were about to scream. "Oh, there's plenty I could have told you! But I didn't!" She sucked the air in between her teeth, making a slushing sound. "Hand them to me right now, please, Frances! And what were you doing poking around in the drawer anyway? *Sleeveen!* You've no business going near my personal stuff. Didn't I tell you I'd get it for you when I was good and ready?"

Fran conceded and handed her the certs which her mother put in the pocket of her housecoat.

"Just wait till your father gets home. And don't you take any notice of what it says on that piece of paper." She tapped her pocket. "The registrar on the day was a gomey!"

All this did was to frustrate Fran further. "I don't believe you. Explain that cert to me, Mother!"

Brigid's shoulders dropped.

"You knew very well I'd be needing my birth cert for the Civil Service. So what were you going to do? Change the dates on it? Cos I wouldn't put it past you, Mother!"

Moments later her frustration turned to pity when she saw the look of anguish on her mother's face.

"*Aah*, Mammy! It's no big deal. Honestly."

When her mother made no attempt to defend herself, the pity Fran was feeling faded fast.

"So you were expecting me before you got married? So what? Why all the secrecy? I don't care – you and Daddy got married anyway."

Then she decided to go easy and drop the subject. It was no laughing matter. There was no mistaking the look in her mother's eyes.

Later, downstairs in the kitchen, Brigid made a flippant comment saying that Fran had been two months premature. She said they celebrated her birthday on her due date and it had stuck. It didn't convince Fran in the least. Two months were missing. Lost in time. She'd often heard her Granny Gaffney saying what a chubby baby she'd been at birth. Ten pounds ten ounces, she'd said. A badge of honour to produce a baby that size. Ready to go to school.

Fran told her mother that she wasn't stupid enough to think that a premature baby born at seven months could weigh in at over ten pounds, or anything like it. Brigid went quiet when Fran reminded her that she had overheard her telling her aunt above in Galway that her pelvis had nearly split in two with the size of Fran.

Her mother then refused to engage with her, brushing away Fran's attempts to delve further. Her father wouldn't be home until after eight. She could take it up with him then.

Brigid busied herself at the sink, peeling potatoes, her back turned to Fran who was sitting at the kitchen table.

"Go on outa that, Fran!" she suddenly said, still peeling. "If it didn't matter for eighteen years, why should it bother you now, eh? You have what you were looking for, so send it off. And change your birthday back as well, do what you want, cos it's all water under the bridge at this stage. You're all grown up so start acting like it. Do whatever you see fit. Remember, back in them days people didn't talk about that stuff. They just got on with it."

"Mammy, I've been celebrating my blooming birthday on the wrong day for eighteen years. All those birthday cakes, blowing out all those candles and all on the wrong bloody day. And ye singing 'Happy Birthday' to me. And I like a fool lapping it all up. What the hell were you thinking? I couldn't have cared less."

Fran was not about to give up even if she had her mother wound up. She deserved the truth.

Brigid stopped what she was doing, the potato knife in her hand.

"What odds, Frances? Jesus, what are you making such a bloody racket for? Dragging up dirt from years ago. Your father is your father through marriage, and that's all you need to know. Now give it a rest, Fran!" Brigid banged the knife down and stormed out of the kitchen.

Well, yes, Fran thought, of course he is. Though her parents had married after her birth, her dad was just as much her dad as if they had married before.

Fran adored her father who had never raised his voice to either her or her mother. He wasn't the type of man to respond straight away when tempers were frayed, when people were letting off steam, even if he was opposed to what was being said. He'd say "The world would be a lot better to live in, if people would just shut their mouths and take a breather." Fran's dad was a master at it.

She'd always found it easy to talk to him – it was to her father she went when she needed a calm response. For now she'd let it lie. No point in saying anything to him, while her mother was acting so weird.

When she had him to herself in the kitchen a few days later, Fran broached the subject. Dan was reading the obituaries in the newspaper as he did most evenings after a long day. Brigid had gone to lie down with a migraine.

She sat down opposite him at the kitchen table. "Daddy, put down the paper and talk to me."

Her father gave her a look that told her he knew what was coming. She told him how confused she had been when she'd found her birth certificate in the drawer, explaining that she was now even more confused, given her mother's reaction.

"Tell me, Daddy, why does my birth cert say I was born in January, if my birthday has always been celebrated in March. It just doesn't add up. Was I or was I not this big bouncing baby at birth – or was I seriously premature, like Mammy's trying to make out? I'm not an eejit, Daddy, so please don't take me for one. And I know you can tell me it doesn't concern me, but believe me it does. I just want to be told the truth. That's all. I'm sick and tired of being shooed out of the room and treated like a baby." Feeling brave, she decided to go even further. "Is my name even Gaffney? And, while I'm at it, I've often wondered – how come I'm an only child?"

Fran didn't feel at all comfortable. Whatever her father was going to say would be serious, if the look on his face was anything to go by. His shoulders were raised, his two hands clasped together under his chin. His usual smiley face was nowhere in evidence. His brow tightened causing three deep furrows. He gave the newspaper a shake to close it before putting it down on the table.

"Fran, your mother is in an awful state. It's been a difficult few days. You were bound to find out some day, so it may as well be now."

Fran looked intently at her father, trying to read his face. He took a deep breath before exhaling quickly.

"Your mother laughs most everything off, as you well know, except that this is no laughing matter. She's twisting and turning in the bed alongside me for the last couple of nights. Ranting away in her sleep. What I'm going to tell you is the honest truth and I want you to let it lie with your mother, until she's ready to talk and, if she's not, come back to me. Just accept it. Please, love. No crime has been committed here."

Fran had never seen her father this serious. He reached across the table and placed his hand on hers.

"You're my daughter, Fran. But not by blood."

Fran's heartbeat quickened. She couldn't believe what she was hearing. She looked at her father in horror.

"What? What are you saying, Daddy?"

"You heard me well enough, love. I've no great speech to make, but there I've said it and you have it now. And if you want to upset the house by dwelling on it and raking up the past, then that's up to you. But I beg you not to be tormenting your mother. Or yourself, love."

"But . . ." Fran felt the blood drain from her face as she pulled back her hand and slumped back in the chair. She couldn't believe what she was hearing. "But . . ." Had she even heard him right?

Her father tried to hold her gaze, but she couldn't look him in the eye.

"No buts, Fran. No need for buts. You heard me. I'm your father. But not by blood."

Fran began to cry, huge heavy sobs that she had no control over. "So who ... who is?"

When he spoke his voice was measured. "I don't know, Fran. I never demanded any details. Let me tell you what I know. I've loved

72

your mother since the first minute I laid eyes on her coming out of Gorman's shop. As you know, she came down here to Ballygore when your Uncle Will got her a job hand-stitching aprons from the room she had rented. She couldn't stay with Will at the time because he was staying with an auld bachelor uncle out the road until he became well up enough in the job to get his own place. I met her in the shop below, and from day one we became the best of friends and I was mad about her, but she didn't give me a second look. I guessed her *grá* was elsewhere. And who was I at the time, only a common labourer with a few acres abroad the road? So when she confided in me that she was alone and in trouble, I didn't give it a second thought. I would have done anything for her. My Galway Brigid. She knew no-one in the town outside of Will. Although she has well made up for that since." Dan took a deep breath and offered Fran a weak smile. "No-one in her home-place was any the wiser about her predicament. If Will was clued in, he paid no heed. Don't ask me how she managed to hide it, but she did. She wore a class of a man's tan shop coat and worked away sewing the aprons, until it became too much. And I was there the whole time to get whatever messages she needed and to keep an eye on her. Will would call up to her flat now and then to drop the leather or collect the aprons, but you know what us men are like. He was more bothered about a mug of tea and a bit of soda bread that she'd give him in his hand, than he was in examining her. And if he did suspect, what was he going to say? Will was always a gentleman. You were to remain on in the hospital after you were born, until such time as they found a home for you. But her heart was broken and there was nowhere to go for support back then. You were born on a Sunday and she ran out of the place on the

Wednesday. She was so broken-hearted we had to go back to get you on the Friday morning. And the rest, love . . . is history."

"But why didn't you marry her, Daddy, when you could have?"

"Because she wouldn't have me, Fran – not until the very day that she told me she wanted you home. She said she'd made a big mistake and could do with my help. Up to then she told me she didn't feel that way about me. Your grandparents were kept in the dark – she was in contact with them only by letter, which wasn't unusual back then. And they had enough to be trying to make ends meet on that auld wasteland of a farm. So no-one in our own families knew, or that you weren't mine to begin with, apart from me and her. We got married six weeks after you were born, and introduced you to your Granny Murphy when you were three months old, and your mother swore Will to secrecy. We told them all we'd eloped this long time and told no-one. Not a word more. Times were tough for people back then. Your mother told them all you were born in March and who was I to argue? Will took it that you were mine and he knew I was going no-place. It was a different world back then – people got away with things they wouldn't get away with today." A smile appeared on his face. "And one look from your mother would soon put them back in their places, if anyone spoke out of turn. You're a Gaffney, love, and that's all there is to it. Your mother never offered any details other than what I've told you and I respected her enough not to question her on it. As they used to say long-go 'What you don't know won't trouble you'."

"Daddy, I can't take this in. It sounds like somebody else's life."

"In fairness, love, in all these years it's never been a problem till now. And why would it? The only place she had to face it was on your birth certificate. She doctored one or two of them, no doubt. It never mattered, love."

"*But it does matter!*" she screamed back at him. "*Of course it matters. It matters to me. To me, Daddy! To me! Frances Gaffney. Or Frances whoever the bloody hell I am!*"

She banged her fist on the table, angry with shock, before breaking down in tears.

"And that's just it, Daddy. I'm not a Gaffney after all, am I?" She felt sorry for him but could not stop her reaction. She wanted to hurt him. Hurt the man who wouldn't say boo to a cat.

Her father stood up and walked around to her side of the table. He pulled out the chair beside her and sat down.

"Fran, love, you're my daughter and you'll never be anything other than that. Believe you me, there's plenty of children born into families here in Ballygore, and every other goddamn town and city in Ireland, where there'd be skin and hair flying if the truth were to be known. And, to answer your other question, we weren't blessed with any more children after you were born. You were more than enough for us."

He smiled his usual warm smile before standing up and walking away, leaving Fran alone to take in what he had just told her.

Later that evening, as she lay on her bed in the dark, she came to realise how lucky she had been. Things could have turned out very differently for her. It had been anything but an easy conversation for her father. She would apologise to her mother in the morning and promise to never bring the subject up again. Her father was right. Who knows who anybody is? So the big secret was out. So what? But it became stuck in her head at the same time.

She decided to say nothing more about it for the moment. Her mother and father loved the very bones of her – they had smothered her with love and at times that's exactly how she had felt. Smothered. Her father had worked hard all his life making sure that they had the best of everything. She didn't need to know any more than that. She would concentrate instead in getting into the Civil Service and moving to Dublin.

But it didn't stop her mind from wondering whose blood she had running through her veins. Was it local blood? Was it someone she knew? Someone who looked like her? She certainly didn't look like anyone in her own family.

It played on her mind as the weeks passed. She had grown up with the security of knowing that she belonged to Brigid and Dan Gaffney from Ballygore, but she couldn't stop the stray thoughts from creeping into her head when she least expected. Thoughts she could handle as long as she kept them to herself. And she did keep them to herself, because she knew not to upset her parents.

Slowly Fran's perspective changed. She began to feel a sense of importance. So she wasn't boring old Fran Gaffney anymore. The Fran who had tried her level best to be included in the school yard. The Fran whose very best friend Delia Blake had run off on her, without the common courtesy of saying goodbye.

She had a secret. A story. About her. And she, Fran Gaffney, was playing the leading role. Knowing that everything wasn't quite as it seemed gave her an edge she had been craving. She began watching people, random people who passed her on the street, wondering if they were related to her. Racking her brains to think who might look like her in Ballygore. Who had similar features?

She'd find herself staring at people. Wondering if her birthfather was tall or small, or if he wore glasses or not? Had he ever married?

What would he think of her? Had she grandparents? Had they the same leg complaint as she had?

The notion that she might have sisters and brothers living in town, going to the same school, excited her. Some of the "Populars" even. Or maybe she had family in America or England? Or some other far-flung place which she might get to visit one day? Sometime in the future, she would have to ask her mother who her birthfather was.

She wondered what Delia Blake might have to say about all this.

Chapter 12

MALCOLM

1965

It was on a wild October morning that Malcolm Clarke was carried out through the factory gates towards the waiting hearse. The impressive mahogany coffin was suitably adorned with enough brass to signal the passing of one of the wealthiest men in the town.

The workers downed their tools and gathered in the leafy yard, to pay their respects to the man who had kept the factory going during the worst years. And long since afterwards. They said he had given many a family a dig-out during tough times and never made a song and dance about it. A hard man with a soft heart, they said.

While he had never openly been in favour of employing women in the factory, Malcolm hired enough of them over the years to work from home. Stitchers. And most of them had shown up to pay their respects. Brigid and Fran were amongst the crowd who bowed their heads as the coffin came through the gates.

Malcom had had a heart attack. He must be in his middle to

late seventies, the locals supposed. He wasn't a bad man at all. Having to live with a missus who was fond of the drink and a young one who had lost the run of herself wasn't a bed of roses. It had all taken its toll on the poor man. The antics of the young one had finished him off altogether, they whispered.

Caps in hand, the workers got in line at either side of the factory yard, their heads bowed to say goodbye to the boss-man on his journey to the church. The wind slapped against the legs of the women outside the gate, as they stepped back to let the coffin pass. The sky darkened as if on cue, and a low cloud descended.

The locals, some with sad sombre faces, blessed themselves as the hearse passed by, more were sneaking a look at the lonely figure of a woman sitting on her own in the back of the gleaming black car. Short grey hair, wearing a black two-piece suit. Gloves. She wore a thin lavender scarf around her neck which had been neatly tucked inside the jacket of her suit. She had rarely been seen outside the door in years. Her two sons walked with the crowd behind the hearse on the short journey to the church. Knowing that she hadn't had an easy time of it with the drink, most gave her a pitying look as the car passed. Others nudged each other.

Many of the townspeople had already called to the house to say their final goodbye to Malcolm. To pay their respects. "Sorry for your trouble, missus." And "God be good to him. He's in the best place now." Eunice nodded in response. "God bless her," some of the women said. Others commented on her appearance. "Did you see the costume and it hanging off of her?"

The priests who had arrived to celebrate the funeral Mass sat in a semicircle around the pulpit. Ten in total. The local parish priest and the curate, another down from Galway, a cousin home from the missions, a monsignor back from the States, a Redemptorist from Limerick as well as a Jesuit from Louth – the top man in the order. Each celebrant was robed in the finest of vestments. Priests from the surrounding parishes took part in the Mass. Old and young. One or two asleep. Heads bent. Bodies slumped. Different orders. Grey pants. Black pants, visible under the gold and silver vestments.

Malcom Clarke was given the full rites.

The back of the church was packed with men, caps in hand. Some knelt in the back pew and more didn't. Some stood up along the sides behind the marble pillars, and some waited outside the front door of the church after flicking the holy water back at themselves from the font inside the front door. Coughing and spluttering. Big funeral.

Headscarved women were seated towards the middle of the church. Watching. Plastic rainhats on some. Heads together, entering the church reverently. God bless us. Dipping their hands in the holy water font in front of Our Lady's statue, making the sign of the cross. Shaking the rain off their umbrellas before leaving them to drip in the corner. Carrying shopping baskets with purses inside. Prayer books. Women who had stopped in on their way down the town for the messages. And no need to ask why so many had turned up for Malcolm Clarke's funeral.

The Clarke boys knelt in the top pew to the right-hand side alongside their mother. Arthur, the older of the two boys, had his left arm under his mother's, supporting her. Dermot the middle son knelt close by her other side.

The front seats to the left-hand side and three rows back were full of well-dressed people. Men and women. No-one knew who they were but they supposed it was the sister in Dublin and the brother in Mayo. Or her crowd. Men in well-cut suits and overcoats. Women in fine wool coats, wearing hats. And nuns in black habits saying the rosary.

And not a sign of the daughter, Ramona.

And Gretta Cummins' bicycle parked at the side of the house all those years and not a sign of her at the funeral.

The Clarke brothers didn't stay around the graveyard for long after their father was laid to rest. They linked their mother towards the waiting car. Straight back to the house. Eunice and her boys and a few more of the black-coated, black-gloved strangers. And the religious along with them.

There had been no mention of refreshments offered from the pulpit and all the money they had. Not a shilling left in behind the counter of Stapleton's pub which most of the factory workers frequented. The locals got the message.

In the week that followed, the factory was the talk of the town. People stopped each other on the street to enquire.

"Any news?"

"Not a word."

In Stapleton's pub on the Mill Road and every other public-house in the town, the factory was top of the conversation agenda. Many of the workers had a slate going in Stapleton's. The word amongst the customers standing at the counter was that the factory would be up and running in no time. No point in being negative about the whole thing when there were pints of porter to be paid for. And Johanna Stapleton, the landlady, perched on her high stool inside the bar, taking it all in.

No one knew what was going to happen to the factory. An emergency meeting was called. Not many were willing to keep the place going without some certainty that their wages would be paid at the end of the week. Will Murphy and Alice Coyne and a few more did what they could out of respect for old times. People made clicking noises with their tongues as they passed the yellow sign with the blue writing attached to the wall outside, beside the gates – now secured with a heavy metal padlock – saying the boot factory was shut.

As far as many were concerned the Clarke boys, men now, were getting on with their own lives in Dublin. No one seemed to know much about the girl. Ramona. Whether she was dead or alive. She hadn't been mentioned at the funeral, apart from those who muttered their suspicions between themselves. That she had opted out of university in Dublin and taken off to some hippie place with some fella in sandals that she met in a park in Dublin.

People had more to be concerned about than to be wondering why the Clarkes' youngest hadn't turned up at her father's funeral. She must be twenty years of age or thereabouts, a grown woman, and 'twasn't as if she'd be in the running when it came to reopening the factory.

Would there be jobs at all? Would the place shut down and fall asunder? A crumbling ruin. A hundred and eighty workers facing unemployment. And the home-stitchers without a wage packet coming in.

Will had been at the factory for over twenty years at the time of Malcom's death. He was chosen by the workers to be the best man to make the call to Dublin to find out what the hell was going on. Whether he liked it or not.

There was little point in Will calling to Malcolm's widow, Eunice, for an update on the factory – everyone knew that she would be the last to know. If she were sober enough to know what was going on around her. Making contact with Gretta the housekeeper was out of the question. She was as odd as two left shoes. She had cycled through the factory gates most days of the week, parking her bike against the wall for all those years, barely offering the time of day. An ignorant bitch, they said. Or a bit of an odd ball. Maybe a bit of both. And people had pride.

Will got it into his head to wait for a while to call Arthur Clarke from the office phone. Until things had settled down. Arthur had winked at him above at the church, holding his hand for longer than was necessary, eyeballing him, nodding his head slowly. A wink and a nod. A sign. Alice reckoned he must have imagined it. The man was probably just acknowledging him.

Will made the call to Arthur Clarke three weeks to the day his father was buried.

To his surprise, Arthur announced that, yes, he had tried to get his attention in the church, that he would come down to Ballygore that same weekend to meet with him. That he had had a chat with his mother, seeing as his father had died without making a will. The factory was in her name. He said he tried to convince her to go back to Dublin with him, but he was coming up against a brick wall. He said she was still a bit shaky on her feet. That Gretta was staying with her most nights, but she had her own mother to consider at home. He said that his wife Lucy was expecting their second child any day now, so the timing wasn't great but he'd manage.

He told Will he'd been thinking about the factory a lot, now that the old goat was gone. "I'll be down on Saturday so, Will.

Many thanks for the call. Keep the place running in the meantime as much as you can. There'll be no jobs lost, not if I've anything to do with it. But I'll need you there by my side, Will."

When Will repeated part of the conversation to Alice, she said he must have been hearing things. Using that kind of language about his own father. *An old goat!* Such irreverence and downright disrespect. Will said he had heard him alright, but refrained from adding the rest of the conversation which he knew Alice would not appreciate. Man talk.

Arthur had the factory up and running three weeks after meeting with Will. He had a maturity about him when it came to planning ahead. Resigning from his managerial position in the jam factory in Dublin had been easier than he'd thought. Too easy, he had admitted to Will. He had expected some level of resistance from the company, but it hadn't come. Three weeks' notice and a bruised ego and he was gone. But the good news was that his mother had given him the go-ahead to run the place.

Arthur stayed in Ballygore during the week, taking the train back to Dublin at the weekends. There was no shifting his mother, he told Will – now that she had the place to herself she wouldn't budge. Gretta was worth her weight in gold, he said. He'd given his mother an ultimatum. Move to Dublin with himself and Lucy for the time being, or she'd better start thinking about nursing homes. He'd laughed when he said it, but wasn't laughing when he told Will the response she had given him. She told him to go to blazes, that she was going nowhere. She had Gretta to sort out a cold plate for her and that's all she needed. She didn't need minding. Arthur said he'd no choice but to move his family down to Ballygore in the end. He couldn't run the factory from Dublin.

News of his arrival back in town soon got around. Arthur had arrived back in Ballygore just before Christmas, driving his father's silver Triumph, a fat Cuban cigar that he found in the glove compartment sticking out of the side of his mouth – accompanied by his wife Lucy who looked as if she were about to deliver her child there on the street. A small boy got out of the back of the car. All dressed up in a coat and hat. The locals talked about little else for a week. Having the factory house occupied by the younger Clarkes was a strange sight for the workers, who had got used to the more sombre habits of Malcolm and Eunice.

Arthur Clarke changed the way the boot factory was run from day one. Having spent his school holidays working there, he knew his way around. His managerial experience in Dublin stood to him.

Will was impressed with just how much he did know as he listened to his new boss's progressive ideas. He admired his vision for change, his plan to move the factory along with the times. He had a five-year plan. Something he said he had churning around in the back of his head for years. Once the old fella had retired.

He planned to double the workforce over the first three years, giving the town of Ballygore a much-needed lift, providing more employment within the local community.

Arthur said they needed women in the factory. Malcolm had refused to hire women outside of those who worked from home. He had been of the mind that women were best suited at home rearing their children, while the men earned a living for their families.

Within the first month, Arthur had formed a management team with himself at the helm, which they all thought was a bit of a joke. Mightier than thou. But he insisted he wanted to incur a team spirit starting from the top down. So Arthur took up the position of general manager. The management team after that consisted of Will the most senior craftsman and four others, two foremen and two supervisors who knew a lot more about the business of boot-making than Arthur himself did. The running of the office was left to Alice.

Arthur confided in Will that he had always loved being around the factory as a boy. It had always been his ambition to one day take it over, whereas his younger brother Dermot had no interest in the place. He said that Ramona, his sister, couldn't be contacted in time for their father's funeral, as she was off-grid – living on a farm in Israel, that she'd get in touch in her own time. No more was said.

He disclosed to Will that his father had blocked him along the way when he wanted no more than to be shown the ropes in the family business, after qualifying with a management degree from university. His father told him he didn't have what it took to run the factory, that he wasn't nearly experienced enough. That his balls hadn't dropped yet and when they did to let him know and he'd find something for him. Malcolm, in his son's mind, had been a hard, single-minded man.

Arthur had been preparing for the day when he would take over the factory. That day had come.

Within months Arthur's plan was taking shape. The first of the women to walk through the factory gates created a stir amongst those who said that women had no place in a male-dominated workplace. Apart from Alice.

Arthur told them they'd better get used to it. He called a meeting where he expressed his intention to expand production towards more cost-effective imported synthetic footwear, alongside the manufacture of quality leather boots, which his father had insisted were the soul of the factory.

With the expansion into plastic-coated patent leather, Arthur's vision was on the way to fruition. The women were to work initially in the finishing section, gluing the latest nylon insoles into the finished footwear, packing the products for retail, until they were skilled enough to take up their soon-to-be-designated positions. Malcolm had refused to consider using glue as an alternative to hand-stitching his product using fine waxed thread.

The introduction of a new modern twenty-station conveyor belt would speed up production. Two machines were bought in from a factory in Cork. Machines that formed the soles, before moulding them directly onto the uppers. Previously they had to be made separately, far more time consuming and expensive to manufacture. The new machines would pay for themselves in no time.

Arthur liked to introduce Will as his right-hand man, particularly in a meeting where he needed back-up. Will nodded – but knew his place. Wearing the new factory coats designed for them by Arthur's wife Lucy, who had taken to dropping into the factory with the pram, unheard of in Malcolm's time.

Girlfriends, wives, sisters, mothers, daughters were hired, changing the dynamics of the old factory. Within that first year Arthur had expanded the business beyond all expectations. The atmosphere changed.

People liked Arthur, remarking that he was a lot like his father, but unlike his father he had the foresight to move forward with the times. Malcolm, they said, had become stagnated and set in his ways in the finish. Arthur had changed all that.

Chapter 13

FRAN

The Journey

By the following spring, Fran was more than ready to move on. She had sat the Civil Service exam in Limerick and was waiting to hear. No matter how many times her mother plagued her about staying at home, she needed to go. She went to the church, where she lit as many candles as there was room for on the stand in front of St. Anthony. Light now and pay later. She put an I.O.U. in the slot, written on the back of a holy picture she found tacked to the kneeler, promising to settle her dues. She remembered Delia telling her that's what she used to do. Pray first and pay later. Nothing for nothing.

Nineteen-year-old Fran would pray her way out of Ballygore, doing as many novenas as she could handle in the meantime. And once she got her dream job in Dublin, she'd return to the candle stand to put five shillings in the tin box to cover her debt, along with a few bob to cover Delia's.

When she got word to say that she was high up on the national list for Civil Service entrants, she prayed that bit harder, and two weeks later she got a letter to say she had landed the job. The prayers had worked and it had to have been St. Anthony, because she had been at the church most days kneeling at the foot of his statue.

She was going. She was moving to Dublin. She got her start date for the Department of Justice.

Fran was beyond terrified once it hit her. Her story was about to begin and she wondered would she feel homesick. She was excited and terrified at the same time, but she knew it was time for her to leave home and become independent.

Her mother cried for a whole week before she was due to leave Ballygore. Begging Fran to change her mind, telling her that she'd be lost without her. That she was her whole life. Her whole world. She said she would never have seen this day coming in a million years. She had always expected that Fran would remain on in Ballygore and get a job in the boot-factory office which would have been big in itself. She said she couldn't believe that her only child was off to the city. Off to join the rat race above in Dublin.

But the fog had cleared in Fran's head and no matter how upset her mother was, there would be no going back. She had her mind made up. She had no intention of getting a nice job in the boot factory.

The thought of walking down the street with the factory workers every morning for the rest of her days and home again in the evening made her feel weak. Coming home to her mother for her breaks at lunchtime. And she looking for news. Back in time for her tea, ready at six on the dot. Her father's favourite, liver and onions. She wouldn't have to do a tap in the house as long as her mother was around – as it was, she could do little more than make toast and clumpy porridge which stuck to the saucepan most times. And that was about to change.

Her father had put his arms around his wife in an attempt to console her. The uncomfortable conversation of the months before had taken its toll.

"Brigid, you've been looking after our girl all these years. It's her turn now. She'll be fine and you'll be fine. Just the two of us on our own for the first time ever. We can take a trip away or you can get yourself a little job if you like, and you needn't bother if you don't feel up to it."

Fran had seen the look of indignation on her mother's face at the very mention of her looking for a job.

"I'll do no such thing, Dan Gaffney, is it mad you've gone? No such thing at this hour of my life. I'm heading for forty years of age, for Christ's sake!"

"Brigid, she'll only be up the road in Dublin and she'll be back home at the weekends with the bag of washing for you. Won't you, Fran?"

"Of course I will. I'll be back every Friday on the bus."

Her mother seemed to accept it after that. The awkwardness between them faded in the days leading up to her departure.

Brigid hugged Fran at the bus stop after handing her the blue weekend case she had bought for her. She would be home again on the bus at the weekend. No need to be taking a suitcase full of stuff until she got settled in. All in good time.

Brigid followed Fran onto the bus.

"Mind yourself up there now, peteen."

Fran was mortified.

Her mother ignored the driver who told her he was taking off in two minutes, with or without her on board.

Brigid hugged Fran one more time and made her way towards the front of the bus, stopping to talk to a woman a few rows from where Fran was sitting.

Fran could hear her mother clearly.

"Excuse me? Are you going the whole way to Dublin? Do you see my daughter a few seats back there . . . in the light-blue coat?" Her mother began pointing back at her.

Fran turned her head in towards the window. Mortified.

"I wonder would you be so kind as to keep an eye out for her. She wouldn't be used to travelling so far on her own."

Fran had heard enough. Taking out a book she had bought for the trip, she pretended to be engrossed in it as the bus headed for the main road. She was getting out of Ballygore – she would stand on her own two feet at last. And on her head if she felt like it. Her father had arranged digs for her in Ranelagh.

Her Uncle Will had made her an extra pair of shoes, saying that once she got settled in Dublin the choice would be hers. He gave her the name of a shoemaker in the city centre, warning her to keep in touch with the hospital for check-ups.

Independence.

She was looking forward to her future in the city where she would celebrate her next birthday. And on the very day she had been born. The thirteenth of January. She was starting out in the job on six months' probation, after which time she would be made permanent. And if she met a fella up there in the meantime, well and good.

When the bus reached the quays in Dublin, Fran breathed a sigh of relief. She had been in Dublin many times over the years at hospital appointments, the city wasn't unfamiliar to her – but she was nervous all the same. She would get off the bus just after the Halfpenny Bridge and walk down the quays to get the bus that would take her to Ranelagh. She had the bus routes written on a piece of paper in her handbag. The 62 or was it 11? Or did both buses take the route? Opening the clasp of her bag to check, she took out the navy leather gloves her Uncle Will had given her as a gift from himself and Alice. Soft as butter, her mother had said.

When the driver stopped the bus and announced "O'Connell Bridge!" Fran panicked. Should she have got off sooner? Nervous at the thought of finding the right bus to take her to Ranelagh, her mind was preoccupied.

Closing her handbag, she quickly put on her gloves and lifted her weekend case off the floor. She stood up and walked up the aisle towards the door, following the other passengers who were getting off at the same stop. Fran did her best to appear confident. She stood at the top of the bus, turning sideways to thank the driver, allowing the passengers ahead of her to get off the bus. There were people behind her. Keep moving.

Just as she stepped down off the first step she felt unsteady. Jittery. Carrying her weekend case over her left arm, she clutched her handbag in the same hand as she stepped onto the lower step. She felt for the rail with her other hand. Immediately Fran knew what was coming. Her ankle was going from under her.

She put her foot straight into a puddle. Into a dirty oily pothole. She felt her ankle tear against rough concrete, causing it to twist back underneath her. Her handbag fell from her hand as her foot became wedged beneath the concrete. The bus-driver jumped off his seat to catch her.

Too late, she went down.

Then she heard it. *Snap!*

Mortified, she tried to get up. The searing pain prevented her from moving. One leg was stretched out in front of her – it was the leg underneath her that was causing the intense pain. She heard someone saying, "Don't move her!" so she sat where she was, in the puddle, resting her elbow on the bottom step of the bus while the passengers behind her did their best to squeeze past.

When she tried to get up again, the pain shot through her. Her foot was wedged in underneath the stony concrete.

The driver made his way off the bus past her, the sweat dripping down his forehead. He was holding her new box handbag on his arm. Crying, she had no option but stay where she was, while people gathered to have a look at the girl sitting in the oily puddle in the middle of O'Connell Street. Her weekend case beside her was splattered with dirt. She noticed blood slowly swirling with the shiny blue oil in the puddle. A passing garda told the driver to stay put, in case he was needed as a witness. Someone pointed to the warning sign which had been turned backwards. *Pothole.*

Fran was taken by ambulance to the Mater Hospital, where she was taken straight to theatre. Later, once they had assessed the damage, they told her that her ankle was badly broken. Messy. An open fracture. Her muscle tissue was exposed, where it had been torn by the layered jagged edges of the asphalt concrete, which had ripped across her ankle, crushing the bone. Fragmented. This was far more complicated than a simple fracture. The bone would have to be pieced together. Re-aligned. A plate, metal screws inserted. She would remain in traction for weeks, after which she would need a long time to recuperate, given the fact that her other leg was already compromised.

Her parents arrived at the hospital the very next day. A nun at the hospital had called the convent in Ballygore to get a message to them.

The pained look on her mother's face when she saw Fran lying in the bed with her leg raised in traction, would stay with Fran forever. It would be a slow process, they told her parents. Most of what they said from then on went over her head. All Fran could think about was the fact that her dream of a new start in the city had turned sour.

So she left it to her parents to figure out.

Her father said, "Now, now, it could have been a hell of a lot worse. We'll get through it, love."

She was far too upset to accept what had happened. There would be no first day in the Civil Service in Dublin Castle for her. No bus ride out to the digs in Ranelagh. No need to present the landlady with the two small China ornaments for her mantelpiece that her mother had sent up. No need to sweeten the landlady with the packet of loose tea she herself had bought in the American store. There would be no need for her to be nervous on her first day at work, and no sense of achievement and pride that she had finally taken the first step to leave home.

She could hear the medics talking around her.

"Might be an interesting case study for the students."

"Nurse, we need to start working on a care plan."

Fran lay in the bed in traction as the doctors came in and out, discussing her case just as they had done since she was a child. Over her head. Words. More words. Snippets of conversations to be remembered.

A continuous gait analysis would be carried out to ensure the best outcome. Posture retraining would be of the utmost importance in the future. They were worried about her hips. Fran could not take it all in, especially when they mentioned the long stretch in the rehabilitation hospital in Dublin after months of being confined to bed in traction. She would be sent back to the hospital in Ballygore, before being sent home to be looked after by her mother.

No birthday candles to be blown out at the digs in January. And definitely no dues to be paid back to St. Anthony. Because he owed her big-time.

Chapter 14

FRAN

Boomerang

Eight months later, Fran arrived back in Ballygore having been discharged by the rehabilitation team in Dublin. They had done all they could for her. She had worked hard during her time there. She'd miss the camaraderie she had shared with some of the patients and staff, but she'd keep in touch.

She was brought back by ambulance to recuperate in St. Mary's Hospital, before being allowed home to the care of her mother to convalesce. She was to spent at least six months vigorously exercising, following the outreach programme adapted especially for her, after which she would return to the hospital in Dublin for a full review.

Once home she would attend the local hospital for physiotherapy. The district nurse would call to her at home.

Fran struggled to come to terms with it all. The one move she had made towards independence had failed her.

The day she was brought home in the ambulance she wanted to grab hold of the driver as he helped her into the wheelchair to be wheeled past her waiting parents through the front door. Her father coughed onto the back of his hand. Her mother's head was tilted to one side, her eyes wide open and pinned on Fran like a contented bird who eyed her young in the nest. Safe in knowing that the fledging was unable to fly. Unable to leave.

Fran wanted to cry out. The tears gathered in her eyes. She smiled instead. The neighbours were standing at their own front doors, arms folded, looking up and down the road. Watching. Waving. The fussing had begun.

Once Fran was settled in an armchair, the wheelchair was folded over. It would be kept under the stairs when not in use.

There was no mention of the good pensionable job she'd had to forsake in the Civil Service. No mention that she wouldn't be moving back to Dublin any time soon. No mention that Uncle Will's fancy new shoes may have been a factor when she was stepping down off the bus. And no mention of the fact that her mother had her life back in Ballygore already mapped out for her. A job in the office in the boot factory.

"All in good time, loveen. Mind you, we'll have a bit of legwork to be doing up and down to Thornton the solicitor in the meantime. I've been up to see him already, to have a quick word, but he says seeing you're over the eighteen, he'd better see you himself. The government or the council or whoever else is responsible better cough up for this one. Stepping off that bus straight into a bloody pothole and it well camouflaged, full of dirty auld oil. By the time that lad is finished with them, they'll know all about it."

Fran was too overcome to contradict her mother. So she went along with it. She made a vow to herself that she would do whatever it took to get back on her feet and straight out of Ballygore.

"He's completely on your side, you know. Thornton. Your whole life ruined and all because them buckos up in Dublin couldn't be bothered filling in their bloody potholes. Tell her, Dan! Tell her!"

Fran's father shook his head from side to side. "Leave me out of it now, Brigid – you're well able to do the organising of all this between yourself and Thornton."

Fran recognised the look of annoyance on her father's face. He wanted nothing to do with the insurance claim. Dirty money, he called it. Her mother was of a completely different mind.

"Well, there's the loss of her good job to consider. Life-changing. And the fact that she had to come home to be minded full-time, never mind the year and a half that was stolen from her life. All of our lives. Also there's the fact that I was planning on looking for a job myself. Now that's all gone up in smoke too, so there's that to consider also. Then there's the fact that 'twas the good leg that got injured. And never mind the costs involved with all the traipsing back and forth to the hospital. And what, may I ask, do you think companies are paying all that money in insurance for, if not for something like this?"

Fran spent a full year at home convalescing. Her mother said it was best in the long run to take her time. She said that the longer Fran was seen to be at home recuperating, the better for the claim. She said Thornton hadn't said as much, but she knew what he meant the way he had looked at her when she happened to mention it to him. Stalling for time.

"Thornton reckons we'll get in the region of five thousand. A sum not to be sniffed at."

Fran let her mother focus on the claim, while she tried to focus on the future. Her future. A future with or without the compensation. She didn't care about the money. She wanted to explore a future far away from Ballygore.

Thornton had said it might take a few years to be sorted. Fran should sign on the dole in the meantime. When she applied, they told her she wasn't eligible because she was living at home. They said to come back in ten weeks.

"We're in no hurry, pet, to settle. Maura Kiely up the road told me that when her man fell and cracked his head wide open on the water pump, they settled on the steps of the courtroom, rather than be questioned on the stand like criminals."

"I'd say 'twasn't the first time that bucko put in a claim. He's notorious for it," added her father.

"It was all a sham, and the Holy Bible in her hand and Maura lying to bate the band. They said he was as drunk as a bloody skunk the same night, in behind the pump doing his business, when he slipped and fell on the moss. There's no good at all to come from all them lies and trickery. We'll take the stand and tell the truth about all we've been through."

Finally over the shock of the accident, Fran took a long hard look at herself. She had been lucky. Standing in front of the full-length mirror at the back of her bedroom door, she made a list.

Starting with her hair, she wrote down everything she'd like to change about herself, no matter how insignificant or out of the ordinary it sounded. Then she broke the list down in two halves to everything she could change and what she couldn't change.

She had two choices. Feel sorry for herself and let her mother plan out her life for her. Or she could take control of herself and do it her own way. She choose the latter.

When her mother saw the improvement in Fran, she began hinting that she should put her name down for the time being at the boot factory.

No.

Brigid said that the factory owed them and when she enquired as to why, her mother said that only for her Uncle Will the place would be on its knees. That he alone had had made the factory a success, since the old fella Malcolm had died.

"So hold your head up in the air and leave it to Will to sort out. That Arthur lad wouldn't have the thriving business he has today, if it weren't for our Will and the boys. Fran, love, you may as well put your name down. I know how much you wanted to be in Dublin and that might well happen in its own good time. With all the money we spent up and down to see you and everything else besides, we could do with the extra few bob coming in until the claim comes through, and in the meantime we have that Credit Union loan to be paying back. Thank Jesus your father is earning. I'd hate if he had to put the few acres up for sale. Would you not think about applying to the factory? It'll be just for the time being, mind."

Fran grew tired of listening to her mother's constant whining about her applying for a job at the factory. She lost her patience. Over breakfast when Brigid had once more broached the subject. Fran dropped the spoon into the bowl, causing the porridge to splurt out onto the tablecloth.

"Mam, I haven't a notion of looking for work at the factory. Will you stop! Just imagine what they'd be saying?" Fran's voice became animated. "Poor Fran Gaffney and the notions on her. Look where they got her!" She glared at her mother. "You'll never understand what it was like for me growing up, Mother. All I ever wanted was to be one of the gang. One of the Populars . . . ah, never mind. The truth is that I struggled the whole way through primary school. Until I met Delia." Fran felt the tears build up in her eyes as her voice weakened. "I need to live my own bloody life."

Her mother wasn't hearing her. She tossed a dishcloth across the table. "Wipe that up. 'Twas good enough for me when I came down from Galway during the hard years and I ended up working from the bedsit on Peter Street. Old Malcolm only let two women inside the door of the factory in them days. One to scrub the floors and our very own Alice to keep his books.

"*Blah!*"

"Don't be so cheeky, Frances. All your father and myself have ever done is look out for you. They weren't laughing around the town when you landed the good job in the Civil Service. Jealous is all they are."

Brigid came around the table to put her arm around her daughter. Bending over Fran, she lowered her voice.

"And while you're making your mind up, I'll have a chat with your Uncle Will to see if he can't pull a few strings. Didn't I hear him say only the other day that his Alice was nearly killed with all the work she has to do, since the new man took over? So maybe, Fran, you're just what they need there, in the office."

"His Alice? Mam, will you give over and listen to yourself." Fran pushed her mother's arm away from her shoulders. "Alice Coyne is no more his Alice than mine. They're friends is all. Just because they go out together on a Sunday evening doesn't mean he owns her. Anyway she's as old as the hills, for God's sake!"

"*Hmm* . . . he must be going out with her for the bones of fifteen years or thereabouts and –"

"And you don't know what he sees in her! I can read you like a book."

"That's not true, Fran. I was just about to say there's no sign of a ring."

"Did it ever dawn on you that they may not want to get married?"

Brigid grabbed the dishcloth off the table and backed away towards the kitchen sink, talking back at Fran. "Every woman wants to get married, Fran. Alice is alright, you know. Not much older than me, I'd say. I remember her when I started the aprons – she was a right clever clogs when it came to totting up what was owing to me. But I'll give her her due, she gave me the work right through and never for one moment mentioned –"

"That's our Alice, Mother . . . boring."

Wiping her hands on her apron front, Brigid took a deep breath through her nose before sitting herself down across the table from Fran.

"Ah, they're a good match all the same and you'll see – they'll surprise us all one of these days. She might even ask you to be her bridesmaid, Fran. Although I'd say Will better get a head-start on her wedding shoes. Did you ever see the feet on her, they're like –"

"Mother, stop it! That's not nice and I'm certainly no one to talk about feet, now am I? And there you go, laughing it off again. And, by the way, I wouldn't be caught dead standing beside Alice Coyne above at the altar. I'm half afraid of her as it is, and I was never one for the limelight, as you well know. I'm going to concentrate on me for a while, so you can march up the aisle with them yourself. Cos by the time they do marry, if they do, I haven't a notion of being around, so you better get used to it. And at the rate they're going, yourself and Daddy won't be either."

Brigid slapped the tablecloth with both hands before standing up.

"I don't know what's got into you lately, Frances. There's no need to be so bloody . . . impertinent. For your information, there's nowhere like Ballygore, but you won't realise that till you've up and left. So off you go with your wild notions. We'll be here waiting for you when you come back down from your high horse."

Fran knew she had gone overboard but she was fed up of trying to please people. Time to please herself.

"Mammy, sit down. Please."

Her mother did as she was asked. Sighing.

"For as long as I can remember, Mammy, I've been prodded and poked at by doctors who half the time didn't even acknowledge me. Talking over my head as if I was a dummy. As if I wasn't there. Stretching my leg out and me crying with the pain. Having me lie on this table and on that table with the palms of their hands at my feet. Moving my hips this way and every other way, and me standing on the wooden blocks. And all the bloody X-rays. And people staring at me all the time. And no one thought to ask if I minded having students wearing white coats that were miles too big for them standing there, watching me, taking notes and yawning at the same time. As if I were a thing. Being constantly reminded that I was . . . I don't know what. And even when I wasn't being reminded of it with every step I took, I felt it on the inside."

"Give it a rest, there's an awful lot of people out there with real problems." Brigid rolled her eyes.

But Fran hadn't finished. She had her mother to herself – she wasn't about to let her off that easy.

"And me out in the yard at school doing my best to keep up when I was small. But I couldn't, could I? I couldn't run like they could. And God knows I tried. I couldn't skip with the lads on the road, or ride a bike until Will made the shoes for me and even after that I was half afraid to get up on it in case I fell off. I had to go through the embarrassment of falling off so many times. Oh, I remember it all. Only for Delia, I'd have been miserable altogether. If I knew where she was, I'd contact her right now. She would understand."

"Fran, that's enough of it. Delia Blake, my arse! You were like her bloody shadow back then and where did that get you? And you had a lot more than some people I know around the town."

"Mammy!" Fran was fast losing patience with her mother. "Are you listening to me at all? Do you ever listen? I'm not talking about anyone else right now and I'm not feeling in the least bit sorry for myself. What I'm trying to do is explain to you how I feel. Me. Just me."

Fran could see that her mother was tiring of the conversation.

Brigid got up abruptly and went back over to the sink. She began wiping the dishes that sat on the draining board.

"You've already dried them, Mother," Fran said.

Slamming the dishcloth down, Brigid turned around to face Fran.

"That's enough, I said. You've had the all clear from the hospital, so that's all that matters. It'll all work out in the end. All part of God's plan. All I'm asking is that you have a think about taking a job in the bloody factory and leave the rest to me."

"The all clear, my backside, Mother. That's just it. I'll never have the all clear, will I?"

"Oh, sweet Jesus, will you give over, Frances? I don't know what's got into you lately. Jesus! Me – me – me!"

"*Me* is correct, Mother, about time I concentrated on *me*. Me with the short blooming step, me with the other one held together with bolts and screws. Or pins or plates or whatever the bloody hell they call them! And they're saying that my hips will give me trouble in years to come. But I'll be damned if I'm going to hang around Ballygore for the rest of my days!"

Her mother cleared her throat and stormed out of the room.

Fran had learned a lot during the past year. It wouldn't be quick or easy, but her mind was made up. She would be leaving Ballygore as soon as the claim came through. In the meantime, she would make sure that she was in the best shape possible.

Over the coming months Fran worked harder than ever before, doing the exercises given to her by the physiotherapist, putting in more time and effort, sticking rigidly to the plan she had drawn up for herself. She was walking steadier than ever, and she had never felt better. Balance was what it was all about.

That's what the physiotherapist had said and that's what it said in the fashion magazines, so Fran worked on her balance. Walk tall and straight and walk some more. And Will had been right. The leather lift he had made for the inside of her shoe had made a huge difference.

"Lass, you know, I think for some reason your accident and all the work you've put in might just have evened things out for you. But don't take my word for it until you go back to the experts to be measured. I'm a shoemaker, not a medic."

Her mother complimented the change in her. Fran was upbeat and in great form. Brigid did say that she was a bit concerned at the same time, after hearing what Thornton had to say, that if the judge clapped eyes on Fran in the courtroom, he'd be hard pressed to believe she'd ever been as bad as they were making her out to be.

Thornton advised that they accept the offer that had been made outside of court, for fear the judge would say 'twas surely a scam and they could well end up paying the costs. The solicitor was full of compliments at the transformation in Fran.

"Jesus, I never thought I'd see the day!" Brigid said. "You look like a model no less. The difference the blonde hair makes, and the centre part suits you. And the slim hips on you. Just keep an eye when you're out and about though. Like Thornton said, we wouldn't want them to think you were faking the claim and end up being done for fraud."

Her father shook his newspaper and clicked his tongue. He still insisted he wanted no part of it.

Fran hadn't bothered to mention that she was only waiting for the claim to be settled before taking off again. She felt they'd all know soon enough once the time came.

Will had been right in what he said. All the work she had put in had been worth it. The orthopaedic consultant had given her the best news.

"It's not outside the bounds of probability," he said. "It does happen. Your leg has healed in a shortened position, due to the fact that your fibula had more than the one fracture, with the muscle tissue being exposed – so it has all worked in our favour. "

He said she'd always need to keep an eye, That she wasn't out of the woods but, from what he could see, the accident and intervention along with the work she had put in had evened things out. They'd see her again but, from what they could see, all she needed for now was to continue to wear the slight lift inside her shoe and they'd see her in six months. No more thick soles. Fran couldn't have been happier.

Chapter 15

DELIA BLAKE

1966

Delia Blake arrived back in Ballygore on a bright May evening. She got into the back of a waiting hackney car from outside the station, asking to be taken to the nearest guesthouse. The driver took her straight to Philly Manson's.

People on the street turned to look at her as she got out of the cab – she didn't mind in the least.

Once inside, the men were eyeing her up and down – there was hardly a woman that she could see. It had been five years since she'd left for London and from what she had seen so far, not a lot had changed.

Most of them wouldn't recognise her as a local girl, and if they did it certainly didn't register on their faces. She thought she recognised a few from back then, but so much time had passed she couldn't be sure and she wasn't of the mind to be drawing them on her.

When she received the note from her aunt saying her mother was in the hospital, that she might only have days left in her, her heart wanted to drop everything and rush home. To say goodbye. But her head wouldn't let her. She didn't reply to the note. Her aunt knew how to contact her. Delia had trusted her with her address two years before on a Christmas card, knowing that she would never divulge where she was, because she had fallen out with her family years before. Bad blood. When Delia got word from her to say that her mother had passed, she felt she had no other choice but to return home. To face him. Her brother couldn't make it back. He had left his contact details for Delia to get in touch.

Delia had no intention of displaying her vulnerability. She dressed as Delta would have dressed. But the child inside of her was screaming to be released. Pining. Scraping at her heart, hoping for recognition. Accountability. The child with the plaits in her hair who had been preyed upon. By him. By the bastard man who was ten steps ahead of them all. The bastard man wearing a Pioneer pin in the lapel of his coat – who walked up to Mass of a Sunday flanked by his wife. The bastard man who had taken advantage of a child for his own sexual gratification. The bastard man who destroyed her innocent life, then hid behind her, and made out 'twas all her doing.

But the child had grown up and here she was. Her lips painted a scarlet red, bright blue eyeshadow painted across her eyelids. Heavy black kohl pencil. She wore Delta's best wig. She would answer to no-one. The brazen huzzy who had run away five years before without as much as a goodbye, leaving her poor mother distraught and never as much as a Christmas card, was back in Ballygore. She had thought about it often enough. Thought about what they'd say about her. What he would have to say. What she would say to him. How she would ignore the quickening heartbeats and the trembling of her body as he approached her.

Philly Manson stood at the end of the bar, gaping at her. Delia waited for no man. When he wasn't quick enough to respond to the click of her fingers, she called out in her best London accent.

"What about some service here, if you please?"

Philly responded immediately. "I'll be with you in a minute."

When he approached, he looked her up and down. She knew by the look on his face that he didn't know what to make of her. Delia was used to men and their egos.

"I'd like a room for two nights. Delia Blake is the name. If you wouldn't mind letting the boss man know. I'll have a vodka and orange while you're here."

She walked off to find a seat, leaving Philly Manson staring after her.

"I'll meet you outside at the desk!" he called after her.

But she sat down and waited for her drink to be brought to her.

When she finished her drink, she stood up and headed for the door. All eyes were on her. She walked past the men drinking at the corner end of the bar, beckoning over at Philly. She heard the men laugh at whatever Philly had said as he lifted the counter to follow her out to the foyer to sign her in.

"Lads, are those cameras in your pockets? Go on, take a picture, that'll make it last longer for ye!" Leaving a lingering trail of perfume behind her, Delia left the lounge.

Philly signed her in. She'd pay later. She wondered if Franny was still around. It had been five years. She went up to her room and never closed an eye. She had a long day ahead of her. The day of her mother's funeral.

She didn't know what the locals had been told about her reasons for running away before she had turned sixteen. And she cared less. They wouldn't have been told the truth. Her mother would have covered up for him and told them all sorts. She had called her a whelp and a liar and a common tramp. And Gary so good to them.

It had started off slowly. So slowly that there was nothing in particular that she could point to. No beginning and no warning and no right time to shout: *STOP!* She imagined she must have been eight when he first started giving her the money, telling her 'twas their secret, a shilling at first and a half crown one time after that, and she wasn't to say a word to her mother and she didn't, because she wanted the money for herself and her mother had ever only given her pennies. Or halfpennies and they were no good. So every now and again he called her out to the front room and handed her a coin, pointing his index finger to his face, and she'd give him a kiss on the cheek and he would turn his face so fast it would land on his lips and he'd laugh and say, "*Shhhhh!*"

She bought ice cream and chocolate bars and Juicy Fruit chewing gum and ate them all up and got rid of the wrappers in case her mother found out. And when she saw something she wanted in the shop, she knew she could have it. Eventually. It was their game and their normal, and it went on for as long as she could remember after that, until it all felt more than stupid and she was fast growing up.

He gave her five shillings for her twelfth birthday and asked if she wanted to play a game of hide and seek, because it used to be her favourite game and it was. She had sniggered at him and said she was far too big to be playing hide and seek. He gave her a threepenny bit the week after and told her it was her loss. The same the following week. When he asked her the week after that if she wanted to play the game, she said yes straight away because she knew in her heart and soul that if she played his stupid game he would give her more money. And Delia had got used to having the money. And so had Franny because Delia shared the stuff she had bought with her. So she played a game of hide and seek and thought it was a bit of a laugh. Then he told her there was no places left to hide downstairs that he wouldn't catch her in ten seconds flat. So they went upstairs and she felt like a fool, but did it anyway.

"Rules are important," he said. They weren't allowed play the game in the main bedroom because it wasn't fair on her mother for them to be messing it up. And they'd never hear the end of it if she found out.

Delia told him not to be so stupid because that only left her bedroom, the small room and the landing. He told her she better be inventive then, because for every ten minutes he couldn't find her he'd give her a shilling. Delia asked him could they not play in their bedroom too to give her a better chance and he agreed as long as she swore on her mother's life that she'd keep her mouth shut. If that's what she wanted, he said, and she said it was. It had to be dark, he said, or there'd be no point, so in the winter they played the game in the evening time after school and before her mother came home from cards, and in the summer they pulled the heavy curtains on the small window upstairs, and they could hardly see a thing.

So they took it in turns to hide and when he caught her she had to give him a kiss on the cheek for the count of three and he'd twist his head sometimes and she'd wipe her mouth and shudder. When she found him, he'd laugh and tell her she was a great girl and hand her the money. And she thought he was an awful fool, and she a much bigger one to be playing such a stupid game at her age, but the money made a difference, and he seemed to be enjoying it and she didn't want to be the one to disappoint. And people were strange.

It had all gone too far and he was easy to find, because he always hid in his bed, or in her bed. And when he asked her to lie with him, she did it for the money. When he told her he wanted to make the game a bit more challenging, she agreed, because it was easy money and all a bit stupid. She couldn't tell anyone that she was playing hide and seek with her stepfather – not even her best friend Franny, for fear she'd laugh and tell her to cop the feck on and grow up for herself. And she was supposed to be the tougher one.

He said he'd had an idea. That he'd hide money underneath him or around him and she'd have to find it and the thrill would be that it could be any amount, even a pound note, or more, but that would depend.

"On what?" she asked him.

And he said "On you!"

True to his word, he hid in the bed under the covers when it was his turn and it nearly always was, because she was getting fed up of thinking up places to hide and it was so stupid, so she let him at it. She had to count to ten and find him and then root for the money in around him and in his pockets and she felt like a proper fool at twelve years of age and she feeling around him and under him in the bed. And she after making her Confirmation. But the game had become so familiar by then it didn't faze her as long as it was him doing the hiding. And seeing as her mother had taken all of the money she had collected for her Confirmation and used it for God knows what, she went along with the stupid game for another while.

Then she began to save the money he gave her because she wasn't enjoying the chocolate any more, or the ice cream. There was no joy to be had from his money. No joy to be had from the stupid game.

By the time it got serious and she didn't want to do it anymore, he said it was too late because the rules had changed. He insisted that it had been her idea in the first place to come into her mother's bedroom to play the secret game in the dark. Not his. And she knew there was a certain amount of truth in what he was saying, because it had been her idea, but the game had gone too far and become all twisted and dirty and she didn't know how she would explain it all, but she knew she had to, if she wanted it to stop. And maybe someone else could make sense of it, because she knew it was wrong and she didn't know how to make it right.

It hurt so bad. She cried and pushed him off. She told him to fuck off away from her, but he said he'd tell her mother the minute she came in the front door and she'd throw her out because she was a nothing but a tease. A tease, he called her. A dirty tease that had led a decent man astray.

He said she had a sick, distorted mind. He warned her that he'd go to the priest about her and it would all come out in the wash and 'twould be the end of her mother.

Then he asked her if her friend Franny would like to have a bit of fun. He said he might have to have a word with her, and maybe she'd like to play the game with them. He had been thinking about it for some time and what a gullible child Franny seemed to be. Delia knew he was right because Franny could be proper gullible at times.

It was then that she told Franny that she wasn't allowed call to their house. *Ever.* They'd meet at the corner shop at the end of the street and Franny accepted what she had said, because she knew her own mother wasn't exactly courteous to Delia at the front door. Franny never asked why the hell not?

Delia knew she was snookered so she brazenly asked him for more money and he threw his head back and told her to watch her mouth, or he'd up his game and she wouldn't want that. She made up every excuse she could think of until he copped on. And she knew at that very moment what she would use his dirty rotten money for. She would save it up until she had enough to run away.

Because Delia felt shame and blame inside her head. She knew what she was doing was wrong but she didn't know how to talk about it. What was she to say if she did talk? That the bastard man had been at her for so long she'd forgotten what was right and wrong, but it didn't feel right and she blamed herself for letting him do it to her. In the beginning she had been chuffed with the money. For what? For playing his game and he hiding in the bed under the blankets when her mother was out. It was gone too far and she was all confused. Because she wasn't sure if she had been the giver or the taker and he had never attacked her, but she wished he had attacked her and beaten her black and blue because then she could have run screaming from the room and gone straight downstairs to wait for her mother to come home. She could have pointed out the marks and told her about the game and ask her if it was right and proper because it sure as hell didn't feel like it. But the ugly bruises weren't on the outside. They were buried inside.

Then she got brave and decided to tell the priest in the confession box that she played hide and seek with her stepfather, but it wasn't any ordinary game, and he told her she was a good child, to keep it up.

The game of pain.

Her mother, when she plucked up the courage to tell her, was horrified, She told Delia to shut her mouth and never utter such filth under her roof again. That she was a demon whelp of a child for concocting such a tale. She threatened to wash her filthy mouth out with soap and water. She wasn't to be saying such things about the very man who wanted nothing from life only to take care of them.

Then her mother went back and told him what Delia had confided in her, and the two of them got the priest to have a word with her. She didn't like the new priest with the bushy eyebrows and the stare in one eye. They said it was wrong not to like a priest. A holy man. Everyone liked the priest and if they didn't then there was something seriously wrong with them. Because nice girls didn't go around making out that their stepfathers were interfering with them, or insinuate that the priest had a funny look in his eyes.

Her mother said Gary was thinking of going to the Guards to make a statement, just in case she made trouble for him down the line. He wanted it on record. Delia pleaded with him not to go to the Guards or the whole town would find out.

Her mother told her that she'd give her two weeks to think about it, and if she didn't come back and admit that she had made it up, and apologize to poor Gary, she wouldn't be welcome under their roof and she could do what she liked after that.

So she waited the two weeks and became terrified, and during that time he never came near her and she began to wonder if it had been all her fault. She decided to apologise to her mother first and admit to being confused about everything. She apologised to the bastard man in the sitting room, in front of her mother. And they all had a horrible hug. They said they were relieved and would never mention it again.

But the atmosphere in the house was terrible.

Later the same night, when her mother ran up to the neighbours for a cup of sugar, he ran after her up the stairs and into her bedroom. "I'll see to you later, miss, when your mother is out cold and you'll say nothing. And if you as much as open your mouth we'll call the Guards and sent you off to an institution where they send slappers like you and who'll believe you now?" And he started laughing at her and pushed her against the door. His hand grabbed her breast. Hurting her. She didn't reply. He ran down the stairs and was back in the sitting room just as her mother arrived in the front door with the sugar. And she knew he wanted to play the game.

Her mother called up the stairs when she saw that Delia wasn't in the front room. "*Delia! Delia, come on down and make us a cup of tea! Come on with you, girl!*"

Delia listened at the top of the stairs with tears in her eyes, as her mother gave out about her. To *him*.

"Oh, that one will be the death of me!"

"Go easy on her, Marge. I thought we agreed to put all this behind us."

After he left her room later that night she cried and cried, muffling the sounds under the blankets. The dirty blankets that smelt of him. The sound of his silence. And no money left on the bed.

She had no choice. *Run.*

The following Saturday morning she was up, dressed and away just as the milkman was leaving the milk at the door.

"Morning, Delia, you're out early!"

She never answered. The note she left on the table would no doubt be taken by him as he left for work.

I'm gone and if you ever as much look at Franny G, I'll be back to tell it all.

She put a second note into her mother's housecoat pocket hanging on the hall stand.

Mam, I'm off to England because you didn't believe me. He did it again. Delia

She had taken his dirty money and left from the station outside of the town. She was never coming back and they could do what they liked.

Delia blamed herself for not knowing what he was at all those years. She took it to be her own fault and the only way was out. So Delia took off to London and thanked her lucky stars that she had no real memory of the wonderful father that her mother said she'd had. Because she had been too small when he had died and her brother had no memory of him either.

She headed off on the mailboat that night, after a trip to the bank the day before to change her money. She was far too upset to say goodbye to anyone, even to Franny. Especially to Franny. She figured that once she was gone, things could go back to normal at home and her mother could get on with doing whatever the fuck she had to do. As long as Franny would be left alone. He could go to blazes. She never wanted to see him again.

Chapter 16

SADIE PRATT
Retribution
1960

Sadie Pratt bolted upright in the bed. It took her a few seconds to work out where the banging was coming from. The house was shuddering. Someone was trying to break in. Or was the house on fire? In a panic she knocked over the small clock on the locker. Leaning over to pick it up, she could barely make out the time. Squinting. It was half past seven in the morning. There was little light in the room.

The hammering continued. Sadie leapt out of the bed.

Who in God's name was belting on her door at this hour of the morning? No time to straighten herself, she hurried to the window. Her long thinning hair which was seldom on display outside of her bedroom door clung to her back. She pulled the curtain back. Releasing the stiff window-catch she removed the stick used to hold the window in place when open. She eased the window down before stepping into the deep windowsill to stick her head and shoulders out. Feeling the morning chill on her bare arms made her shiver. The lintel above the front door below was blocking her view. Whoever was hammering at the door below her was not giving up.

"Who's making all that racket? Show yourself!"

When the man in the dark uniform stepped back she guessed what was coming. A second uniformed guard stood back and looked up at her. Sergeant Rice.

"It's not eight o'clock in the morning, Sergeant! And you'll break the door down. Stop, will you! What do you want with me?

"Get down here right now, Sadie Pratt, or we will most certainly break the door down."

"*Aah* . . . I'm coming . . . I'm coming . . . give me a minute till I cover myself, I'm here in my shift."

"Not a minute more, if you're not standing before me in thirty seconds flat your door will need mending."

Sadie stepped out of the windowsill. Tugging her grandmother's shawl from the end of the bed she hurried down the stairs in her bare feet. She had barely pulled the heavy bolt back on the front door when the young guard burst in on top of her, knocking her back against the table.

Sergeant Rice strode in after him. Tapping his truncheon on his left palm, he made no eye-contact with her.

"You sit over there, Sadie, and don't move, or we'll cuff you to the railing outside. We're here on foot of a complaint. You've been accused of carrying out illegal interventions here and at addresses in the town. Your grandmother before you was well-known to be involved in the same game in her heyday. There's a young lady in a bad way and your name has come up. The apple doesn't fall far from the tree, Sadie Pratt."

Sadie did as she was told and sat on the wooden chair by the small table. She had to stop herself from grinning as she addressed the sergeant.

"Oh, Sergeant. Here on foot of a complaint, is it? Well, if you'll excuse me for saying so, but there's nothing in this house that could incriminate me. If I were guilty, of course. So root away, let ye, ye'll know what you'll be looking for . . . I suppose."

Sadie smiled as the disgruntled sergeant issued orders to the young guard, pointing around the room. *Search.* The young garda did as he was told. He went up the stairs, his head bent.

"Mind your head there, Guard!" she called out. "'Tis a low enough ceiling!"

Sadie wasn't fearful of what they might find. She hadn't survived in the business for this length of time without learning how to protect herself. Most of her duties were performed away from home, so she had little to worry about. And in the event that a girl called to see her, there was no proof. They were away out the door most times before the bleeding started.

Sadie had two essentials for her work. A small leather pouch containing three instruments. Implements that she had covertly removed from the obstetrics unit at St. Mary's hospital. Obsolete, Matron had told her. To be upgraded. Get rid of them.

Sadie had not disposed of them – she took them home for no other reason than to seek ownership of them. She liked to look at them. They looked far more professional that the knitting needle her grandmother had used back in the day. And she liked the leather pouch bound by a thin strip of leather. Faded. Used. Made her feel important to have such implements in her home. Linking her to the profession she knew she was born to serve in.

The second essential that served Sadie in her work was her journal. Bound in oilskin. The journal held just enough detail to rattle a few men in Ballygore. Or anyone else that might take it on themselves to accuse her. Or deny their involvement in matters, should she feel under duress.

The oilskin journal had been intended for her nurse training. She'd had her eye on it in the shop window for some time. Then it disappeared and when she went in to the stationary shop to enquire about it, she spotted it wedged in at the side of the cash register behind the counter. The man in the shop had all but snapped at her when she asked could she see it. The orange notebook. Looking out at her over the rim of his glasses and his nose all crinkled, as if to say 'twas out of her league, beyond her means. The man told her that it wasn't a notebook, but a journal, that oilskin covers were expensive, that he kept a few of them on order for certain customers, but he didn't think she'd want to be spending her money on that particular one. Removing it from where it was wedged, he wiped it down with the palm of his hand before turning it over to show her the back of it. Plain brown. It wasn't orange at all, he said. It was damaged. It had been brown to begin with, but had faded from sitting far too long in the shop window. The wife's fault, for failing to ensure it was in under the yellow plastic to protect it from the sun. He turned it over again in his hand and grimaced and said if she wanted it he supposed he could offer it to her at half price. But no return. So she bought it and took it home and let it sit in her own back window facing the sun, until the back cover and spine eventually turned a shade of orange too. And when it did she was well pleased. She loved her orange journal, there was no other like it. She cared for it, minded it, because no else would have bothered.

It had a raw leather strip wound around it, twice, to keep it closed, and a narrow red ribbon inside to mark the pages. Sadie thought it was the most beautiful thing in the world and so many pages, far more than she'd be able to fill in any given year. It would hold all the wonderful words that she would hear during her training in London, she would read them over and over again at night in her bed in the nurses' quarters when she would recall her day. She would jot down things she might feel would be of benefit in the future. Important medical notes. Sketches even.

She had gone back to the man in the shop and bought a fountain pen to slot into the elastic loop inside the front cover. She bought a card of four ink cartridges, leaving the slim black cardboard box that the pen had sat in to the man behind the counter. She wrote, *Property of Nurse Sadie Pratt,* on the inside cover when she got home. She flicked through the empty pages of the journal, imagining them filled with all sorts of exciting detail. She had high hopes for her journal. High hopes for herself. Her grandmother would have been so proud.

But it never happened. Because Matron put a stop to it.

The orange oil-cloth journal never left the house even for an overnight and neither did Sadie.

Her life had been turned upside down.

Matron had destroyed her nursing career.

In time, she used her precious journal in the best way she could. She would use it to document information pertaining to the only line of work she felt was open to her. Insurance, her granny would have called it.

Included in the journal were the names of every girl she had helped. Where Sadie was given a name, she recorded it. She did her best to get the names out of them, asking the question just at the right moment when they were at their most vulnerable. Legs apart. Probing. And the names came out. Out of the mouths of misfortunates at the height of their pain. Sadie would make a mental note and jot it down. Later. The dates of her house calls. The names of certain men who had paid cash for her services.

And here was Sergeant Rice about to search the house looking for it, because Sadie had been slack with her mouth and mentioned it where she shouldn't have mentioned it. She should have kept her mouth shut when she heard the girl ended up with a ruptured bladder. She knew that they were pointing the finger at her. She had told them to point elsewhere and referred to the names in her journal. Evidence where needed.

Sergeant Rice had a knowing look on his face. Guilty.

There were names that had come up more than once. His own name for one. Alongside the names of the misfortunates.

Sadie remembered the way the schoolteacher used to look at her. Her head bent to one side with her lips pursed as if she were about to pat a wounded animal. Unsure. Reaching out, but half afraid at the same time in case 'twould bite her. Well, Sadie was not wounded and she certainly wasn't an animal.

She knew well enough what the locals thought of her. The names they called her. They had no idea that she knew. But Sadie knew. The remarks they passed when they saw her coming. Branded with the same nickname as they had given her grandmother before her. The Knitting Needle.

All she had ever wanted was to help out. Left with no alternative, she had finally realised her vocation. Accepted her gift. The vocation that her grandmother had realised back in her younger days.

Except that Sadie's instruments were a class above what her grandmother had used. Sadie used surgical instruments to help those who saw no other way out.

The poor girls – and Sergeant Rice and his ilk. Malcolm Clarke from the boot factory and Davie Keogh from the garage, and other men, if you could call them that. Men who shared the same condition. Lust. Scattering their seeds around with no regard for the poor girls. Seeds that would never germinate into seedlings and, even if they did, they would never get to blossom in their birthfathers' gardens. Along with their blood line. No. The girls that Sadie helped were at the mercy of men like Clarke and Keogh and the notorious Sergeant who would do whatever they had to, to protect their own good name. Men who believed themselves to be invincible. Men whom Sadie had no regard for. And their dirty secrets carefully logged in her journal.

The notebook hadn't disappointed. It had paid for itself in kind a hundred times over. She'd had to mention it a few times when things were not going as intended. Protection against those she knew would stop at nothing to bring her down. But she'd never had to produce it. If she had, many a family in the town would have felt the brunt of her wrath. Big wigs who thought they could get away with everything. Men with power of sorts who pounced on stray young women. Wearing dry-cleaned suits and long woollen overcoats. Who thought they were above everyone else. Men who turned heads. At Mass on a Sunday wearing the finest of wool scarves and leather handstitched gloves. Gifts from their adoring families. Making ample contributions to the church. Buying their place in heaven. And behind their devout masks they had no conscience in choosing one child above another. Men who took what they wanted and hid behind cloaks of respect. The church on a Sunday was full of them. Family men whom the townspeople knew were fathering more children than they were taking credit for.

"*Found it, Sergeant!*" The young garda came back downstairs with a smug look on his face. A notebook held aloft.

He handed the notebook to the sergeant who sniggered at her and beckoned his colleague to open the front door.

Sadie put her head in her hands. To stop herself from laughing.

And they were gone. Out the door. And only then did she throw her head back and shake with laughter.

Decoy. Names taken at random from the newspapers. Surnames juggled around. Dates and times made up. And there were a few more lying around should they decide to come back. Sadie enjoyed using her fountain pen to create. They'd never get their hands on her precious journal.

The following day she would make it her business to go up to the post office to make a couple of phone calls. And she knew exactly who was first on her list. Time to shake things up. Retribution.

Chapter 17

DELIA

Life Lessons

On her arrival in London, Delia had found a room to rent from a notice pinned to the wall at the Tube station. A single room in a three-storey house in Soho in the heart of the West End of London.

The landlady was short and stern with a square jaw. White hair, white face. Small eyes. Steel. She spoke in broken English. German, she said she was. She told Delia the room was cheap, to take it or leave it. A month's rent in advance. Delia took it because she didn't know what else to do. She lay on the bed, hoping to sleep. To sleep and wake up and find that she was dreaming. That she had imagined it all. Her eyes would not close so she stared at the door blindly, allowing her thoughts in. Telling herself it had been the right move.

The room was cold. Delia was shivering. She had felt warmer out on the street. Grabbing her bag she left the room just as it was getting dark. The noise on the street was louder than she remembered it hours before – like nothing she had ever heard. A thousand different sounds.

Absentmindedly running her fingers through her hair, which hadn't seen a brush in days, she stepped back onto Charing Cross Road, facing the busiest street she had ever seen in her life. The clock above her head read eleven. Neon lights flashing everywhere. Red. People rushing about, laughing and talking and linking arms. The aromas from the restaurants made her stomach rumble. She didn't remember when she had last eaten. The pace at which people were moving about frightened her. But nobody seemed to take any notice of the Irish girl standing on the street corner. Nobody here to tell her off for being a brazen hussy for doing what she did. Nobody here to call her a brazen whelp of a child. The tears burned her eyes as she looked around her. *Panic.* What had she done? Coming here to a strange city on her own. She was far too scared to move. She began to sob. The tears slipped down her face. Down her neck and she let them fall. Clutching her bag to her chest, Delia waited.

There were girls everywhere and twice as many men. When a man approached her and asked how much she charged for a hand-job, she pushed him out of her way and ran to the next street corner. Panting. Straight into the arms of a decent-looking fella who led her up a dark alleyway and into a doorway and she thinking he was helping her, but he wasn't and it was all over in a few minutes and he asked her how much, before fixing himself and running out of the doorway. She put the fiver in her pocket. She had sold her wares without meaning to. She straightened herself and went straight to the shop on the corner and bought herself a half pound of sausages and a small pan loaf that reminded her of home, and she stayed another night in the freezing cold room. Laying the food out on the brown-paper bag it had been wrapped in, she boiled her sausages in a pot on the one-ring gas cooker. And she slept like a baby in the clothes she had on her and counted her money and put it down her stocking for safe keeping while she slept, because the paraffin heater was only half working and she was far too cold to take her stockings off.

The following morning, after a bad night's sleep, she surveyed the room from the bed. The paint on the ceiling was covered in mould, a gaping hole showing the rafters in the ceiling over the door. The wallpaper on the walls was curling down in sections, exposing more of the same mould. The brown lino on the floor had been sticky to walk on. The small cooker she had used sat on top of a chest of drawers. Just as well as there was only one cooking pot in the place. An enamel mug with a plate to match. A knife and fork and a spoon. A dirty curtain hid the space which she supposed was a makeshift wardrobe. The lampshade was faded pink. The shared toilet was on the floor below. She could wash her delph there. The only good thing she could think of were the top and bottom heavy bolts on the door. It would do for now.

She got up to start her day, not knowing where to go except back to her corner where she had earned the fiver the day before. Not knowing what else to do because she wasn't staying in the room.

"Love, are you all right? " The voice came from a girl who had stopped on the street to check on her. "Barb, I'll follow you on — tell Audrey I'll see her later." The blonde girl waved at a woman before putting her hand on Delia's arm. "You alright there, love. You look like you've lost your mommy."

Delia recognised the look of concern. "I'm OK. What do you want?"

"I'm only saying you're new around here, ain't you? Haven't seen you before."

"Well, you needn't be saying anything. I'm well able to look after myself."

"OK! I best leave you where you was at then."

The girl had walked a few steps when Delia caught up with her.

"Miss . . . I'm sorry. I *am* new around here, just getting my bearings till I find a job. If you know of anywhere?"

The girl giggled. "Thought as much. You've only just arrived over then. My nan was Irish as it happens. We get a lot like you around here. Running away or looking for excitement, which is it, lovey?"

Delia didn't answer.

"I'm Jenny," said the girl.

Delia nodded.

"Have you a place to stay then? I'm on the way for a cuppa if you wanna come?"

The street corner where they stood was thronged with people. It was near lunchtime and the smells from the many cafés in the area wafted under their noses. Jenny took Delia by the arm.

"Come on with me to the café and we'll grab a nice cuppa and have a chat."

Delia pushed her arm away roughly, before taking a step back.

"OK, that's it, I'm off," said the girl. "And if you want me to help you out, darlin', you'll have to come find me."

And she was gone.

Meeting Red Eddie ten minutes later changed everything. He crept up and was standing beside her before she knew it, his two arms stretched out, palms flat against the wall behind her, blocking her in. She panicked and pushed against his chest but he didn't move. His stringy dark hair was greased back over his head. Curled at the nape of his neck. Wearing a navy suit with a pink shirt, he looked dapper. Said he'd been watching her. He'd copped her the night before in the alleyway with a trick. And he'd seen her with Jenny earlier. He told her there wasn't much going on around that he didn't make it his business to find out about. When he said that he could take care of her, she listened, because she thought she saw the kindness in his brown eyes. He told her that it was illegal for working girls to solicit men on the street. She would, not could, be arrested. He said he could protect her and keep her safe. That he liked her. He brought her for a coffee and croissant to an Italian place and she went knowing that she was far too naive for her own good. The place was busy and she had never heard of a croissant before.

He warned her about the Maltese gangs who'd pinch her off the busy streets – if the cops didn't get her first. And no one would take a blind bit of notice. The Maltese would make her work for them, and make her do all sorts with other girls and other men who'd hurt her. And move her around and dope her up so she wouldn't know who she was, or where she was. Some of the pimps could rough her up and if they caught her working their patch like he had caught her doing, they'd slice her throat, dump her body in the Thames and that'd be the end of her.

As they left the café, he said he had a work flat on Greek Street, if she was interested in taking a look. Said it was a two-minute walk from where they were standing. He whistled across the street and a blonde girl with backcombed hair and a white mini-dress appeared within seconds. Just in case she was nervous, he said, the girl would accompany them.

He said he liked the look of her. He had a job for her there if that's what she wanted. He wouldn't let anything happen to her.

She nodded her head and said she'd have a think about it, knowing that she'd have to take a risk if she wanted to make a life for herself. And the girl who tottered along beside them giggled.

Delia fell for Eddie from the very first day. He had a sense of danger about him and she liked it. Honest danger. He seemed straight up, unlike her stepfather at home who couldn't tell the truth if his life depended on it.

Eddie said he had runners working for him who kept an eye on the street. They sent the punters up to the girls' flats – he managed another work place in Charlotte Street, near the Fitzroy. And two more flats on Dean Street.

Delia took him up on his offer and went to see the work flat on Greek Street and went home to the room she had rented from the German with the square jaw and decided to stay there until her rent was due at the end of the month. Red Eddie had given her cash and told her to go smarten herself up.

She met Jenny and the girls on the street the very next day and became acquainted with them. She told them she was off to buy a few bits because she had work sorted for that very evening. Jenny and Audrey took her to the Lady Jane boutique.

They met for coffee most days on their breaks and life became easy. She had a man to look out for her and the money was rolling in. And she had friends. She thought a lot about Franny and how she must have felt when she heard that she had taken off.

By the end of the month Delia could stay in the German's house no longer. The room had become unbearably cold as the October winds rattled against the window panes, leaving the draughts in. The papers she stuffed around the rim were of no use. They were squelchy and dripping wet in no time, adding to the misery of the room.

She moved into one of Eddie's flats on Dean Street. She had plenty of money because she worked all day most days and into the night and she put the money in a hidey-hole and she lived well.

Eddie began to stay over and, before she knew it, they were a couple because he was there most times. Life was good and Delia was happy knowing that she had Red Eddie to look out for her. She felt like they were special and she was special. And she worked hard to make life easy and coughed up the money to buy him whatever he fancied, because he was her man and she was his woman.

Delia settled in Soho and made money and lived her life without shame and sold the only part of her she felt certain had value.

She was Red Eddie's girl which gained her a certain respectability because no one messed with Red Eddie. He had spivs working for him on the streets, selling cigarettes and knocked-off watches, or whatever else they could get into their suitcases which would be slammed shut in seconds. And off they'd run with a bobby chasing after them.

Delia answered to no-one outside of Red Eddie and, when he slapped her the first time, he told her it was for her own good. To keep her mouth in line. The second time, he punched her in the face and she got up and walked out.

The third time, she stood up to him. She made it clear to him that she'd slit his throat in his sleep and leave his balls dangling from his mouth if he ever tried that again. She meant it and he knew she meant it. She slammed the door and left.

By the time she got back the morning after, she knew it was now or never and told him no one was going to treat her like that again and expect to get away with it. He began to treat her differently after that, but she saw it in his eyes. The way he treated her and the way he held her wasn't like it was before. And for some time things improved – but not for long.

He told her that if she wasn't his to do as he said, then she wasn't his at all. That was just the way. She thought that he loved her but realised that Eddie wasn't the sort of man to be seen to be weak. And he told her that's how it looked when he had her swinging off his arm and she acting all cocky. No one would take Red Eddie seriously if his moll was a mouthpiece. That was how it worked, he said, and he was under pressure trying to keep his business afloat and he couldn't do that if his treacle tart was laying it on the line for him. Eddie said he wouldn't be taking any crap from the skivs. Yet here he was taking crap from a squeeze. An Irish squeeze at that. He told her not to bother turning up at the work flat on Greek Street either. She had two days to clear her stuff out of the flat they shared and if she didn't do as he asked, she'd be left without a face. So he threw her out the door to find her own way after giving her a shiner and breaking two of her ribs for good measure.

An Italian woman who lived in the next building took her in when she found her leaning against the window on the street outside. She made her sit down and she minded her. She said she reminded her of herself when she first arrived. She fed her chicken soup with noodles in it and helped Delia get back on her feet.

And when she did get back on her feet she started out again. As Delta.

The Italian woman introduced her to her son Enzo, whom she said might be able to help her. He owned a few places around. The

133

woman said her boy was afraid of no-one. That he would look out for her as a favour to his mama. He agreed when he met her in Bar Italia on Frith Street. As long as she worked for him and paid her dues he'd make sure she was left alone. He didn't want to see her hurt. He wasn't shy in telling her what could happen if she crossed the line. She got the drift and moved into a room he owned above a strip club on Carnaby Street. He said he had a maid looking after things for him in a walk-up on Frith Street who managed the business side of things and made sure everything was on the straight and narrow.

Flip was that woman's name. From Croydon. Short and skinny and no nonsense. Flip reported directly back to Enzo. It all worked out. Flip had been working for Enzo since her husband had died. Delia knew she had no option but to keep her head down. Once Delia had familiarised herself with her clients she had a steady stream of regulars.

Enzo knew that his mother was fond of her, so he left her alone. She visited his mother every now and then because she liked the old woman who had warmed to her. Delia brought her sweet almond cakes and they drank grappa out of bone-china cups and before long Enzo's mother let it slip that Enzo had plans for her. Big plans. She then widened her eyes and told Delia if she wanted out now was the time. She drained her grappa and warned Delia not to trust Flip.

A few days later, Delia bumped into Jenny on the street. Jenny told her that she had heard in one of the clubs that Red Eddie had got in over his head – that he had been lifted and his body had been dumped near Epping Forest. Jenny said that she had heard that Enzo was getting a bit of a name for himself in the wrong quarters

– if he wasn't careful the Eastenders would get him too and Delia along with him. Jenny said she had rooms on Brewer Street if Delia ever wanted out. She'd keep an ear out in the meantime and keep her up to speed. Delia said she'd think about it, that she would bide her time and work it out. She knew her life would be in danger if she double-crossed Enzo.

Chapter 18

FRAN

The Claim

Brigid handed the white envelope to Fran. It had already been opened. No point in saying anything – her mother would no doubt come up with some excuse.

"It's all yours, Fran, and you deserve every single penny of it, after what you've been through. Losing your job and all. So we decided, your father and myself, that we won't be looking for one penny out of it." Leaning closer to Fran, she lowered her voice, making sure that Dan was out of earshot. "Unless you decide to throw the small change my way, loveen. I won't object." She grinned, putting her finger to her lips. "*Shhhh!*"

Fran ran straight past her mother up the stairs to the privacy of her room. She kicked off her shoes and lay on the bed. Holding the cheque out in front of her with both hands she could hardly believe her eyes. *Five thousand two hundred pounds.* A fortune. All those noughts, and in her own name.

Chatting to her mother over tea a few hours later, Fran admitted that she was half afraid of owning so much money.

Dan, her father, walked in on the conversation, leaving his boots outside the back door. Removing his cap, he sat at the table, the newspaper laid out in front of him, ready to read the obituaries page. He would leave the rest of the paper until later.

Fran knew by his face that he wasn't going to get caught up in a conversation about the money. He would no doubt have already heard enough about it from her mother.

He looked out over his black-rimmed glasses and smiled at Fran who sat there staring at the cheque. "You know I don't believe in all this claim business, but I hope it brings you luck, love. Just remember, money wherever it comes from won't bring happiness with it. Take your time before you go off spending it."

"Daddy, for God's sake, I barely have the cheque in my hand! Let me enjoy looking at it for a while longer, before I decide what I'm going to do with it!" She turned to her mother. "Mammy, could I buy a house with this much?"

"Well, what do you think, Dan? Could she buy a house with that much?" Bridget was anxious for Dan to stay in the conversation but he was clearly having none of it. "You know what, Dan, we'll have a drink to celebrate!"

Fran's father rose and went to the press. He handed Brigid the bottle of sherry. Her mother poured herself a drink in her teacup and did the same for Dan who moved the cup away from him. Fran wasn't offered one, neither did she want one. Not in front of her parents.

"Dan, for God's sake, don't be taking the huff. Come on! Talk!"

"I suppose you could buy a small house," he said to Fran. "But what would you be doing with a house, love, a single girl like you and you barely only after getting the key of the door here. Your money would be gone and all you'd be left with would be bills. Travel is what I'd advise you to do. Travel the world, love, and educate your mind."

Brigid threw him a warning glance. "Read the paper there, Dan, and tell us who's dead."

Her father did as he was told. Opening the newspaper he folded it over on the obituaries page and, straightening his glasses, began combing through the death notices with his finger. Reading aloud. "*Friday April 29th, Margie Blake (Moss), Peter Street, Ballygore, after a short illness.*"

"Jesus, I meant to tell you, Fran, when I heard it in the shop earlier," said Brigid.

"So she went in the finish," said Dan. "Margie Blake. And her present husband's name 'Moss' in brackets beside it. *Hmmm*, she must have held on to the first husband's name. Strange that."

"The two children are Blakes – maybe that's why," said Brigid. "I suppose Mrs. Margie Moss is a bit of a mouthful. 'Tis all the one anyway, cos she'll be buried with the first man as is the way. And he's a Blake. She hadn't been well at all and took a turn for the worse before the weekend and never came out of it. Read on, Dan. When is the funeral?"

"Wednesday coming, arriving at the church for seven. That's the day after tomorrow, isn't it? Burial on Thursday below at the cemetery. What day have we? I wonder will they wake her above at the house?"

"Indeed-in they won't be waking her above at the house, or anywhere near it. Well, that's according to Molly Dempsey, and nothing goes on around the town that she doesn't know about. Margie will be going straight from the morgue to the church.

Apparently himself told Molly weeks ago that he couldn't bear to be looking at her lying in a coffin in the middle of their front room, with the Child of Mary cloak on her. He'd rather remember her sitting beside him on the settee. Did you ever hear such bullshit in all your life? He'd rather think of her on the settee long-side him!"

Dan shook his head slowly.

"Poor man," Brigid went on. "Anyway, if Molly Dempsey is to be believed, there's rumours of Gary Moss putting the house up for sale as soon as the funeral is over – he'll be taking off to wherever he came from. They said she knew she was on the way out for some time. They had all them years together, I suppose. Bit soon though to be making them kind of decisions and poor Margie barely cold. Cork, I think she said, although he hasn't a trace of a Cork accent on him. 'Tis done up like a palace up there, according to Molly, although with the state of her own place she wouldn't have much to compare it to – the shed out there would look like a palace. Jesus, there's a house you could put a deposit on, Fran, and the place all done up."

Fran didn't reply. She had removed herself from the conversation. She was staring at the cheque in her hand.

"'Tis the very same as our own here except for the add-on at the back," Brigid continued. "Whoever will get it will be lucky. They'd such pride in the place. New lino from top to bottom. I believe, the thick plastic covers are still on the settee from when they bought it years ago. I don't know how they sit on it, do you, Dan? You'd be stuck to it. Molly said she sat on it and 'twas squeaking that much 'twasn't a bit comfortable. She had to excuse herself in case they thought 'twas letting off wind she was." Brigid didn't wait for a response. "That's what happens when you're such a good-living creature like Margie Blake. Never touched a drop in her life. All that clean living and now she's gone." She paused and frowned at Fran. "Of course, yourself and the Blake young one were great with each other. Fran! Wake up there! Margie Blake is dead. Delia's mother. There was only her and the older boy. Dan, would they be Gary Moss's half-children or stepchildren?"

Dan didn't answer. He nodded over at Fran, waiting for her to respond.

Fran looked up. "Yeah. Delia was my best friend who upped and disappeared. Some friend she turned out to be."

"I warned you about her. Margie told me herself that she went off to work in England, that one of her uncles was home and took her back with him. He got her fixed up with a job. God, that must be well over five years ago now."

"I wonder will she be home for the funeral?" Fran suddenly asked before putting the cheque down on the table.

"Oh! So you *are* tuned in, miss. Jesus, of course she'll be home for her mother's funeral. We could run up to the house later on to sympathise, and we'll have the job done and you won't have to be going anywhere near the church. I wonder will they have soup and sandwiches after the Mass, Dan?"

"Probably over in Manson's lounge bar, seeing as 'tis this end of the town. They'll hardly cross the river and give the turn to the hotel."

"Fran, you'll nearly have to introduce yourself at the door, you've changed that much," said Brigid. "He's a gentleman, that Gary, he treated her like a queen, they said. Someone said he was married before he met her, in England somewhere. The wife must have died. Poor man."

At seven o'clock that evening Brigid and Fran walked up to the house. A black crepe cloth with a card detailing the funeral had been pinned to the front door.

"House private, if you don't mind. Family only. You'd think that they'd at least let the neighbours in to sympathise. Wouldn't you? 'Tisn't as if they're a big family."

"Maybe 'twas what Mrs. Blake wanted, Mammy."

"Never mind, Fran, come on away from the door. We'll have to go to the funeral Mass on Thursday morning, and you can run over to Manson's afterwards, to see if they're in the lounge bar. I wouldn't darken the door myself after the way that Philly Manson spoke to me years back when I dropped the butt of a fag on the street as I was passing. He told me to pick it up and take it up home to my own bin. And he not two hands higher than a grasshopper looking up at me. I can't remember what he said exactly, but it was enough to stop me from going in there. Just as well your father isn't fond of the pubs."

Chapter 19

DELIA

The Funeral

The morning of the funeral Delia arrived at the church in Ballygore before anyone else got there. In plenty of time to have a word with her mother, who lay in the closed coffin at the top of the church. She hadn't seen her, and didn't want to see her – too much on her conscience to be looking down at her mother in her Children of Mary shroud and she all ready for heaven, if she weren't there already.

Delia placed her hand on the coffin and lowered her head. Whispering.

"Mam, I came back to say goodbye and to tell you how sorry I am that I wasn't in touch. You didn't believe me at all, Mam. I was only eight years old when it started and my heart is broken but I see it now. You were blindsided by him. Tell my dad I said hello if you can find him up there. I've often wondered would he have believed me? You can ask him if you find him. Bye, Mam."

Delia moved away from the coffin just as people began to arrive in the church. She wondered if they would recognise her. Probably. Gone were the bright red lips, replaced by a softer shade of peach. Her eyes she left bare, apart from a double set of false eyelashes. She was about to leave a lasting imprint in the mind of the bastard man who had stolen her youth.

Sitting towards the middle of the second pew at the right-hand side of the church – Delia didn't acknowledge her relatives as they excused themselves to pass her by. Those who had judged her. She kept her eyes fixed on the coffin. She pulled her cony-fur coat across her chest, her white box handbag sitting on her lap. The bastard man sat in front of her at the edge of the seat. Delia didn't look at anyone else – they were mostly women. His crowd. From the back he looked about half the size she remembered. She had expected to be brazen enough to face him, but when she saw him again she began to shiver and shake and her heart was belting against her chest and she thought she was going to collapse in a heap.

"Delta, help me out here," she whispered to herself. Delta obliged.

After the funeral Delia returned to Manson's, sitting at a table on her own just inside the door. Her aunt from her father's side sat at the table beside her, along with a few more of her relations.

Philly Manson walked around, handing out plates of withered sausages and ham and egg sandwiches, while the barman ran up and down the bar serving customers.

Delia ordered a double gin. Neat. Her aunt gave her a sideways glance from the next table, but said nothing. Delia was disgusted with them all for eating the offerings of the bastard man. Then her aunt broke the silence by leaning over, pointing at the sausages.

"Can't you pick away at them, Delia, or we'll have them all eaten?"

"No, thanks – I'm fine," was all she could muster. She clicked her fingers at the barman, gesturing for another drink.

The bastard man sat hunched over at the table across from her. His two sisters like guard dogs around him. Sisters of Sorrow with hankies in their hands.

People were coming in and out to sympathise, to offer a few words of support to the grieving widower. Faces she recognised. Nudging. Squinting over at her. The sound of handbag clasps closing, belonging to those who had taken their glasses out to take a closer look. At her.

She had her life in London and as soon as this was over she'd pay her bill and be gone. And the men around the bar counter could have a good look at her on the way out. And they eating the food paid for by the bastard man wearing the narrow tie and black armband.

Fran took a deep breath as she walked across the street towards Philly Manson's lounge bar. She stopped to read the notice taped to the door, making it obvious that she was there for no other reason than to join the funeral party. Women weren't encouraged in public bars.

The glass-panelled door led to the spacious lounge section which was a lot more comfortable than the bar. A hatch on the wall between the two made it easier for the men to send a drink through to the ladies, if they weren't of the mind to come through with them themselves.

Fran spotted Delia immediately. She was sitting at a table on her own to the right of the door. Delia was smoking a cigarette, blowing rings up in the air, her two legs brazenly resting on the stool under the table, her feet sticking out at the other side. Big hair. Very big hair. The table next to where she sat had a few people around it. Fran nodded at Delia's aunt.

There were people scattered around the lounge, some standing at the food table at the far corner. The counter was busy. Men moved in and out from the bar, more were having half-ones at the counter while they were waited for their pints. Noisy. Fran recognised Delia's stepfather Gary sitting with two women she thought must be his sisters. People were over and back to them to have a few words, some carrying paper plates of food.

Fran took a deep breath and approached Delia.

The girls eyed each other awkwardly.

Delia was the first to speak. "*No way! Franny Gaffney? No way!*"

Fran bent forward and smiled. "Delia, great to see you. Sorry, I know it's not . . . I mean . . . are you on your own? I was very sorry to hear about your mother. I only heard about it two days ago. How are you doing?'

"Oh my God, but you're a sight for sore eyes. Jesus. I can hardly believe my eyes. No way is this you! I met your mother at the church. I asked if you were around and she never answered me. What's new there?"

"I was there, Delia, but I never like going up to sympathise, so I stayed in the seat."

Delia stood up. Towering over Fran, she gave her the biggest hug.

"Jesus! My old buddy! I wouldn't have known you if you hadn't come up to me – I wouldn't have recognised you in the middle of that crowd. Here, sit in here beside me, girl, quick, and have a drink before any more of them arrive over! The rings are dug into my fingers with all the hand-shaking. Look!"

Delia was wearing two gold Cladagh rings, one on each thumb.

The other fingers were adorned with colourful rings. In her ears she wore flat yellow button earrings. Her wrist jangled with hard plastic bracelets to match.

"Not many of that crowd will come over near me. I probably have the plague."

"Sorry, what?" said Fran, distracted by the jewellery.

"Oh, never mind, Franny. I'm glad you showed up." Delia patted the red leatherette seat beside her.

Fran sat down.

"What'll you have? Tell me you're not a flaming Pioneer! I've enough drink in me to down a ship – they're not coming as fast as they were though. They've slowed up. Be a dote and go up and order – Philly can bring them down. I remember him well but he didn't know me from Adam when I booked in here last evening. Ignore that shower over there with that bastard. Just pretend they're not there."

Fran wasn't sure how to respond.

"Look, some of Mam's crowd are on their way through. They're looking for the food. Here . . . move that bloody stool out of the way before some of them plonk their arses on it. "

Fran looked over but didn't recognise anyone.

Delia nudged her. "Look at Mam's cousin from Wicklow in the suit and the legs of the pants riding up around his ankles. I had to tell him to button his fly earlier. And the fella beside him, some other cousin far out, and he crying like the rain and I never laid eyes on him in my whole life."

Fran didn't know where to look. She was delighted to be in the company of Delia, but was unsure of what to say to her old friend who was checking the empty glasses in front of her, putting each one in turn to her mouth to drain the last drops.

It could have been anybody's funeral the way Delia was acting.

Fran headed for the counter to order the drinks. Two double gins and a bottle of bitter lemon for Delia. She'd ask for two mixers and a small gin for herself. She turned to look back at Delia whose legs were once again stretched out in front of her. Delia's aunt must have left in an awful hurry. The table next to Delia's was being cleared.

Fran muttered under her breath. "Jesus."

She thought better than to pass comment, given the day that was in it. Delia's hair was piled high on her head, a mass of curls at the top. Like a nest. She figured it had to be a full hairpiece, much too glossy to be real. Much too full. She never remembered Delia having such a full head of hair. She wouldn't say a word. It wouldn't be right.

She headed back, doing her best to avoid looking at the table in the centre of the room.

Delia beckoned towards her. "Franny . . . tell the landlord to drop us down a few sandwiches, if there's any left up there. Better still bring them down yourself, or we'll be waiting all day."

Fran obeyed.

Delia reached up and grabbed a sandwich before Fran had a chance to put the plate down on the table.

"Egg. Jesus! I hate bloody egg sandwiches. Had they no ham up there? Oh God! Here's what's his name on the way out from the bar!

Delia kicked the stool she had been resting her legs on out from under the table. It landed upside down on the floor. Delia ignored it and told Fran to do the same when she moved to get up to put it back. People were looking over at them. The stool was picked up within seconds.

Fran had to control herself or she'd burst out laughing. Delia Blake was a breath of fresh air, even in these awful circumstances. She was such a laugh. Answerable to no-one.

"It must have been an awful shock for you all the same, Delia? Are you sure you want me sitting here with you? Would you not go over and join the rest of them? Did your brother not come home for the funeral?"

"No and no, Franny. Two bleeding no's. Terence was home to see my mother a few weeks ago. He's based in Toronto. And the second no is a bigger no. I definitely won't be going anywhere near that shower of fuckers. I've met most of Mam's crowd and half of them would rather I hadn't turned up, but Delta came, didn't she?"

"Delta? Who's Delta?"

Delia tapped her own chest.

"Is that what you go by now?"

"Yip . . . that's me. Delta is my alter ego if you like. She steps in when I need her support. Never mind. I wasn't on good terms with Mam since the day I left. It's a long story, I'll tell you some other time."

Delia leaned forward to look directly across at her stepfather.

"*And I don't speak to that bollocks over there and I won't be either!*" she said, raising her voice.

Fran looked across at Delia's stepfather. His face had turned grey.

Delia banged on the table with a bottle. "*Bollocks! Are you listening to me?*" she screamed across at him. "Oh . . . you can be sure he's badmouthed me all over the place, Franny, but *we'll see about that . . . won't we?*" Leaning forward, she gave him the two fingers.

The room quietened as people turned to see where the commotion was coming from.

Delia was still shouting across at her stepfather, using choice language.

Fran's eyes opened wide with shock. She couldn't believe her ears. She could not believe that Delia was making such a show of herself. The way she was talking and her mother only after dying. So angry. She certainly didn't seem to be that put out that her mother was gone and, if she was, she was hiding it very well. And people were leaving. Fast.

Fran looked at Delia and felt a chuckle rising in her chest. She was beginning to feel a bit giddy. She had to check herself. Force herself to think of Delia's mother. Sad. Delia was anything but sober. Fran was terrified that she was about to burst out laughing. Her body was beginning to let her down. She began to shake. Stifling her giggles, she lowered her head so she wouldn't have to look at Delia. Once more she tried to concentrate on something serious. Nothing was coming. It got worse. When she snorted out loud she didn't know where to look. But the moment passed and she began to relax.

People were looking over at them. Philly the owner was standing with one arm resting on the counter. He was glaring straight at them. Ready to pounce. Just when Fran thought that Delia's rage had simmered down, she started off again.

"Look at the other fucker over at the counter and the tea towel over his shoulder. Let him stare away, he won't dare come near me. They're spending big money out in the bar all day so he can hardly open his fucking mouth. *Can he?*"

Philly pulled the tea towel off his shoulder, turning his back to them.

Fran leaned back in the seat as more people began to make their way out the double doors. She felt sorry for Delia who was only making matters worse for herself.

"Delia, I'm not telling you your business, and I don't understand what you're on about, but can I just say it might be best if you keep yourself to yourself for another day. It's not really appropriate at your mam's funeral. Whatever is bothering you can surely wait?"

She regretted opening her mouth the instant she had spoken, with the look that Delia gave her. Fran leant in closer and grabbed her arm.

"I'm sorry . . . I really am. I'm here for you and you can tell me anything – but, please, just leave it alone for now."

No response.

Delia opened her handbag. Taking out a perfume bottle, she sprayed it on her neck before offering it to Fran. "Try it, Franny."

Fran did as was asked of her. She took the perfume, spraying it discreetly on her wrists.

"Chanel No. 5, Franny, the smell of clean soap." Delia leant forward and roared across at her stepfather. "*To wash away the filth!*" She sat back closer to Fran and picked up the perfume bottle. "And plenty more where that came from."

"Oh, it's really lovely, Delia, the real good stuff."

Delia seemed to have stopped her rant. For now.

"You know, Franny, if someone were to ask me what it is I remember most about you, I'd say I remember how you always had a good word to say about everyone, even the two bitches who were taunting you and slagging you off. You never fought back, did you? Remember the Populars? I found out later that it's a real word after all. And we didn't even know it."

Fran felt sorry for Delia but she also felt proud to be sitting beside her even if she was shouting and making a complete show of herself. There was no-one like Delia.

Some people nodded towards the table as they passed by, but no one approached them. Fran knew they were half afraid to come near Delia in case they got her started off again.

Her stepfather hadn't moved. He sat stony-faced, drinking a cup of tea.

Then Delia began talking about her mother, becoming morose. Fran held her arm and said she was delighted to be sitting there beside her on such a sad day.

"Mothers, eh? I suppose yours is the same as ever?"

"Still the same, Delia. The best in the world, but as stubborn as they come. Still treating me as if I were a kid. I always thought your mother was such a lady."

Delia's voice broke. "She was, Fran, and innocent along with it. But she hurt me more than she ever knew when she took his word over mine. She blocked me out and refused to listen. She said I was telling lies, that I was jealous. She took his word against mine and did nothing about it, and I had to run away and now she's gone and he got away with it. Long story, Franny."

Fran didn't know what to say. Took his word against her? Got away with what? She could see the tears building in Delia's eyes. Delia was well on. Her words were beginning to slur. Fran wasn't sure what she was talking about. Whatever it was, it sounded serious.

"Nothing about what, Delia? Look, I'm not entirely sure what you're on about, but I'm here for you. Now that we've met up again we'll stay friends. God knows I could do with one myself."

Delia put her arm around Fran, pulling her towards her into a tight hug. The smell of her perfume was divine. Fran wouldn't dare ask what she was working at that she could afford such a luxury. It could wait. It could all wait.

They talked about everything and nothing. Fran wanted to tell her about her father not being her birth father and she only after celebrating the wrong birthday all of her life but now was not the time.

"Franny, look over there behind your one in the purple turban – see that good-looking guy – over there at the corner bar with the black hair? He keeps staring over at us. I remember him. He's one of the boot factory, isn't he? Old Clarke's son Arthur! Remember his sister Ramona? A bitch she was, and as snooty as they come. They were all packed off to boarding school when they hit eleven, in case they'd be contaminated by the rest of us. Jaysus, when I think about it!"

"He'll be my boss soon enough if my mother has any say in it – she has me tormented so she has. She wants me to stay on in Ballygore and start below in the factory. In the office. You remember Ramona then? She eloped with some fella she met in Dublin, and ended up in a kibbutz in Israel. The family weren't at all pleased. They say it was the cause of Malcolm Clarke's death of a heart attack only a year or so ago."

"Is Arthur married then?"

"Married to this one from England. Mam says she's a snooty bitch, but in fairness Mam says that about everyone. But do we want to be talking about all this and it the day of your mam's funeral?"

"And what should we be talking about then, Franny? My tears are all dried up. I cried so much after leaving here, I thought I was headed for the Thames. But here I am. Keeping the best side out. I never told anyone what went on at home. I couldn't, but now I don't care who knows when I see the way they're glorifying him.

And do you see the way they're staring over at me, as if I'm a piece of shit stuck to their shoes. Nobody believed Delia, did they? They were too quick to judge her." She glared around the bar. "I mourned my mam a long time ago, living on my own in a right dive in London at the time. She had left me on my own to face more of the same, so I ran away. That's the truth and I won't lie about it and why should I? Anyway I don't want to be all misery here. I wouldn't give him the soot. Promise me you'll keep in touch with me now that we've met up, and you'll come over to visit me in London. Yeah? I'll put you up and wait till you see the new pad I just moved in to. Proper posh it is. And wherever I am they'll always be room for my old buddy Franny." She leant towards her, her voice becoming even more slurred.

Fran was over the moon to be invited over to London. She said she'd love to. This could be the chance she'd been waiting for. She'd never been on a plane, or even a ferry. The thought of having Delia Blake as her best friend once again made her feel happy. No one would undermine Delia in her company. She would definitely go to London. She had plenty of money. She could go where she liked.

Fran didn't stop Delia when she picked up her drinks as well as her own. It suited her. She wasn't used to alcohol, but she wouldn't dare admit it. The three drinks she'd had were more than enough. But not for Delia, who now said she felt like throwing up. It was the hard-boiled egg sandwiches, she insisted. When she belched loudly in the direction of her stepfather, Fran excused herself and went to the counter to order a soda-water for her.

Philly beckoned her to one side. He said he'd be serving no more drink to their table. Take it or leave it. Drink up and leave.

Most of the funeral crowd had left. Philly was dismantling the trestle tables, giving the odd glance over towards the two girls. Delia had slumped to the side almost on top of Fran.

Fran saw Delia's stepdad out of the corner of her eye, coming towards the door, the women she thought to be his sisters walking behind him. Warning Delia with a dig from her elbow, Fran kept her head down. But Delia was too far gone to react. Fran gave her another dig, harder this time, until Delia sat bolt upright just in time.

"What the fuck, Franny?" Delia found herself facing her stepfather. "Well, if it ain't the big man himself!"

Fran heard the first hint of an English accent coming through.

"The excuse of a wanker who's going to walk straight out that door without stopping. Or I might just announce to the whole place what he done!"

Her stepfather walked straight ahead, his sisters shuffling along behind him, throwing darting looks back at Delia.

"Wanker is all he is, Franny, a bloody wanker!" Delia gave him the two fingers. "Come on out of here, girl. I need the toilet. Time for some shuteye. Just let him off first."

Ten minutes later Fran helped a staggering Delia to straighten herself as they prepared to leave the lounge. It had been easy enough to get her out in the end. Philly was standing inside the bar, shaking his head.

Walking out towards the double doors, Delia broke away from Fran, heading straight for the wooden piano to her left, banging the palms of her hands down on the keys several times. *Hard.* Fran pulled her away, mouthing the word *sorry* back at Philly who was hurrying towards them.

He pointed crossly towards the door. "*Out!*"

"A good sleep is what you need now, Delia, but don't lie on your back in case you vomit, and choke. I'll call over to you around twelve tomorrow before you leave. We can have a bite to eat together and chat about me coming over to London."

Delia stumbled up the stairs, the key of the room dangling in her hand.

Brigid had the tea on the table by the time Fran arrived home.

Her father sat in his usual spot reading the newspaper at the head of the table. "Have you a few taken, pet? Certainly smells like it."

"That's just the smell of fags from the lounge bar, Daddy. And Delia Blake's Chanel No. 5." Then she got brave. "Actually, yes, as it happens, I do have a few taken. The gins were coming out of everywhere and we drank them all as they were lined up on the table." Feeling braver, she threw her mother a look. "So ask me all the questions now. Oh! Just so you know, Mother, I've been invited over to London to visit Delia . . . and I'm going. We're meeting up in the morning to make the arrangements. Delia's treat in case you're wondering. And no . . . I didn't open my mouth about the insurance money."

"Frances, are you taking leave of your senses? Jesus, Mary, and Joseph, you'll do no such thing as go to London to see that strap! And the cut of her? She was dressed up like a bloody slapper at her mother's funeral above at the church. She'd more bangles hanging off her than you'd see on a gypsy fortune-teller. I'd say the poor priest had to go for a lie-down after witnessing that spectacle. Common as bloody muck is all she is, wherever she got it from, because I can tell you here and now poor Marge was an out-and-out lady!"

"Well, Mother, there's nothing you can do about it – me and Delia were always friends and always will be, so there! Criticising what she was wearing at her mother's funeral is a bit low, don't you think? Even for you." She could see that her mother was ready to explode. Her lips were pursed with temper. Fran was tired and not in the mood.

"Well, it wouldn't take a genius to work out what she's at over in England. The fur coat on her and the skirt up to her arse inside the coat – she looked like a prostitute with the get-up of her. My heart went out to that man, and his poor wife only after dying, and he having to put up with that one. He's at first Mass every morning, rain, hail or snow."

"And how would you know that, Mam? Unless Daddy sees him on his way out to work and reports back to you." Feeling braver still, she continued. "Delia hates him with a vengeance for some reason, and there was always something fishy about him."

Fran had never thought there was anything fishy about Gary Moss. But the way Delia had behaved in Philly's, there was definitely something fishy about him now. And if Delia hated him so much, there must be good reason for her doing so. She'd find out more when she saw her the next day.

Fran went to bed, leaving her parents in the kitchen. The room was spinning when she lay down so she doubled the pillow against the headboard and kept her head raised until the dizziness went. She was happy that she had met Delia. The two of them had hit it off, as if the five years in between had disappeared. They had so much to talk about, so much in common and, no matter what her mother said about her, she was thrilled to have Delia Blake back in her life. Fran couldn't wait to see her the next day.

The following morning Fran was up early, excited to be meeting Delia, whom she imagined would be making a lot more sense without the drink. Trying on different clothes, the pile strewn on the bed could wait until she got back. Most of what was in the wardrobe had either been made or altered by her mother. She looked forward to going shopping now that she had her own money to spend. She might even wait until she got to London. Deciding on the sleeveless navy dress with white collar and bow, she wore her white cropped bolero over her shoulders. She crossed the road and walked down the main street, turning left, heading for the hotel. It was just noon – the bells in the church were ringing for the Angelus. People on the road were blessing themselves. She could feel the heat of the May sun on her head. No need for a cardigan.

Philly was standing at the front door leaning on his sweeping brush.

"Morning, miss."

"Morning, Philly, well, 'tis afternoon now, I suppose." Fran was feeling confident.

"Miss, if you're looking for the young one of the Blakes, she's gone. Left this morning first thing. All packed and out the door with her. Said she was in a woeful hurry to catch the train. Paid her bill in cash and ran off down the street. And good riddance, I say."

Fran was shocked. "Left? No, she couldn't have. We were supposed to … Philly, are you sure? Can I go up myself and check?"

"You'll do no such thing, miss. The cleaner is above cleaning out the room so leave her at it. Aren't you the lassie that had the bad fall in Dublin some time ago? I'd be half afraid to let you up there, in case you'd fall on the aul stairs – they're not great."

Fran could feel herself blush.

"I can't tell you any more now, miss, other than she's gone. And if you want my tuppence-worth, you'll be having nothing more to do with that one. She's a bad egg. The carry-on of at her mother's funeral yesterday, God rest her soul." Philly blessed himself. "Her father called back late last night looking for her. He had a nice few on him and I can tell you 'twasn't in my place he got them either. I never saw him take a drink before yesterday but wherever he went after here, he was mouldy drunk. There was no way I was going to let him anywhere near that young one's door, or all hell would break loose the way she was roaring at him earlier in the day. So I sent him off home to sleep it off. Maybe he could tell you more if you call up to the house."

Philly continued to sweep the footpath.

Fran walked away. Rejected. She felt like a fool. She really believed that Delia had wanted her back in her life. That the two of them would take off where they had left off. And she hadn't even told her about the claim. So much for her placing her faith in other people. For believing that people actually meant what they said. They didn't. For all she knew now Delia's anger for her stepfather was drink-related. Lies. Fran had dressed up to the nines and Delia hadn't even the courtesy to wait to say goodbye to her. Or good riddance. The second time that Delia had run away without saying goodbye. She wouldn't get the chance to do it a third time and that was for sure.

Not wanting to face her mother's "I told you so", Fran marched straight down to the factory to put her name down for a job.

Chapter 20

FRAN

The Boot Factory

1966

Fran started in the factory office two weeks later. She arrived at the gates at eight o'clock sharp. She had lodged her check in the bank the week before, withdrawing enough money to keep her going until payday. She gave her mother two hundred pounds – just to shut her up.

Her father insisted he wouldn't touch a penny out of it. No luck to be had from that kind of money. Her mother gave him a look as she put the crisp banknotes in the pocket of her housecoat, mumbling that she'd put some of it away in the Credit Union for a rainy day.

Wearing her new green-and-lemon-print shift dress, Fran felt confident as she headed towards the factory door. At least she wouldn't have to wear the brown work-coat, or one of the heavier aprons that some of the workers had to wear.

She spotted Lucy Clarke, Arthur's wife, standing over at the front door watering her pots. She waved at Fran who waved back.

Growing up, Fran remembered looking in at the factory house through the gates. She had often wondered what it would be like to live there. Everyone in town knew the house. A large imposing two-storey house with sash windows, standing in the gravel yard to the right of the factory, without a flower or a sign of a garden surrounding it. Two stone lions, sitting at either side of the front door. Protecting it from what? Fran used to wonder. The house had always looked cold.

But Lucy had changed all that. Everything about it looked different now that Fran was inside the gates. There was a softness about it. It was summertime and the smell of flowers wafted across the yard towards her. She recognised the scent of lavender. And when she got closer to the factory door, she noticed a stone wall had been built around the back of the house, with small clumps of blue campanula peeping out of the crevices. The old lady's lace curtains had been replaced with blinds which Fran thought looked very smart.

Her own house on Peter Street was smack in the middle of a row of twenty houses that ran the whole way down the street. Four small windows to the front. A tiny hallway leading into the kitchen, a scullery and bathroom to the back of the house, stairs on the left in behind the front door, front room to the right. Three small bedrooms upstairs. Most houses had a bathroom built onto the scullery since the houses were built. Some of the older tenants still relied on an outdoor toilet.

The kitchen would be wallpapered by Fran's mother in time for Christmas every other year, leaving the wallpaper of the previous year behind on the wall. Her father would mix the paste in a plastic bucket, applying it to the wallpaper, folding it over before handing it up to her mother who stood on the kitchen table waiting with her sponge to hang it on the wall. And the atmosphere was always warm. Upstairs and everywhere else could wait until Dan had the time.

Fran knew Lucy from seeing her around the town. Everyone in Ballygore knew Lucy Clarke to see. English. Tall, slim and elegant, blonde hair tied back in a ponytail that swished from side to side as she walked through the town. She had a way about her. Fran heard her Uncle Will say that Lucy Clarke had a light heart. Fran had liked the sound of that. She decided that she would like to be described as such.

"Oh that Fran, she has such a light heart!" Except that she didn't have a light heart and Delia Blake certainly didn't have one either.

She admired Lucy's flair, her style, her well-cut clothes. Her attention to detail. She reminded her of President Kennedy's wife, Jacqueline. Except for the hair. Boatneck dresses, well-cut jackets, shift dresses in the summertime with bows to the front, large sunglasses. And pearls. Wintertime a well-cut coat over denim jeans and a French beret. She must have loads of them, Fran thought, she seemed to have a different one on her every time she saw her. She knew because she had made a note of it. Green, red, navy, blue, black, so she must have at least five. Lucy's trademark. She sometimes wore a coloured neck square but Fran didn't bother to keep track of them. She wore leather gloves. Stylish. Expensive lipstick applied perfectly on her full lips. Pink and shimmery. Lucy always wore comfortable shoes. Fran noticed. Because Fran always noticed shoes.

Lucy had her own car which hardly ever moved from the yard. She walked everywhere, making friends with the locals who warmed to her. Fran imagined that it couldn't have been easy for her moving in with her mother-in-law, who everyone knew had a fondness for the drink. Uncle Will had told her mother that they had built an add-on for old Missus Clarke at the back of the house. A granny flat with her own front door. He also said that Lucy's mother-in-law was a lot younger than she looked and that she hadn't touched a drop of drink since Old Malcom had died.

Lucy walked the children to the park, introducing them to the other children. She took it on herself to break the Clarke tradition, now that Malcolm had passed. She made it known that her boys would attend the local school just like everyone else's children – there would be no boarding school. She wasn't shy in telling people that Arthur and his brother hadn't been happy at boarding school, that Dermot had all but disengaged himself from the family ever since. But that Ramona had taken to boarding school like a duck to water.

Bloody Ramona Clarke who had punched Fran right in the stomach when they were children.

There was something about Lucy Clarke that made her stand out, apart from the light heart and the way she presented herself. She had confidence and she had charm. And she waved back at people on the street, so she was nothing near the snob that Fran's mother tried to make her out to be. When they met in the yard or on the street they chatted about this and that. Fran asked where Lucy had her hair styled, where she bought her clothes. She looked forward to meeting the polite Englishwoman who wasn't shy in sharing her style tips. Fran figured that Delia and Lucy would have nothing at all in common. If they met.

A month later Fran Gaffney was happier than she'd ever been in a long time, maybe ever. She loved her new job. It mightn't be anywhere near as exciting as working in the Department of Justice in Dublin Castle, but it was the next best thing. It would do for now. Life couldn't be better. She had tons of money in the bank, as well as a wage packet coming in every week. The time she had spent working on herself had not only made her physically strong, she had grown in confidence. Fran would be beholden to nobody from then on.

And Delia Blake could go to blazes.

Up every morning and out the door, looking forward to the day ahead. As the days passed, Fran thought less about Delia, though she still did creep into her mind at times – Delia and her empty promises. But Fran had more on her mind. Passing the floor workers out on her way to the office on the first floor made her feel good. For the first time in her life she fitted in. She liked working in the office with the dark panelled walls and wood ceiling. Two desks facing each other. The bigger of the two was Alice Coyne's.

The days were flying by. Fran had settled in so well, she barely gave moving from Ballygore a second thought these days. The attention she was getting from the boys on the factory floor, made it all the more enticing to stay. So she wasn't transparent after all. The looks she got from some of the girls when she got promoted to wages clerk were not congratulatory by any means. Rumours went around the canteen that her Uncle Will had got her the coveted job in the office. Fran ignored them. It came easy to her.

Poor old Fran Gaffney was no longer someone to be ignored or disregarded. She had become the talk of the factory girls.

Fran held her head high. And she looked taller. She had her hair professionally coloured in Limerick by Lucy's stylist, touched up every six weeks, bright blonde, her green eyes danced in her head as she walked through the factory floor, wearing the very latest in stylish shoes she had bought in Todd's in Limerick. The neat leather insert placed inside her shoe was of little consequence to her anymore. Nobody could believe the transformation in timid Fran Gaffney, who all of a sudden had become the trendsetter in the factory.

The managers and senior staff sat at the yellow table to the right of the canteen for their tea breaks. Up two steps, elevated from the rest of the canteen, where they had a bird's-eye view. A rite of passage for the more senior staff. The biscuits were paid for by the boss and it wasn't unusual for Arthur himself to sit at the yellow table with a company rep. The odd time.

When Arthur did appear, the workers below would be mindful to lower their voices. Alice and Fran sat at the yellow table – no questions asked. They took their breaks together. The office door would remain locked until their return.

Alone at the yellow table, Fran peeped out over her magazine. Alice had been summoned back to the office. The canteen was empty apart from Mary B. Welsh and Rhonda Baker who sat side by side on the bench below, each wearing a tan factory coat. They were staring over at her. Both were well known in the factory for not having a good word to say about anybody. Fran wasn't sure if they realised that she could hear every word with the echo in the room. Perhaps the conversation was strictly for her benefit. Mary B. was smoking an untipped cigarette. Rhonda sat beside her. Closer than two people would normally sit on an empty bench. Pretending to be engrossed in her magazine, Fran listened.

"Jaysus, Rhonda, I can't believe the change in your one all the same. Can you? Talk about a transformation. Everyone at school treated her like the eejit she was, and she running up and down the yard like a flipping megrim, trying to butt in where she wasn't wanted. And here she is all dressed to the nines, looking like Lady Muck."

Rhonda leaned closer, all the while staring straight over at Fran.

"She got big money from the accident in Dublin, and by the looks of it I'd say she's going through it at an awful pace. Nice get-up all the same. She gets her tips from the boss's wife, the Lucy one."

"Nice get-up, my arse, Rhonda – in this place. And the lads outside on the floor gaping at her as if they'd never seen the likes. I saw the Tommy fella having a right gawk up the stairs after her this morning. Although I wouldn't take much notice of him. And the home-made dye job on her. I'd say her aul one throws the dye at it, cos that's what it looks like – as if 'twas fired at her head."

"And the yellow top on her last week and it matching the hair. Did you see her this morning on the way in and she all smiles over to the Lucy one. Licking her arse, she was. She hasn't given me the time of day since she set foot in here. Has she with you?"

Mary B. shook her head and whispered, "No."

Rhonda nudged her. "Jesus, will you talk up, Mary B., she can hardly hear you from over here. I wouldn't give her the soot, would you? I don't know who she thinks she is, but I'll tell you this much. I never in all my life saw the likes of it. One minute she's a right dozey mare and the next she's acting like Lady Muck herself."

"I wouldn't give her that much . . . and will you stop pucking me, Rhonda, or I'll be black and blue from you. She's like a fuckin lemon!"

The two girls looked at each other and broke into a fit of giggles.

"Mary B., come on, quench the fag. Quick, they're all gone back except us. Dump the butts over in the bin. Come on, will you? Will Murphy is coming down to check my machine."

The two waved cheerily across the room towards the yellow table as they walked out the door. Smiling.

Chapter 21

FRAN

First Love

August 1966

Roy Wallace was the new agent sent down from the leather suppliers in Dublin. He would be calling to the factory every six weeks on Arthur's insistence. Orders or no orders. Arthur had of late refused to place any orders over the phone given the amount of inferior leather that had slipped through the factory stores in the recent past. The clickers had brought it to his attention that the quality of the leather had been slipping. Never would have happened in Malcolm's day, they said. Arthur told the suppliers that he would be dispensing with their services if they didn't pull their socks up. Plenty suppliers around the country that would be glad to supply their best hides to the boot factory in Ballygore. He had been well impressed with Roy when he arrived down from Dublin to compensate him for his losses. To smooth things over.

Curly reddish hair. Straight teeth, big brown eyes. A straight back. Fran had no real experience of men but she liked a man with a confident stride and a straight back. Not that she'd been asked out by many men, stride or no stride. She met him at the yellow table with Arthur and when he asked her to join him for a drink in the lounge bar at the River Hotel, she was more than nervous – but said she would. Her first real date.

Wearing her new black-and-rose-patterned skirt with black boots to her shins, she admired herself in the mirror. Her new pink twinset with the tiny flowers embroidered around the cardigan was perfect.

She thought she'd die walking into the hotel. Women didn't walk into bars on their own, unless they weren't of a mind to care what people thought about them. It had been different at Delia's mother's funeral as that was after the Mass, during the day. And the sign was on the door.

Fran imagined what Delia would have to say if she knew that she was going to the River on a real date. "You go right in there, girl, and don't give one flying fuck what anyone thinks!"

Fran walked straight in.

He was standing at the counter. There were a few men around having a drink. Dressed in his perfectly pressed pinstripe suit with multicoloured tie, he stood out. He beckoned Fran to sit at the table in the corner.

He brought her a Babycham with a pint of porter for himself. He hadn't asked what she might like to drink, but she didn't mind because she was nervous. She didn't know what she wanted. She drank it faster than she might have done. Had she known that the bubbles would go straight up her nose to her head she wouldn't have drunk it quite so fast. She spluttered and spilled the drink all over the table. When she sneezed, he laughed and went back to the bar to get her another, telling her to put the empty glass in her handbag as a memento. She said she wouldn't dream of it, that the glass was lovely at the same time with the picture of a deer wearing a scarf on it. She let it be.

The last time she had drunk alcohol was the day of Delia's mother's funeral when she had downed the gin with Delia, but she wasn't going to tell Roy as much. She had downed three drinks that day and gone home with her head spinning.

Roy talked about Dublin mostly, about the government. He talked about De Valera and Jack Lynch and Seán Lemass. Fran was well impressed with the knowledge he had. She herself knew just enough to comment now and then – so she let him talk away and talk he did. He told her all about his job, how he was on the road quite a lot, staying in hotels all over the country. That the boss in Dublin was giving Arthur Clarke his full attention given that the previous agent had taken his eye off the ball. She said it sounded very glamorous, getting to stay in all the fancy hotels – she had never stayed in a hotel in her life. He said it was far from glamorous, that it was an awful lonely life and he was glad she had agreed to go for a drink with him that he really enjoyed her company. He told her he was an introvert. Sort of shy. That he was full of chat but quiet on the inside, he said 'twas her lovely smile had given him the go-ahead to ask her out on a date.

The Babycham was going down well and by the fourth one she was enjoying herself so much she lost her inhibitions. When it went up her nose for the second time she got a fit of laughing. Laughing and giggling with Roy steadying her as he helped her into the driver's seat of his car. Fran had never had so much fun. When she said there was no need to be dropping her home, that she only lived across the road and up a bit, he said they could sit and have a chat in the car and not move at all for a while. Which is what they did. Opening the passenger door for her an hour later, Roy asked if he could see her again the following night. She agreed and let him kiss her on the cheek.

She had drawn a love heart in the condensation on her bedroom window that night.

The following day at work he winked at her through the glass partition as he passed the office on his way to meet Arthur. She blushed and felt her heart flutter.

The second date that next evening went even better than the first. He said he'd thought of taking her to the pictures, but took her for a drive out the country instead. He said it was far too nice of an evening for them to be stuck inside the picture house with all that smoke. He wanted to talk and not to be wasting time staring at a screen in the dark. When he told her that he was half afraid that if he sat too close to her in a darkened cinema house, he might get all sorts of notions, Fran was beyond excited.

They didn't get out to admire the view when he stopped the car. He pulled a blanket from the back seat and said there was a chill in the air, that he'd rather sit beside her and have the chat. So they sat in the car, looking down at the foggy green fields below, and he said he really liked her. That she was different. When she asked him what exactly he meant, he took her hand and laughed and told her what he meant was that she was different to all the others. He said she was intelligent as well as beautiful and he felt privileged to be in her company. Fran was well pleased.

When he leant across and put his arm around her and searched for her lips with his own, she forgot to breathe, and when he moved away he said her lips were soft. There was something classy about her, he said. And she thought of Arthur's wife, Lucy, being classy. Then he kissed her a second time and for longer and he put his hand up under her top and she got an awful land. No one had ever touched her breast before and she'd never been kissed like that by a man until she met him. She was glad she had her new white bra on. He pulled away so fast she asked him what the matter was, and he said he was sorry that he didn't know what came over him. That he would never in a million years take advantage of her. That he wanted her to be his girl and he'd take it at her pace, but she wasn't to be surprised if he forgot himself every now and then. With a body like hers he said 'twouldn't be easy to keep his hands to himself. Respect, he said. It's all about respect and he told her he had the utmost respect for her, as long as she knew that she was driving his senses wild. Then he said that a man needed a sign from a woman to let him know that he wasn't wasting his time. That it wouldn't be fair to be leading a man on and he hoped that she wasn't that sort of a girl.

He asked her to give him a sign when she felt she was ready, so she said she would and wondered what kind of a sign she would give him. She laughed and told him she'd surprise him when he least expected it and he put his arm around her and drew her close to him. When he put his tongue in her mouth, she didn't know what to do for a few seconds. She was glad he couldn't see the colour of her face, because she knew she was blushing, but she opened her eyes wide and got brave and rolled her own tongue around his, until her tongue got too tired and tasted tobacco and she didn't like it too much. But she did it anyway and said nothing. His breathing quickened and he pulled back from her and wiped his mouth with the back of his hand and apologised and said she was far too much of a lady for him to be taking advantage of her. That he wouldn't do that in a million years. Then he looked at his watch and said he was taking her home before he'd lose the run of himself. He said he had never been kissed like that before in his whole life. She wanted to ask him what was so great about the kiss. To tell him that she hadn't been sure what to do at all, but she didn't and was left with the feeling that she must have done it the right way, or he wouldn't have got so excited. He stepped out of the car to straighten himself – pulling out the front of his pants. Shaking his leg. He got back into the car and told her she shouldn't be having such an effect on him. She smiled and gave him a kiss on the cheek and put her hand on his thigh. That was the sign – she wondered should she tell him or would he automatically know.

Fran went home feeling confident. She said nothing to her mother or she'd be tormented with questions – she definitely wouldn't be telling her Uncle Will, because he'd tell her mother as well as Alice, and before she knew it the whole place would be talking. She might tell her father that she'd been out on a few dates with Roy, because he'd leave it alone and wouldn't be pestering her every five minutes.

She decided that when the time was right the whole world could know that Fran Gaffney was doing a line.

She brushed her hand against her breast in bed that night, getting the same feeling that she'd had when he had squeezed it hard. So she circled the nipple on the other breast and then she squeezed the two of them together and her breathing got deeper and quickened and she was happy. And a low buzzing current went through her body and she squeezed her legs together and it felt better than good. She had never before known that such a wonderful feeling could come over her and she couldn't wait to have the feeling again.

When he rang her the following day at work, he told her it would be at least a month before he'd be back in Ballygore. He said he'd had to leave in a hurry but he'd be back. Back for her. He said wild horses wouldn't keep him away and, now that he had met her, he wasn't about to let her go. She was beyond disappointed. A whole month.

He said he had to go up the north for a couple of weeks, and he would be staying up there in a guest house with an elderly widow woman to get all the business up there done at the same time, and in the meantime he'd be thinking about her every day and alone in his bed at night and he'd call her every few days at the office, to make sure she hadn't forgotten about him. He said he'd call her every single day if he got the chance, but given the fact that he'd be busy working all hours, she wasn't to fret if she didn't hear from him. It wouldn't mean that he wasn't thinking of her. He said he'd have to force himself from thinking about her every minute of every day, or he wouldn't get a stroke of work done. She didn't tell him how he made her feel.

She spent every spare moment the following day running her tongue over her lips, licking them, remembering the kiss, remembering the sensation she felt the night before. She shuddered at times.

Fran was happy. Anxiously waiting for the phone on her desk to ring, she decided to pull herself together or she'd get nothing done. She jumped at times when the phone on her desk did ring, but it wasn't Roy. She felt funny every time she thought about him and

Alice must have known there was something up.

Roy called the factory the very next day asking to speak to Alice and Fran thought her heart would stop beating when she heard his voice. It fluttered in her chest and her stomach went funny, but he didn't recognise her office voice and, when he didn't acknowledge it was her, she was put out.

He called her a few days later, to tell her that he hadn't had a minute to himself. That sometimes he might be calling the office, and wouldn't be saying too much to her, because he had work in his head. He told her not to be thinking that she wasn't on his mind, because he thought of little else – he had to concentrate on his job or he'd get the sack and they both laughed at that. He told her he never would have thought that he could get the sack from loving a woman – and she thought her heart would burst out through the wall of her chest, with what he had said. She said it was fine, she understood. She felt exactly the same about him.

She nearly fainted with the shock when he surprised her by turning up at the factory the following week. He was in town for an overnight, he told her. He said he couldn't wait to see her. He had to see her, he said. He said it was his birthday and he wanted to spend it with her and nobody else, and when she said she had no card for him and no present he joked and said she could give him his present later and she blushed and decided to give him another sign.

The date was even better than before. He took her to the River Hotel for dinner and she saw people she recognised looking over at them. She was embarrassed, but beyond excited at the attention. The dining room was full. They drank white wine which she had never had before and, when she tasted it, she wanted to spit it right out. She made a face and screwed her lips together and held her nose and swallowed it, like she had done with the horrible red medicine her mother had made her take as a child. The wine didn't taste anything like gin or Babycham. She found it sweet and sickly. She didn't like it. He told her its name meant "lady's milk" in German and suggested she try the red, but she didn't like that either.

Over the course of the evening, Fran told him about her short leg and the accident. She told him that the fall off the bus had been a blessing in disguise, because the bolts and pins had evened out her problem to a great extent. When she pointed out the shoe with the insert, he said he didn't know what she was talking about and it looked all the same to him and wasn't she the prettiest lass in the factory, so it was all the one, he said, because her head wasn't full of fluff like some women he had met on his travels.

He said he could only stay for the one night, that he had come down specially to see her – he missed her too much. He told her the next time he would stay in town for three nights and the time after that he would arrange for her to be introduced to his family up in Arklow. He told her he had two sisters and they were dying to meet her.

She told him not to be daft, that they had plenty time for all that, they didn't know each other that long to be getting so serious. Then he told her that he knew it was love the very second he laid eyes on her. She told him she understood, because she felt the same.

After having a few drinks in the bar he said the place was getting too noisy and he wanted to concentrate on what they were talking about and not to be distracted with all the goings-on around them. They sat into his car which was parked around the corner on Spring Street, and they talked some more.

When he said his tummy was a bit upset, but he had Maclean's stomach powder back in the hotel room. She said of course she would go back in with him – he could hardly leave her sitting in the car in the dark on her own. He sneaked her up the stairs after him. Giggling. He said they could chat better in private and he wanted to know everything about her and he'd be better off relaxing in the room in case his stomach acted up again. He'd walk her up the street to her house in a little while once he was feeling better.

She sat on the chair beside the bed. He said to take off her shoes and put her feet on the bed. She said that she never took off her shoes until she was getting into bed and he joked and said she could if she liked. Get into the bed. She told him to stop fooling around, that she meant her own bed, and he said he had dreamt about being there with her the night before.

Sitting on the bed, he removed his boots and lit a cigarette. She felt awkward sitting on the chair so she moved over to sit beside him on the bed. He lay back against the pillow, tapping the space he had made beside him. She felt a bit dizzy as she bummed her way up towards the pillow. She said she couldn't stop herself talking and the two of them laughed. He took off his watch and left it on the nightstand beside the bed and finished his cigarette. He said he didn't want it to scratch her when he'd put his arms around her to hold her.

He told her to keep talking, that he could listen to her for hours and that he felt so sorry that she had been bullied when she was younger. He said that bullies were cowards with problems. He said that most bullies were victims themselves and it all made sense to her. He listened intently to her and held her hand and said she didn't have to be on her own, that she had him now. She told him how she felt when her mother pushed her to join in with the others on the road, but she couldn't, because she couldn't keep up with them. That her mother was a strong woman afraid of no-one. That her father was a quiet man, a gentleman, who wouldn't say boo to the cat. That he had come in from the country to live in the town and it hadn't changed him. That he rolled his R's and wore wellington boots most times and took everything in his stride.

She told him her Uncle Will Murphy had made her shoes and still made them the odd time, even though she no longer needed the thick sole, and the difference it had made in her life to have an uncle who wasn't afraid to stand up to her mother, because her father wouldn't dare. He said he knew Will from the factory but that his dealings were mostly with Arthur. Her boss. He said they were the best of friends.

She told him about the birth certificate, that she didn't know who her birthfather was, but that her real father was Dan, because he had raised her and stuck by her mother. He said she was so lucky to have parents – that he was an orphan raised in a Home. He said he didn't want to talk about it and she put her hand on his chest and said she understood. But she felt confused because he had told her earlier that he'd love her to meet his two sisters and his mother in Arklow. She put it to the back of her mind and talked some more and told him everything she could think of about herself, because he said he wanted to know everything about her and she wanted to tell him everything.

She told him about the day she spend in the pub with her best friend Delia Blake, who had returned from England for her mother's funeral and invited her over to visit and then fecked off the following day without saying a word . She told him she would have gone over to London only for Delia bailing out on her. He said that was lucky because she might have stayed over there and he never would have met her. And he wouldn't be making the plans that he was making right now in his head.

And when he turned to kiss her she thought she was in heaven. She could smell his aftershave and she loved it. And the feeling she had inside was warm and she was beaming. He knew how she felt when no one else knew. Her mother whom she loved all her life and would always love didn't seem to understand how she had felt as a child, like an outcast. Ignored and left behind when all she ever wanted to do was belong. To fit in. Her mother who would have babied her for as long as she got away with it. Roy told her that she was his baby now.

He began running his hand up and down her shin, telling her what lovely legs she had. When he went above her knee she got a strange feeling. A nice feeling. It was hot in the room and she said as much and wiped her brow. So he helped her remove her cardigan. The one with the pearl-seed buttons. It was without concern for Fran who was more than willing to do whatever it took to give him a sign. And the room was very warm and he told her she had the loveliest arms and he kissed her right arm the whole way down to her fingers. She felt the fastener flip on the back of her bra when he put his arms around her – his hand had slipped in under her top. It felt strange and loose and she wasn't so comfortable. She pulled a face behind his back. He moved her bra upward out of the way and found her breast which had escaped the security of her bra. She felt a bit awkward with her top sitting on her shoulders and one of her breasts exposed. She told him she felt a bit dizzy. That she wasn't used to the drink. He told her to lie down, that she'd soon feel better. He was breathing very fast. He said he couldn't control himself, that she excited him so much. He said he didn't feel too good himself, that he'd get in under the covers beside her, if she didn't mind. So he did get in and, when he tugged at the covers underneath her to let her in too, in she went because she wanted to cover her exposed breasts and she felt a bit stupid lying there with one breast out and the other one half hanging out under the loosened bra. He told her he'd never seen anyone as lovely as her. He began kissing her breast. Searching with his mouth.

She was pleased and embarrassed all at the same time, but she enjoyed it because no-one had ever got this close to her before. She was even more pleased when he said that she had made him feel so good. *Her*. Fran Gaffney who had fallen off the bus on O'Connell Street in Dublin and landed in a pothole and had to go back home to her mother with her tail between her legs.

The same Fran Gaffney not two years later with her very own fella, lying half naked in a bed in the River Hotel. She felt his bulge against her hip. He said he was sorry but she excited him so much. She told him he needn't stop. She whispered in his ear to keep going, that it was alright. He asked was she sure. And his breathing got heavier.

She told him this was the sign. That she was ready and wanted to give herself to him. He said he'd be gentle. That he wouldn't hurt her and to tell him if she changed her mind and he'd stop straight away. She said she wouldn't be telling him anything, because it was what she wanted. And when it became uncomfortable for her, she knew she had done it because all the fumbling was over and he made a squeaky noise. He had barely entered her when he had fallen on top of her moaning like a wounded animal. It had hurt, but not as bad as her mother had led her to believe it would, the very first time her hymen would be torn. He said it was the best he could ever imagine and reached over for the half-quenched cigarette he had left in the glass ashtray on the nightstand. The smoke was still rising from the ashtray, so he took a drag and it lit up again.

She went into the bathroom to clean herself off. Smiling to herself. She had her man. She'd get over the mild discomfort. She'd experienced enough in her life to know the difference between discomfort and pain. It crossed her mind that she was no longer a virgin. She didn't feel any different. She had imagined she would.

Roy was leaving for Dublin the following evening. He sent her a single red rose in a silver cardboard box. The boy from the florist shop brought it straight to the canteen during her tea break and she was mortified but she'd dry it and keep it forever. Her first gift from her man. Any man. She could see the looks she was getting from the girls in the canteen. Fran wondered if they could tell by her that she was no longer a virgin. Alice had smiled at her, as if she knew. Knew that she was after having it off for the first time and wanted to shout it from the rooftops that she was doing a steady line with her fella down from Dublin. But she couldn't because she knew that if her mother found out that she kill her for giving herself to a man – even if she was twenty-one years of age and madly in love with him. And her mother was no one to talk even if she did find out – because she had done it herself about the same age and she hadn't gone on to marry the man she had gone to bed with. Fran knew it would be different for her, because herself and Roy would get married and make love every single night of the week.

When he rang her two days later and thanked her for the sign, she said he was welcome. She couldn't talk much because Alice was at her desk at the other side of the room, so she coughed twice to let him know. He asked if Alice could hear him and she laughed and said of course not, and then he asked how she was, and she got the feeling back, but not as strong. He told her she didn't need to answer, that he was staying in a hotel on his own in Westmeath, if she'd like to come up on the bus and join him for the night she'd be more than welcome. She laughed and said some of us have work to do and Alice dropped her pen and looked straight at her as if she knew.

Fran pointed to the phone and winked and rolled her eyes. Roy said he mightn't see her for a few weeks, that he was going crazy thinking about her. He asked her if she'd thought about him in bed the night before, and that he had thought about her and had a wet dream. She felt her face burn. She knew what a wet dream was because everyone knew what a wet dream was and she'd seen somewhere that a woman could have one too, but she wasn't too sure what all that was about. So she said she'd better get back to work, that she'd talk to him the following day.

Chapter 22

FRAN

Yellow Boots

September 1966

Fran hung up the phone on her desk. Pushing back her chair, she stood up and headed for the door. Not one for spontaneous reactions, this was a first. She grabbed her bag from the shelf beneath the coatrack, tugging roughly at the tail-end of her coat, bringing the jacket underneath down with it. She had bought the coat to impress him when he had told her bottle-green was her colour.

Alice appeared just as Fran approached the door. She pointed to her jacket on the floor, her eyebrows raised high on her forehead. Expectant.

Fran brushed past her, stepping on the brown-velvet jacket.

After what she'd just been told over the phone, stepping all over Alice's jacket was the least of her worries. She was devastated.

Fran's world had crashed and there was nothing or no-one who could make it better.

A week had passed since she had heard from Roy. Alice had

mentioned that the new leather agent from the suppliers had called earlier looking for Arthur.

"What new agent? You mean Roy?"

"No, Frances, I'm talking about the new agent, Danny."

She dialled the Dublin number when Alice stepped out of the office. She recognised the voice from ringing in the orders. The girl told Fran that Roy wasn't working there anymore. She went on to say that Roy had moved up north with his wife and kiddies. The new agent would be in touch with the boss.

"What do you mean he has moved – he can't have moved anywhere. His wife? No, it's Roy I'm looking for, Roy Wallace. He's not married. This is Fran. Frances Gaffney, his girlfriend."

The girl at the other end of the phone sighed.

"Listen, love. Believe me, it's the same bucko. Our Roy." The voice took on a different tone. A softer tone. "Look, pet, I don't know who you are, other than you work in the boot factory in the country. I probably shouldn't be saying this at all, but that lad needs a good box. Roy is well married and has been for years. He's the daddy to three kiddies. Believe me when I tell you, you're not the first. Anyways, he was only ever going to be covering your part of the country for a couple of months until they trained up the new man."

Fran couldn't speak. The girl continued.

"Come here till I tell ya, love – forget about that jackass, and move on with yourself. Ah sure, 'twas all closing in on him. Are you still there, love?"

Running across the cobblestone yard, Fran opened the side gate back with such force it banged hard against the wall behind, bouncing back on her, hurting her arm. The tears slipped down her cheeks as she fled the factory yard. She was in a state.

Out on the street she collided with Sadie Pratt, who grunted crossly at her, making no sense. In no mood to stand and offer an apology Fran continued on down the street, her coat trailing along behind her. She wouldn't be wearing it again any time soon. He'd said it matched her eyes.

When she heard someone calling her from behind, she thought for a second it was Sadie Pratt calling her back to have another go at her. She had paid no heed to her. It wasn't the first time Sadie had muttered to her in the street. The Knitting Needle, as she was called, was well known in Ballygore for her snide remarks. Nobody questioned the scrawny woman with the sharp tongue. They were half afraid of her. Everyone knew to ignore Sadie, so they passed her by. They wouldn't be seen to be talking to her. Men or women. Sadie's line of work was covert. Behind her own front door.

"Fran . . . Franny, will you wait up? Jaysus, you're in a woeful hurry!"

Suddenly recognising the voice, Fran's heart skipped a beat. She could hardly believe her eyes when she turned around.

There in front of her, large as life, was Delia Blake. Delia her old pal and she hurrying towards her. Who else but Delia had the brass neck to be seen out in daylight wearing what Fran's mother would call whore's clothes. Her big breasts bulging out above her bra, like four breasts, all squashed inside a small red waistcoat that barely covered her sides. Difficult to say where Delia's breasts started and where they finished. She was wearing a hairpiece, different to the last one. Straight black glossy hair, tumbling down over her back. Her own hair was visible underneath, scraped back with a thin yellow plastic band.

She wore pair of yellow, shiny, knee-length boots.

"You came back, Delia!" Fran's torment changed to despair as she ran sobbing into Delia's arms. Any grievances she had felt against Delia over the past four months were put to rest. Delia was back and that's all that mattered.

"There, there, Franny, mind the dribbles on my new top, pet. Jesus . . . if I'd known you were going to react like this I'd have come back a lot sooner. Didn't think my presence was going have this much of an effect on you."

Fran bawled her eyes out, unable to speak.

"What's the matter, lovey? Hush now. Come on, or they'll be thinking I'm bating you up. Hold on a second, will you? Just one second. I'm sweating like a bloody pig here with all the rushing. 'Tis awful hot for September."

Struggling to remove the waistcoat, she managed at last and tossed it towards Fran. "Hold that, honey, while I root in the bag, or I'll pass out here."

Fran took the waistcoat. Taking a blue can from her white handbag, Delia unashamedly lifted the sides of her white top, and began squirting anti-perspirant under each arm.

Fran looked around to see if anyone was looking. Delia offered her the can.

"Go on, have a spray. It's the good stuff, Snow Spray – go on, spray away. I brought it over from London."

Fran shook her head. "No, thanks."

She knew better than to stand on the street lifting her blouse to squirt anti-perspirant on her armpits. Even if it was the good stuff.

She breathed in the air around Delia. It smelt good. Like baby powder. Replacing the can in her bag, Delia rubbed her brow with the back of her hand, before grabbing the waistcoat back from Fran.

Opening the clasp of her handbag again, she stuffed it in.

"Now what's all this about?"

Fran had got her breath back but when she spoke fresh tears welled up in her eyes.

"I can't tell you out here on the street, Delia, but I never want to see the inside of that bloody factory again. Such a clown I've been, thinking that I had finally met a fella who wanted me. A fool is all I am. A big fool," she whimpered. "But he didn't have any interest in me at all. He got what he was after and then he was off."

Fran was far too upset to continue, blowing her nose into the hanky she took from the sleeve of her blouse.

Delia held her by the arm. "Who is he, Franny, tell me? Who is this man who didn't have any interest in you?"

The sobbing continued.

"Come on out of here, for fuck sake! And quit the bawling, Franny." Delia led her firmly by the arm down the street.

"I'm so glad to see you, Delia!" Fran whimpered. "You've no idea how glad I am. When did you get home?" She blew her nose again.

"Two minutes more and you've have missed me, pet. I'm on my way over to Thornton's to sign a few forms. This will business will never be sorted. My appointment is not until four so I've a bit of time." She checked her watch. "I arrived earlier on the train from Dublin, still in my work clobber – no harm, no-one here worth bothering about – apart from yourself, of course, so I'm heading back later on the eight o'clock in time for the night boat. I'd wondered would I bump into you. Come on with me over as far as Thornton's and we can chat away for a few minutes before I go in to see him. Come on, out with it all, Franny. It can't be that bad."

The two walked together towards Thornton's solicitor's, ignoring the attention that Delia was getting from two headscarved women across the street. The women had stopped walking to get a better look.

"What the heck are they staring at?" Delia waved over at them. "Good afternoon, ladies – wait till I cross over and ye can say what ye have to say to my face!"

Fran was mortified. She tried to curtail Delia. "It's just your yellow boots, Delia – there wouldn't be too many wearing them here in Ballygore. They're just admiring them, I'd say."

"They are in my tail-end admiring my boots, Franny, but I couldn't give a flying fuck." Delia gave the women her full attention. Shouting across at the two. "Like 'em, do ye? Wait there till I take them off and you can have one each."

Delia leant against the wall, lifting her left leg as if to remove the boot. The two women hurried at speed up the street. Fran stood there caught between a giggle and mortification.

"That'll shut them up for about two minutes." Delia straightened herself. "*Nosey cows!*" she roared after them.

Fran gently pushed Delia to move her along.

The two girls sat on the bench across from Thornton's office. It was damp from a recent shower of rain. Fran had put her green coat underneath them. It didn't matter if it got ruined – she hated it. Delia opened her mouth to speak but Fran cut across her.

"Delia, by the way, before you go in. Why did you just up and leave the morning after your mam's funeral, when you knew that I was calling over to see you in Philly Manson's the following day? And I had every intention of coming over to you in London for a visit. You made me feel like a right eejit. And, just so you know, all you did was give my mother more leverage against you."

"*Aah*, Franny, give over! Jesus, stop. I was dying with a hangover the same day. Remember I had just buried my mother and made a right fucking eejit of myself in Manson's lounge. I had my reasons to bail out, believe you me. Anyway, it's what Delia does best. *Run, Delia, run.* Your turn. What the feck is going on? With the speed of you coming out the factory gate, I thought you were being chased. And what was that Knitting Needle one saying to you? She passed me wearing the same auld mangey hat I remember her wearing when I was a kid. A dead ferret. She muttered something at me under her breath."

"Don't waste your time going on about the Knitting Needle, Delia. I don't even know her real name, do you?"

"It's Sadie Pratt. She's half mad and a good scrub would do her no harm at all."

Fran nodded in agreement. "She hangs around a lot. Getting worse she is. Mooching around the town with that aul hat perched on her head summer and winter and she muttering away to herself. My mother says her head hasn't seen air or water in years. She grunted at me too, Delia. Feckin' eejit. Or maybe 'tis I'm the eejit."

Delia shook her head and grabbed Fran by the wrist. "You're no eejit, Franny Gaffney – maybe a bit soft at times, but you're far from an eejit."

Encouraged by Delia's comment, Fran sniffled and continued. "Mam says Sadie was no eejit at all years ago, well known for getting rid of a problem. The girls used to come from everywhere, but not anymore, not since she was raided. The guards hid in the laneway and banged on the door with a truncheon till she let them in. They searched the house and came out with all sorts. Some said they got hold of some old book that she had all the names in. People were out on the laneway watching and Sadie roaring down at the Guards from the top window. Spitting venom. Mam said that they didn't do anything about it after, cos the sergeant brought plenty of business her way back in the day. Do you remember him – Sergeant Rice?"

"Indeed-in I do, the bloody creep! If I met him now I'd give him a good run for his money. Ah well, if there wasn't a need for her services she wouldn't be getting the business, now would she? Touch wood and all that. Anyway, come on. Talk to me, Franny, and forget about the flaming Knitting Needle."

"I don't know where to start but I'll tell you –"

Delia cut across her. "As long as you don't go off bawling again, Franny. I'll tell you what, go on home and meet me in the hotel in say – half an hour. Not in Philly Manson's lounge bar though. He'd refuse to serve me after my outburst at Mam's funeral. I'll see you at the River Hotel and I promise I won't leave town in such a hurry this time."

"No, Delia, no way. I'll wait for you right here and we'll go to the hotel together. I'm not letting you out of my sight. Anyway, how can I face going home after just walking out of work?"

"So you walked out of the job proper like?"

"Yep! And I'm not going back. Ever."

Delia stood up and faced Fran.

"*Hmmm* . . . so you're free to come and go as you like then. Are you now? *Hmmm.* Tell you what! Come on back to London with me then. You haven't got a fella here in Ballygore, right?"

Fran pulled a face, shaking her head from side to side. "Don't even think of asking me that again, Delia. The fella I thought I had was not only married. He had three kids and counting."

Delia rolled her eyes. "Fucker! What else is new? Look, tell me later – let me get this business over with first. And, come on – come to London. Why the hell not? What's stopping you? We'll have great fun and it'll all be blown over when you come home. If you do decide to come home."

Fran made a face.

"Look, there's plenty of work where I'm set up over," said Delia, "and you are twenty years old. Old enough to make up your own mind."

"I'm twenty-one, actually. Oh, that's another story I have to tell you, but thanks for the lovely card. *Not*."

"Oh, you're more than welcome and I got yours in January for mine. *Not*."

The two sniggered.

"Seriously, are you bonkers, Delia? How can I just up and leave like that?"

"Because you can, Franny. Because you can. That's why. And that's all you need to think about. When have you ever suited yourself apart from going off to Dublin that time? Just tell your mother you're coming over to visit me for a few days, and she'll be fine with it. But, for the love of Jesus, don't dare say that 'twas I suggested it. I don't want Brigid Gaffney coming after me for exploiting her little girl."

"Oh, you really are on the bonkers side, Delia Blake, and I haven't even seen you for years apart from your mam's funeral. God rest her. What is it now . . . four months? So how've you been really?" Fran felt a pang of guilt that she hadn't mentioned Delia's mother earlier in the conversation.

"Just fine, darlin', Delia is doing fine. Delta on the other hand will always be fine." Her voice softened when she mentioned her mother again. "I have my mother here in my heart, and that's where I'll keep her. If she were still on this earth 'twould be with that prick of a husband she'd be. So yeah . . . I'm just fine."

"But, Delia, I can hardly just up and leave. I've never really been anywhere outside of Ballygore. Except for Dublin with all the hospital appointments and going up to start the job. And we all know what happened there." Fran's voice became animated. "Poor Fran that went up to Dublin for the big job and fell off the bus into a pothole and ended back where she came from! Oh, never mind! You wouldn't understand!" She stopped. "Sorry for going on, Delia."

Fran saw the look on Delia's face. She squinted at Fran.

"Jesus, give over, Franny. Self-pity is no pity and I'm an expert in that field. And I'm well aware of what you've been through — all the way back. I haven't exactly been going around with my eyes closed, you know. You used to walk on your tippy-toes when we were small until you got them proper shoes. 'Twasn't as if I was going to say anything. But I knew by you, and it was hard enough on you, besides me adding to it. You really wouldn't notice a thing anymore anyway, but I do remember." Delia raised her painted black eyebrows, pursing her lips together, she shook her head slowly. "You look perfectly fine to me, Franny."

Whatever self-pity Fran was feeling at that moment disappeared. Delia understood.

"Turns out the break in my ankle two years ago was a blessing in disguise," she said. "Remember I told you in Manson's that I had broken it in three places when I fell off the bus into the pothole? Then again you probably don't remember a whole pile from that conversation. I had to get a plate and screws fitted. 'Twas my hips they were worried about. Well, it turned out that the difference in the length of my two legs is now under the marker to be needing the thick soles. Ever again. That's how they gauge it seemingly. Anything over an inch. So all I have now is an small insert."

"You dirty rotten thing, Franny Gaffney! Talking measurements now, are we?"

Fran laughed. Delia couldn't help herself.

"So now the only time I notice any real difference is when I put the insert into the wrong shoe."

"Ah, we all have something uneven. Look at me, lovey – my right side is a full size bigger than my left side." Delia clapped her hand against her right breast before doing the same with her right hip. "Meet Dolly. And I couldn't give a tuppenny shite . . . so there! I remember them two bitches in the yard in primary school calling you names. The Bates one and Mary B., I felt like bating the crap out of them. No one would say anything to them and you never stood up for yourself. Feckin' bullies. What was it they used to call you?"

The two spoke in unison: *"Tippy-Toes Gaffney!"*

Fran sighed.

"Bitches is all they were, Franny. But they weren't so inclined to be slagging you after I had a word with them. I bet they're still the very same, only whispering about somebody else now. Those kind of people don't change. They think so poorly of themselves that they try to drag everyone else down to their own level."

Fran felt there was no need to tell Delia right away that the same two bullies were working in the boot factory. The word about her and Roy would no doubt get back to them. She could never face them again.

"I better go in here to see this man. Hey, have a think about coming back with me while I'm gone in. Come on, Franny, for God's sake, take a risk! You won't need much, just throw a few things in a bag and I'll cover your fare over on the mail boat. You can pay me back when you have it. Are you owed wages at the factory?"

"They can keep their wages – it's only two days they owe me anyway. And I have my own money. The insurance settlement for my leg. I got a good few bob."

Fran expected Delia to react at the mention of the money. But she didn't.

"Well, you can stay with me over and I'll get you sorted with a little job. There's loads of work going where I am. And if you want to come home again, then do! Simple. All worked out. So what are you waiting for?"

"You know what, Delia! I will go! I will go with you. I'll go home right now and pack a bag and we're off. And you're dead right. There's nothing stopping me from coming home whenever I feel like it. Anyway, I'm sick and tired of being the good girl. Well, no more poor old Fran. A holiday in London is just what I need."

Delia grinned and put her finger to her lips as she headed for the glass door of the solicitor's office.

Chapter 23

FRAN

Defying Mother

Ten minutes later Fran thought her mother was going to have a heart attack, when she announced that she had bumped into Delia Blake and was heading back to London with her for a holiday.

Shouting up the stairs after her, her mother sounded as if she were ready to explode. She followed Fran up to the bedroom. Red-faced, she stood at the door, her hair set in her pink rollers.

"What nonsense is this, Fran? What do you mean you're taking off on a holiday? What about the job? You're only there a few months."

Fran did her best to ignore her mother as she reached for the brown-leather case on top of the wardrobe.

She could see that her mother was only waiting for her to respond before she'd let loose. Fran didn't care what came out of her mother's mouth – she needed to get out of Ballygore and away to London with Delia. She was being spontaneous.

"Delia Blake? And how do you think that's going to look around the town? Well? Look at the holy show that strap made of herself the last time in the pub. I heard after that she was roaring and shouting at her poor stepfather and he just after burying his wife. A bloody slapper is all she is! Did you not see the get-up of her at the funeral?"

Fran did her utmost to remain calm. "It's fine, Mam. I took two weeks' holidays is all and I'll be back again in a fortnight. Maybe sooner if I can't hack it over there."

Fran knew that Will would fill her mother in later – how she had upped and left the office without a word. How she had trampled all over Alice's jacket on her way out.

Fran couldn't bear to look at her mother. She was filling her suitcase with shoes, sandals, and boots. It had always been about footwear for Fran. She pulled her clothes roughly from their hangers before stuffing them in on top of the shoes.

Her mother tried to grab the case from her. "You can't just up and leave like that, missy! You can't. What about your tea? What'll your father say? You haven't even got money changed, have you?"

"Mother, I told you. I'm going for a fortnight, that's all, maybe a week, and when I get back I'll see what I'm doing. Delia will see I'm not short and there's a Bank of Ireland over there I can deal with."

"What do you mean you'll see what you're doing? Doing about what?"

Fran lost her patience. "Jesus, Mam! I walked out of the blasted job and I'm not going back. *So there!*"

"What? What do you mean you walked out of the job? Have you lost it completely?" Her mother flopped down on the chair beside the nightstand. "Where's all this coming from? After your

Uncle Will bending over backwards to get you in there in the first place. And what about this fella of yours that had you all excited and happy? Yeah, I know. Someone saw you at the hotel. *Hmmm* … I wonder what he'll have to say about all this? The Blake one isn't exactly the sort of company he'd want you to be keeping. Some bloody mismatch. I'd be careful if I were you or he'll run a mile."

Fran watched as the blood vessels on her mother's cheeks became more visible.

"Would you, Mammy? Would you really be careful if you were me? Well, I'm sick and tired of being bloody careful, and for your information Delia Blake is the most exciting person I have met in my life. Up to now. She's intelligent and smart and could have been anyone she wanted to be if she was given half a chance. And she doesn't give a hoot what anyone thinks of her and, yeah, she knows that everyone here in Ballygore has her down as a proper tramp. And while we're at it, my 'item' as you call him, has just dumped me. He's married, Mother."

Brigid gasped as her hand flew to her mouth.

"Yes. You heard me. I just found out he's a married man and I never knew it and I let him have his way with me in the hotel and in the car. And here I am, an eejit. And a worse eejit for telling my mother, but there you go. So I walked out of the factory and I'm never going back and you can take that whatever way you like. So who's the slapper now?"

"What? I told you a thousand times a fella won't marry an easy girl."

"Oh, really?" Fran paused. Angry as she was, she couldn't bring herself to accuse her mother of being 'an easy girl' by her own definition. "So, yeah! I'm off to London with Delia Blake, my best friend. My only friend!"

Brigid didn't move. She sat with her hand covering her mouth.

"Yeah, Mammy, three kids he has, and other eejits like me no doubt in every corner of the country. The girl in his office told me straight out when I rang looking to speak to him. You'll have to excuse me for being upset, but I'm sick and tired of being the good girl. The naive fool of a girl. Gullible Fran. Tippy-Toes Gaffney. That was my nickname in school, by the way. Did you even know that? And it probably always will be my nickname for some ignoramuses here in Ballygore, no matter how old I am. Do you know who christened me with the nickname while they tried to trip me up as I passed? Mary B. Welsh and Rhonda Bates, the two bitches I have to pass every morning on the factory floor. I was afraid to tell you because you'd have gone marching up to the school and made everything worse for me. So I put up with it and learned how to deal with it in my own way and told no-one. And the only one who knew what was happening and cared about me was Delia Blake."

"I'd no idea. Why didn't you say?" Brigid looked as if she was going to cry but she didn't. Then she did what she always did. She became defensive. "Well, don't take it out on me! If you'd said something, of course I would have sorted it. Wait till I see them two tramps on the street!"

"No, Mammy, you won't. Not this time. This is my life and I need to start living it. I know you want the best for me and have always tried to protect me, but you can't keep on doing it. I just need to get away for a little while to clear my head. I feel confident when I'm with Delia. I can't explain exactly what I mean but I know I'm doing the right thing. For me."

"I can't believe I'm hearing this. And I don't know where you think you're going with all them sandals in the middle of

September." Her mother began to whimper. "You've only been with her for a few minutes and you're up and leaving for a holiday. You're not yourself, that's all, you've had a shock. I'll have a word with Will. You know you won't find as good a job anywhere else in Ballygore."

"Mother, I'm off to London. Face it. And not that you've noticed but I'm a grown bloody woman. I'll leave my bag under the stairs and come back for it in an hour or so. And that green coat . . . you can do what you like with it. I'll never put it on my back again.

"The coat you paid all the money for in Limerick!"

"I have plenty more where that came from."

"Well, you better not tell the Blake one about the claim, or she'll bleed you dry." Brigid stormed out of her daughter's bedroom, slamming the door behind her.

Fran flopped down on the bed. It hadn't been easy listening to her mother talking to her as if she were a child. She had felt like screaming at her. Like swearing and cursing and screaming and roaring and losing control and telling her mother that all the mollycoddling and trying to protect her over the years had only made her look stupid, no matter how well-intentioned it was. That she had felt ostracised, ignored in the school yard and on the street and on the way home on her own and she walking in near the wall, too afraid to stand out in the open. And they all laughing at her. Until she became friendly with Delia.

They had tormented her and she never told anyone and she couldn't because she was ashamed to say the words that nobody wanted to hear. To be open and honest about what had happened to her on the way home from school. Two girls. Not two boys. Two sisters. Because she was so embarrassed, she couldn't find the words. Because they were dirty words and she was too ashamed to repeat them.

They had pushed her up the concrete steps of an old abandoned house, cornering her in behind the hedge, like a rat. And when she crouched down in fear they sniggered at her and told her to pull up her dress and show them her knickers. The next time they went further and pulled her knickers down and roared laughing. They sneered at her and she was terrified, helpless and alone.

Terrified of the sisters with the sickening smiles, who were well able to conceal whatever had turned them into sick-minded girls who bullied a younger child just because they could. They were rough with her and they ran off and left her feeling exposed and bare. Sneering. They did it again and again and she couldn't remember when it started and when it stopped, because it didn't bear thinking about and she had been terrified. They belittled her and called her a dirty cry baby and pointed at her and pushed her on the ground and she would never ever forget how humiliated she'd felt. She was seven years old. One thin, and the other one twice her size. One with long fair hair and the other with thin mousey hair. They had long since left Ballygore and Fran had often thought of them and wondered if they had married and had children of their own and how they might feel if someone did the same thing to their own precious child. But she wouldn't wish the experience on any other child. But she wished it on them. The sisters. She'd heard her mother mention once that the bigger of the two had become a nurse in Dublin and the other one was in some other job. A respectable family. Fran couldn't mention it to anyone. Even Delia. The very word *knickers* gave her a creepy, cowardly, dirty feeling and triggered a memory in her, bringing her back. She hated the word *knickers*. Fran had kept it to herself, but she might just mention it Delia when the time was right. Delia would understand.

Frances grabbed her suitcase and hurried down the stairs. She threw it in under the stairs with a thud, calling back to the kitchen where she knew her mother would be, behind the door smoking a cigarette.

"See you in about an hour so, Mam!"

She banged the hall door shut behind her just as she saw father parking his bicycle against the wall outside. She waved her hand as she stepped out past him. "Mother is inside, she'll explain. I'll see you before I go, Daddy, so don't budge from the house."

"Go where, love? Are you off out with your young man?"

She dismissed him with a flick of her hand.

"Not now, Dad. Your Galway Brigid inside needs you."

Chapter 24

GALWAY BRIGID

April 1945

Brigid Murphy climbed back over the fence at the same spot she had entered less than thirty minutes before. Feeling her skirt snag on the barbed wire, she pulled it free. Hearing it rip was of no consequence. The tears were scalding her eyes as she pulled her bicycle roughly out of the ditch. Nothing mattered now. She felt dirty. Stained. She needed to get away from where she was.

Away from the man who had coaxed her into the field under the pretence of picking mushrooms. Huge big white caps, he said, ready and ripe for picking after the rain. They were always there at this time of the day. He told her how to cook them in a saucepan of milk with a knob of butter, the way his mother used to make them.

A day out and maybe a picnic, he said. She brought a flask of tea with an extra cup and two cheese sandwiches wrapped in a tea towel tied in a knot. And a tablecloth. He told her he would bring a blanket for them to sit on.

They met on the humpbacked bridge at the far side of Ballygore. He said he'd forgotten the blanket but 'twas very mild for April and they could sit on his coat and the grass was grand and soft. And at least they had the tablecloth.

They scanned the field, searching through the grass, but there wasn't a mushroom to be found. He said he didn't know where they had got to, maybe the cattle had got them earlier. Or maybe the fairies had made them disappear under the ground.

"Maybe 'tis over there they are, behind the tree," he said, pointing. He took her by the hand and led her to the corner of the field, between the hedge and a budding rhododendron bush.

"We might as well lay out the cloth here, Brigid, and have the tea."

She had her back to him, kneeling on the grass, when he pushed her on her side and began tickling her until the two of them lay back on the soft grass laughing, with the sweet scent of hawthorn floating behind them in the hedgerows. They lay side by side. Giggling. When he rolled on top of her and kissed her, she smiled at him.

Until he put the full weight of his body down on top of her and pinned her to the ground, holding her two arms up over her head.

She thought it was a joke at first then shouted at him to stop fooling around. To let her go. She tried to get out from underneath but she couldn't. Her heart was pumping mad with fear. The smell she had got from his clothes before, the one that she couldn't quite describe, now introduced itself as a stale mouldy smell. The smell of damp clothes that had been left in a pile in a cold room. A smell that she would never forget. When she tried to push him off her he laughed and told her to be quiet. He said he knew it was what she wanted. His breathing had quickened. He said 'twas too late now to be changing her mind after goading him and egging him on for weeks. He was fumbling at his pants with his left hand with his right arm across her chest. She kicked at him and screamed at him to get off and he covered her mouth and she couldn't breathe and he began tearing at her underwear and she gave up the fight. She felt the hardness and he wasn't listening to her. He was no more than an animal in a field. She lay there in the end – unable to move. In shock.

He took himself out of her and lay on his back for a second. She turned her head. The flask of tea and sandwiches were as they had left them, sitting innocently on the tablecloth on the grass. Nothing had changed and everything had changed.

He stood up and buttoned up his pants and ran off before she was able to move. Leaving her there to clean herself up. So she did. Through the tears that fell down her face. Blinding her. Feeling dazed and unable to think beyond the moment she was in, she looked around her. She needed to get out of there. The cattle in the next field had gathered at the rusty gate – they were swishing their tails and mooing, staring at her. She wondered if they had seen what had happened and she felt the shame.

Looking down at her mauve check skirt, she straightened it. The skirt she had made herself was turned back to front. One of her stockings was laddered where the steel cap on his shoe had dragged against it when he had pinned her down with his legs. Vice grips. The other stocking felt loose above her knee where it had become detached from her suspender. The top two buttons of her blouse were missing. The pearl buttons that she had sewn on herself to replace the cheap white see-through ones.

Picking loose grass from her hair, she stared transfixed down at the flattened grass, before kicking it with the side of her shoe, wishing for it to go back to the way it was, wishing she could go back to the way she was. Then she ran along the hedgerow to get back out over the fence, leaving the picnic behind her. There was no going back.

She told no-one. She couldn't and she wouldn't. They would have called her a fool for going into a field with him in the first place. Easy. For looking for white cap mushrooms in a field in the month of April.

She had met him when he called to the flat to drop off the patterns for the aprons. He had a scooter. Will had warned her about him. He had told her to stay well clear of him when he came to collect the finished aprons, because he was an ignoramus with a mouth on him like a sewer rat and he didn't like the way he spoke about women. Will told her he had gone as far as to have a word with the boss-man about him. But Brigid paid no heed. She thought he was genuine.

He had courted her for four weeks on the sly and never laid a hand on her, or made her feel in the least uncomfortable. But he had made her feel more than uncomfortable in the end. She became wary of everyone. Scared. Jumpy and suspicious. Flashbacks. The smell of damp from his jumper had stayed with her. Trusting no-one no matter who they were. Blaming herself for weeks on end. Because she had gone out of her way to impress him. She would never again eat a mushroom.

And she couldn't tell a soul. He had said he had clout in the factory and when she found out from Will that he had no such thing, that he was a seasonal worker travelling around the country, it was too late.

Brigid kept to herself in the weeks ahead. And not a sign of him coming near her door. And when he did turn up after some time, she didn't answer – she hid and pretended she wasn't there. When Will enquired as to why she didn't answer the door to him, she said she didn't want to, he was to send someone else, that the man gave her the shivers. And Will knew not to ask again, because he knew well the measure of him.

When she met Dan Gaffney in the shop a few doors down, she didn't give him a second thought. He had held the door open for her and tipped his cap on his way out. Then she bumped into to him the very next day outside the shop, and she got it into her head that he was following her. Stalking her. And she told him in no uncertain terms that she'd tell her brother Will on him, if he didn't stop pestering her.

He said he was sorry, that he'd leave her alone. That he was only trying to be friendly. Later when she thought about it, she realised that she had overreacted. Dan was a shy country lad who wouldn't harm a fly, and she asked Will to make enquiries about him, and he came back and told her that Dan worked as a farm labourer. And when he wasn't at that, he did a bit of painting and decorating. A man who wouldn't baulk at a day's work. He was well liked, according to Will. He had a few acres out the country and he wasn't a bummer. Bridget made it her business to meet Dan on the street – she told him that she was awful sorry for being so rude to him that day outside the shop, that her head had been all over the place. They became friends and no more, because she hadn't a notion of letting a man in on her, until she knew how to choose the good from the bad.

They met twice a week and went to the bingo on a Sunday in the church hall and she was happy enough. When he said it was no matter who said what when he called to the door, she agreed and let him come up to the flat. Will seemed pleased for her that she'd met a decent fella because he didn't have to be worrying about her anymore – he said he had enough to be getting on with at the factory.

Dan was funny. He made her laugh. There was a simplicity about him that she liked. He sometimes called her Galway Brigid. Said she had a lot of Galwayisms in her. She told him from the outset that they would never be more than friends but that she loved his company. She saw the hope in his eyes and she shot it down every time, and he said he accepted what she was telling him, but he wasn't a man to give up even if it took him a lifetime. She was the one. But there wasn't a man on God's earth that Brigid Murphy would trust. Not even Dan Gaffney.

She put what had happened to the back of her mind and carried on, knowing inside that she would never be the same again in her head or anywhere else. That she would carry the shame of it around with her, whether she wanted to or not.

Her sense of smell had always been sharp and when she noticed a change, that it had become sharper, she took it in her stride and thought nothing of it. Then she began to feel sick in the mornings towards the end of May. Running to the toilet under the stairs to vomit, and nothing coming up but bright yellow foam and it floating on the water like a lemon sherbet. She hadn't bled for a while. She put it out of her head, because she remembered her mother telling her that shock could cause all sorts of havoc to a woman's hormones.

Then she knew. The taste of the sour yellow stuff and the intense smells that were making her vomit. Bile. She was expecting.

She mentioned to Will that she was getting fat but what about it? Men didn't want to know about such things.

Then she was five months gone and her clothes were tight on her and Dan was looking at her.

"You seem different, Brigid, kind of distracted and not yourself. Now tell me to mind my own business if I'm intruding on you."

She blurted it out, trusting the very gut that had left her down in the past.

"I'm expecting, Dan. I'm on my own and there's no father and there never will be. I'm having it adopted, and that's the end of it and, if you know what's good for you, you'll follow what I'm saying. And no, before you ask, I don't want a man by my side, or the promise of a ring on my finger. I'll never see you in that light."

She had no choice but get on with it and he knew where the door was if he wanted no more to do with her.

Instead he said, "What of it? We'll work it out. I'm going nowhere."

Brigid had smiled at him then.

She had considered her options. Maybe she would hide away and hire the services of a local woman to deliver the child and tell no one and see how it all panned out. Dan wouldn't open his mouth whatever decision she came to, especially not to Will and if he did he'd never see her again. And if Will started on her he could go to blazes too.

Dan persuaded her to go the doctor and she promised she would. Any day now. And when she was ready she went to the doctor and explained her predicament. The doctor made the arrangements for her to have the baby in St. Mary's. Dan would help her pay towards the baby's keep in the hospital until it was sent to a good home. The baby would be put up for adoption. The doctor had connections with people who had childless couples on a waiting list who wanted more than anything to become parents.

Brigid told Dan it was the best decision, that she would remain on in the flat and work away until she was unable to work any longer. Dan supported her, saying that the cold winter weather would be a right bonus, seeing as she wouldn't be seen outside the door in her frock. The right coat could cover a lot. Whatever she wanted. He would not give up on her. She wouldn't be the first to have a baby out of wedlock and give it up. He said there wasn't a sign of it on her anyhow, and he knew by looking at her that she wasn't the type of girl to swell up. She had laughed in disbelief at his words.

And if she had to leave the flat in the latter weeks and people copped, what of it? Who knew her well enough to cause her distress? The gossips would talk and let them off. As long as she didn't hear what they were saying about her. Dan said that he could have a quiet word with Will when the time was right. If it even came to that. Her family were back in Galway and after that 'twas no one's business. And when Dan looked straight at her and called her his Galway Brigid, she felt his love.

Chapter 25

DELIA & FRAN

The Plan

Delia was sitting on the high stool at the bar in the River Hotel when Fran arrived. She couldn't wait to tell her that she had her bag packed and had informed her mother. Delia was turned sideways talking to someone at the bar. Thighs on full display over her booted legs, she leaned across to take a light for her cigarette. Her breasts were no more than a couple of inches from his face. Fran recognised him as Davie Keogh, a local.

"Sit over there, Franny, in the corner – you know David, don't you? I'll be over to you in a sec. Just chatting a bit of business here. I'll get the drinks in then. Gin OK?"

Fran nodded. Delia winked at her before turning back to Davie Keogh.

"Two large gins, thanks ever so much, David. And two bottles of bitter lemon."

True to her word, Delia didn't delay in joining her. The two sat in the corner by the window looking out at the river. Delia nodded towards the bar counter where David stood peering over at them.

"Look at him, the randy fucker, and he only mad for it. I remember the wife well, I do. Full of notions – he did well for himself with her. All men like him want is a five-minute shag, wherever they get it. No excuses."

Fran looked at Delia, her eyes opened wide.

"*Aah*, so what, Franny? I've been in London going on five years now, so I have. Long enough to know the ways of the world."

Delia pointed to herself, tapping her long red fingernail against her chest.

"We're not too unlike, you know, Franny. You and me are survivors. I ran away to London at fifteen cos I had to. Hadn't a clue where I was going. So I followed the crowd and ended up in London where I met people who took me in and taught me how to survive. People like us, Franny, need to be with people we can count on, people who won't shoot us in the back."

Fran sipped at her drink in silence. letting Delia talk.

"So believe me, I've spent more than enough time getting to know what makes people tick. Before I left Ballygore, I saw myself as worthless. A disgrace. I had no interest in school, until it dawned on me that it was all the shite that was going on at home that was the cause of it. So I had my eyes opened and had to look out for myself. My thoughts and feelings are no different to anyone else's. The way I choose to dress, to speak, to act, the way I present myself is of my choosing. I realised where I was going wrong. I was offering myself up to be judged. So now I play at being me! And I couldn't give a tuppenny shite about no-one. So there."

Fran was mesmerised. She couldn't believe that Delia had so

much going on inside her head. The admiration showed on her face as Delia went on.

"In this life, Franny, as long as you have the proper pedigree, an education, be seen to be moving in the right circles with the right people wearing the proper clobber, walking around with a copy of *The Times* under your arm, you can get away with a hell of a lot more than if you haven't a pot to piss in and spending the day at the street corner, scratching your arse. Who makes the rules, Franny? Society, that's who makes them."

"I'm shocked, Delia. Truly shocked. I always thought you were bright but never thought . . ."

"Thought what, Franny? That the bold and brassy Delia Blake with the skirt up to her arse and a different hairpiece for every day of the week actually has a fully functioning brain in her head. Intelligence isn't exclusive to the educated. I've met some fucked-up professional dumb-asses in my line of work, I can tell you that."

Fran wasn't sure how to answer.

"I like myself these days," Delia went on. "And if other people don't, well, that's fine too. People see what they want to see, they look at the outside and don't bother to go any farther. People judge others from where they themselves are at. Has something to do with 'cultural relativism', if I remember correctly. I can't remember the guy's name, an American. Boas – that's it! So there's a bit of useless information for you. From one who didn't know her arse from her elbow going to school."

Fran stared at her friend with fresh admiration.

"I met my kind of people in Soho, Franny, where the good and the not so good live side by side. And they do. When a pal mentioned that she was taking a few English classes once a week in a room over a chippy in Kilburn, I tagged along on my day off to see what else was there. I got hooked. Philosophy classes, if you don't mind, and I hardly knowing how to pronounce the word. But guess what? I was wanting more and me not having a clue what they were on about half the time, except that I liked the sound of it. So I started reading up on it and it blew my mind."

Fran thought even her mother would be hard pushed to keep up with Delia. The words coming out of her mouth and the books she said she had read. Her mother had been so wrong about Delia. So had a lot of people in Ballygore. She was so much more than most gave her credit for – which was nothing.

The girls formulated a plan. Once they finished the soup and sandwiches Delia had ordered, Fran would grab her bag at home and the two would head for London. Delia would cover Fran's fare over. They'd take the train to Dublin and remain in the carriage bound for Dun Laoghaire. The night boat would take them from there to Holyhead in Wales. Then a seven-hour train journey to Euston Station in London, just a few minutes away from Delia's new flat.

Delia explained that she worked in a flat around the corner from where she lived. Fran had tried her best not to react when her friend more or less explained what she did for a living.

"I'm a working girl, Franny, working in the oldest profession there is. Plenty of work to be had, and as I said the girls in Soho are the best. We're a little family, a community so we are. There's the rough and the smooth, the dodgy and the more than dodgy, but there's the soft and sweet – all in the same little place. So I don't waste time worrying about the dark side of it all. Don't ask me how it works, but it does."

Fran was struggling to come to terms with what Delia was describing.

"Fran, Soho is even smaller than Ballygore. One square mile is all. Like a little village. Well, a very busy touristy little village, but you'll see it all for yourself and I know you'll fit right in. Remember, I'm Delta the minute we hit the West End. I left Delia behind in Ballygore years ago."

"OK, I'll practise and call you Delta, but if I forget, don't bite the head off me. *Em* ... I don't know quite how to put this, but you can forget it if you think I'm going on the game with you. Not in a million years. No way. If I do stay on, which I've no notion of – unless – you know what I mean – I'll have to find a different job."

Delia sniggered. "Ah, Franny, give over! I didn't think that for a second. I have something else in mind for you, but we'll say nothing for now. I need to have a think about it first on the way over. To work it out in my head. There's all sorts for you to do if you do decide to stay on. A good mate of mine owns a launderette on the street behind mine. Not much money to be made in that kind of work, but we'll see. *Hmmm.* There's the clubs. Or maybe not. Maybe the Sunset on Dean Street? There's Raymond's Revue bar in Walker's Court. He has his own girls. *Nah*, maybe not."

"So who do you work for, Delia? A pimp, is it?"

"I work for myself, darling," answered Delia, lifting her chest with pride. "For me. Delta works for Delta. Lots of the girls have pimps and more will tell you they don't, but half the chaps they call their fellas are nothing more than glorified pimps. Ponces, we call them. 'Cept that no one admits to their fella being a ponce, and some of the girls are just too blind to see it. Even I fell into that trap when I came over first. There's Betty, my mate, she used to live in the old flat on the same floor as me with a Swiss guy. He's basically a small-time petty criminal hiding out in her pad. Looks the part. Greased back hair, wears the best of clobber, speaks with an accent. He's living off her and every penny she makes she spends on him. I've told her to cop the feck on, that he's on the make, but she says she loves him and one day they'll have a house and kids together. But he's a ponce. He shares her bed, gives her the odd shiner to keep her in place, and uses her to get what he wants. In every sense."

Fran was gobsmacked.

"I work most nights," Delia went on, "and every now and then I take a night off and I sit at home in my lovely new flat on Wardour Street under my continental quilt, listening to music or reading. Unless I get a better offer, or there's a band I want to see. I paid three months' rent in advance before I came over, so no rent needs paying till end of year. You can pay for your keep if you decide to stay on."

"Three months, I never heard anyone paying three months' rent in advance. You must be earning a pile of money if you're paying all that money out?"

"Have to spend the dosh somewhere, so might as well be keeping a roof over my head. Happens when a lease is up. Short-term renting."

"Does the same landlord own the new flat as well as your old one?"

"*Nah!*" Delia sniggered. "No one seems to know who owns the walk-ups or any of the flats for that matter, but they're either Maltese or Swiss. The big boys. They buy up the buildings cheap to get in on the make and put heads on the payroll while they're off sailing around the world with their families in their fancy yachts. The Maltese have control of Soho this long time."

Fran let Delia ramble on. She wanted to know everything.

"The East End buckos try to rain on their parade every now and then but they're no match for the Maltese. Or the Swiss boys. The Americans are in on the game too. Us West End girls are savvy enough and in the main we're left alone. As long as we pay our dues and stay on our own turf, there's plenty for all of us. So to answer your question – I haven't a notion. The flat I just moved into on Wardour Street has been let, sublet and underlet. The walk-up is the bloody same. No one knows. Confusing, innit?"

"It sure it is . . . but you can't work in that career for ever, can you?"

"I have a plan, don't you worry. Two years tops and I'm out. No second thoughts now, Franny, we're off and that's the end of it. Time you lived a bit and don't you worry – I'll show you what living is all about. And if what you told me is true, you've enough dosh of your own to keep you going. We'll chat again on the ferry on the way across and I'll fill you in some more. Now off up to the hatch with you and get the drinks in. We'll have one for the road. No sign of Keogh to cough up for another round. He went out that door in an woeful hurry a few minutes ago, holding his overcoat in front of him. 'Tisn't only his old cars that need a good service, I'd say!" Delia roared laughing.

Fran didn't join in – she was too preoccupied with wondering about the life Delia was describing.

"Relax, Franny! Trust me, the punters are mainly decent blokes. All the girls have regulars, especially the girls who offer . . . shall we say, a few extras. But that's their own business. It's not unusual to have a punter ask for something right freaking odd, that's not on the menu like."

214

Fran didn't dare ask what Delia meant.

"We don't take risks – that's why most of us have a maid. Well, not a maid exactly, but that's what we call the ladies who keep an eye out for us. Like a receptionist. To answer the door if we're occupied. Yeah, that's it. A secretary. So the maid hangs around while we work, to keep everything running smoothly. She organises the show, if you get me?"

"In the same room while you're doing the … you know, the business?"

"Jesus, Franny, I know I'm a bit twisted but I'm not that fucking twisted. No. The maid shows the punters in when they ring the bell and more importantly sees that they leave again. No hangers-on. Oh . . . and making the tea. Plenty of tea and chat. Making sure everything's in its place. Taking the clobber to the dry cleaner's and all. Some maids are right bitches, but in the main they're decent enough. A lot of them are old biddies in their fifties and sixties – some of them own the walk-ups themselves."

"I didn't want to ask before, but why are the flats called walk-ups?"

"Walk-ups … walk up. Get it. Come on, Fanny. Do you want me to spell it out for you? Walk-up!"

Fran stood there with her bottom lip curled, her eyebrows raised . . . she couldn't think of anything more to say. She didn't want to look like a clown in front of Delia.

"My last maid ran off to Italy with her fella. Imagine! And she's happy to be getting out of the business. She's moving away with a fat bank balance and a new life ahead of her. Great money to be had as a maid, you know. *Hmmm.* Much better money than slaving in a sweaty kitchen somewhere. Or dancing on the stage in a clip joint. Awful boring. Clobber on, clobber off, and the same again."

Fran didn't dare ask what a clip joint was.

"Sweaty bodies, sticky carpets, bad drink, and smelly jacks. That's how some get started when they land, before they find out where the real money is to be had."

Fran was already having second thoughts. "Now you've me well scared. But I trust you. I do. You were the only one in school that I did trust, so I'm going back with you and I won't change my mind." She was unsure of who she was trying to convince, but one thing was for sure – she was not about to let Delia Blake walk out of her life again.

An hour later, after a teary parting encounter with her mother, Fran left.

Her father handed her a ten-pound note in the hall, telling her he'd see her so in a fortnight. That she needed to have a few bob of honest money in her back pocket for good luck. When she refused, he insisted, so she took the note and stuffed it down her bra.

Chapter 26

DELIA & FRAN

The Journey

Delia paid for Fran's ticket at the station as they had agreed. Delia was quieter than she had been over the past few hours. Fran didn't mind so much – she had enough to be thinking about. Part of her wanted to stand up and pull the cord, to stop the train. A braver part of her was curious enough to want to keep going.

The carriage was packed. Delia had squeezed herself in beside a round-looking nun, forcing the sister to move closer to the window. Fran sat across from Delia, beside an older nun who refused to budge until Delia stood up and glared down at her, hands on her hips. Only then did the hard-faced nun move to make room for Fran.

When the inspector came to check their tickets, he told them they were in the wrong carriage: the first two carriages only were bound for Dun Laoghaire. Last stop for the rest of the train was Dublin. So they upped and moved to the top of the train to find a seat.

"Well . . . we're off now, Sisters, thanks for the chat," said Delia.

The dock at Dun Laoghaire was teeming with activity. Men were offloading and loading trolleys of mail onto the boat – the *Hibernia*. Women were pulling their children along to keep check on them. Men leading their women along, dragging heavy suitcases at the same time. Once the boarding call was announced over the tannoy, Delia tugged at Fran's sleeve as they made their way up the gangplank, past a group of black-robed men. Delia told her to get a move on, to head for the bar area where they could sleep for a few hours.

The chairs were taken by the time they pushed their way through the crowd. Abandoned overcoats and suitcases sat on seats as their owners stood three deep at the bar. Delia moved fast, removing two of the overcoats before throwing them onto an already loaded bench across from them.

"Quick, Franny, sit here! At least we'll be away from the jacks. We don't want to be inhaling passing farts after that lot have had a few pints. Don't mind who's looking at you. Just sit. They'll be grand. They're hardly going to move two dolls like us off the seats, now are they? They'll be far too busy eyeing up the merchandise."

They sat facing the bar.

"Sit down and close your eyes and don't flip your lid if they arrive over. Pretend you're asleep. That lot will stay put for the crossing."

Fran looked at Delia, who had put her bag under her head against the side of the tub chair, her jacket around her chest, her legs on full display. She closed her eyes.

Fran was restless, sitting upright every now and then, checking to see if Delia was awake. She wanted to stay alert, to find out more. She was hoping that Delia would fill her in with what she had in mind for her, if she did decide to stay. When Delia opened her eyes to find Fran gaping at her, she wasn't impressed.

"Franny, I need to get a bit of kip here. I'm starting straight in to work once we get back to London in the morning. I've a busy day ahead. Come on, get some shuteye there, we'll have plenty of time to chat on the train down to London."

"I can't sleep until I'm in bed and I get up early. What about you? What time do you get up at?"

"Usually around noon or one, depending on the night before."

"Noon? No way! What am I supposed to be doing until noon? I'm used to early mornings."

"Well, you better change your bloody sleep pattern if you're going to keep up with Delta. Give it a couple of days and you'll see – it'll all work out. Goodnight!"

Delia turned on her side before turning back to face Fran.

"Look, Franny . . . you'll be fine. I'll show you around, where to go and all that. No need to be overthinking it all. You can tear off yourself and see the sights. Remember, I landed over there when I was fifteen. A big eejit. Now, goodnight."

"Goodnight, Delia. Sorry."

A few minutes later Delia shot up in the chair just as Fran found herself dozing off. "*Right!* You can start work with me in a couple of days if you want. As my maid. Only on trial, of course. Just till the beginning of January, mind – until the lease on the flat on Wardour Street is up. No tricks for you, babe, so no worries." She leant back on the chair with a thud. "Night, Franny."

Fran didn't answer. She could forget about sleeping for now. Her maid? Had she heard her right? No matter what way Delia tried to colour it, a maid was a maid. A servant girl. In a brothel? Her? What would her mother have to say about that? Or anyone else in the town for that matter? They wouldn't believe a word of it. She began to panic, thinking about her Uncle Will and Alice Coyne. They must never find out. What had she got herself into? What if she recognised someone from home?

One thing was for sure: her "item", as her mother had called Roy, was fast fading from her mind.

Fran took in a deep breath before bursting into a fit of nervous laughter. She was off to Soho to work in a brothel with the wonderful Delia Blake

Chapter 27

DELIA & FRAN

Flashing lights

By the time Fran and Delia arrived at the ferry terminal in Holyhead, it was gone one in the morning. Fran felt tired, in need of her bed. Delia advised her to stay alert, she could get a bit of kip on the seven-hour train journey down to London. Fran felt like getting sick with the heady smell of fumes. A steamy, oily smell.

Delia led her along towards the railway platform, warning her to stay close as they made their way towards the train bound for London. The station was in the same building as the ferry terminal.

A man in a black uniform ushered them forward. "*Irish mail this way, passengers for London Euston this way!*" he called.

Fran wrapped her coat around her as she followed Delia onto the train. She felt unsteady, as if the ground was moving beneath her feet.

"That's your head playing tricks with you, after being on the boat. Keep walking."

Once they had boarded, they sat side by side on two seats at the end of the carriage, where some of the luggage had been stowed.

They could talk without being heard.

"I'm starving, Franny, so I am. We'll go to the dining car for a bit of grub in a bit. I can smell the kippers from here."

Fran took her purse from her handbag, leaving it on the small table in front of them.

"Delia, I'll pay you back every shilling once I get to a bank in London." She had decided not to mention the tenner her father had given her.

"I know you will, Franny. Don't worry about it." Delia rolled her eyes. "Will you be careful with that flaming purse – it's bulging. It's not the best idea to be having that much dosh on display."

Fran looked around, anxiously eyeing the other passengers seated farther up the carriage. Delia put her hand to her mouth, speaking through her fingers.

"Franny, one bit of advice. Will you stop staring at the fucking passengers? That one up there will throttle you if you keep gawking at her. You're not in Ballygore now."

"I was just looking, Delia. Just looking. No harm in that, is there?"

"Yeah, Franny, but flipping staring straight at people ain't just looking."

"Never mind. I get the picture." Fran bit her bottom lip, lowered her head and stared into her lap.

Delia nudged her gently. "Look. I hadn't a clue about life myself when I left for London. Pretending I was all confident on the outside. Only I was scared shitless inside, and I had no one to give a tuppenny-feck about me. You've got me."

Fran lifted her head. "I cared, Delia. Only you upped and

disappeared if you care to remember."

Delia tried to link Fran who tightened her arm closer to her side. They both became giddy, breaking the tension between them after Delia finally managed to force her arm through Fran's. They burst out laughing, delighted to be in each other's company. Delia leaned to kiss Fran's cheek. Fran responded with a wide smile.

They sat close together, arms linked, until Delia broke the silence.

"Franny, let me fill you in on a few things. My mother and the other bastard didn't give two fecks about me, because I spoke out against that dirty animal. They didn't want to know me. Aunts, uncles, grandparents, all in denial that my mother's bastard husband was touching me up and lining me up for most of the five years since he married my mother, and I such an innocent I didn't know any better. They stopped coming near us. They called me a liar and a troublemaker. A scheming bitch. Just because he carried a missal and sang in the choir at Mass on a Sunday."

Fran reached over to lay her head on Delia's shoulder. She didn't know what to say so she stayed where she was and kept her mouth shut.

"And he asking me to close my eyes and keep them closed, to play hide and seek, offering me a few bob. I thought nothing at first. He was dressed when he 'hid' in the bed, but as time went on he might have his shirt off, wearing his vest, and then his pants and it happened so slowly that I can't remember when I got the creeps the first time. Then it got to the stage that he was nearly throwing the money at me, until it went too far and I didn't know how to say no. The sick feeling in my stomach when I was in the house on my own with him. When I copped on what was happening and tried to stop him, he said if I told anyone he would leave my mother and tell her that I had led him on. That it was my fault for being such a dirty teasing bitch of a young one."

Fran sat up, looking back at her friend, her mouth open. Delia had made it plain enough earlier on that she detested her stepfather. But listening to the detail of what she had experienced repulsed Fran. If she had never before felt sorry for Delia, she felt it now.

"So when I saw him sitting there in Manson's at my mother's funeral, I reacted the way I did, all brave with the drink on me. The only regret I have is that I didn't slice his fucking dick off when I had the chance. Now that's enough about it, I feel like throwing up every time I think about him."

"Oh my God! And imagine I had no clue back then," Fran said softly. She didn't know where to look, so she lay back on Delia's shoulder, not knowing what else to do. There was nothing she could say that would fix things for Delia, apart from reassure her that she believed her.

When she did speak she sat up and looked straight at Delia.

"I was wondering why you were roaring across at him in Manson's. They didn't believe you, Delia. But I do. I believe you."

"So now you know and the only reason I'm telling you is because you're the only person I can trust. You are a pure soul, Franny, and not a backstabbing bitch who'll judge me. Now, if you don't mind, shut the fuck up, Miss Gaffney, or I'll send you in to work the double shift for me."

Fran smiled to herself, knowing that Delia didn't mean a word of it. What she had just told her about her stepfather bothered Fran more than she was going to let on. Sickened her stomach. Her mother had warned her about creeps and dirty old men. But Delia's stepfather? Someone she saw every day on her own street. She had a lot to learn. Preying on children. Children like Delia. Destroying the lives of innocents to satisfy their sick depraved cravings.

She opened the A-Z of London that she had bought on the boat on the way over.

She couldn't see Soho on the map until Delia told her where to look.

"Like I said, it's less than a square mile, hard to see it on the map. Find Oxford Circus and Leicester Square and it's thereabouts. Charing Cross and Regent Street are at either side – Soho is in the middle. It's pedestrianised."

Once they arrived at Euston Station in the early morning they got straight on the bus headed for Soho. Within minutes they had reached their destination.

Fran stared around her. She was mesmerized. All these people. Men in suits and bowler hats on their way to work. Tastefully dressed women smoking tipped cigarettes. Headscarved women carrying their shopping bags on their way to the markets to get the best of the fresh produce. People passing people. Every other minute she was bumping into someone.

The market traders were displaying their wares at either side of the street. The noise. The sounds of banging dustpan lids. The smell of freshly baked bread reminded her of home. Delia said it was the smell of croissants. Fran had never tasted croissants but they smelled of buttery bread and her stomach was rumbling. Barrowloads of fruit and veg were being pushed by boys wearing flat caps. Cabbages for sale sitting on damp newspaper, markets up and down either side of the street.

Delia pointed to the street sign. *Berwick Street.* Brown brick three-storey buildings. People shouting everywhere. "*Melons, melons, get your melons!*" "*Onions, onions!*" from another stall, each stallholder vying to be heard about the other. "*Carrots, carrots, carrots!*" from another stall. Produce neatly displayed by traders intent on drawing attention to their own stalls.

This was certainly not what Fran had expected.

"This is the scene around here from cockcrow every morning, Franny, although 'tis rare enough for me to see it. Soho morning starts at dawn when the streets are swept and the shop fronts washed down after the night before. The streets are full of ice. You'd have to duck or you'd get a right cooling down. They sell every kind of fruit and vegetable you could think of. The barrow boys run the length of the street all morning stocking up until lunchtime when they sell off the fruit. Dirt cheap. The place does be jam-packers then. Smell that!" She breathed in deeply. "It's garlic. Some of them crush it into the footpath around their shops to get the people in, and it works."

Fran had never eaten garlic. She'd never even seen garlic. Neither had she ever seen so much life. Even in Dublin. From what she could see, apart from neon flashing lights and red signs, it looked just like a busy market street about to start the day.

"Look, there's the shoe repair place. You can get anything and everything you want here. See, we have it all!" Delia pointed as they walked. "There's a good drycleaner's on Carnaby Street, up the length of Broadwick street keep going and you'll see the signpost. It's the hub of the place. If you want the latest in fashion, Lady Jane's is where to go, it's only new here – up to that there was only men's shops here. Look over – the girls dress and undress in the window to draw attention from the street. And, boy, does it what?

They dress from their knickers out."

Fran squirmed at the mention of knickers, though she hadn't been taking much notice of what Delia was showing her. She was far too busy reading the signs. *Striptease. Peep show. Sex. Girls. Girls.* Flashing neon signs. Everywhere. On windows, doors, overhead shops.

By the time they reached the flat on the first floor of a building on Wardour Street, there was barely time for Delia to show Fran where everything was before she hurried off towards the bathroom.

"I'm off for a quick scrub in the tub, Franny. I'm doing a few hours payback for my mate Jenny, so put your things into the press beside the bedroom door there and have a snoop around. Jesus, I hope you're not a messy cow like me!"

Fran did as she was told.

"I'll leave the bathroom door open and you can shout in at me."

Fran pulled a face. Awkward. Seeing Delia naked in the bathroom as she lowered herself into the tub was not a sight she was wanted to witness. Delia issued directions as she undressed.

"If you need anything while I'm gone, don't bother with her next door. She's a mad cow. Accused me of stealing all sorts. She's dangerous so make sure to have nothing at all to do with her. Stay away from her, Franny."

"OK, OK. So I'm not to be inviting her in for tea then?"

"Very funny. No. Milk and cheese in the fridge, bread's in the breadbin and tea's behind the plastic curtain in the caddy. I got them in before I went over. Toaster is there in the corner. There should be a few tins of spam in the press above your head. The electric meter is behind the door, there are coins there beside it in the tin box. Check it out. If you need to buy anything just nip to the shop a few doors down. I'll leave some keys for you. There's a Wimpy Bar on the corner of Old Compton Street if you're hungry later and you can drop into the bank to change your money on the way. You can't miss it."

Fran headed for the kitchen where she checked the small fridge. Pulling back a plastic curtain, she called back, "I'll be fine, Delia! It's all here, don't worry about me."

"Remember it's Delta from here on in, Franny."

Fran wasn't fine, she was anything but fine. She certainly wouldn't be moving outside the door of the flat, without Delia or Delta by her side, especially after what she had just told her about the neighbour. And who was this Jenny? First she had heard about her.

Making use of the time, she had a snoop around after putting two slices of bread in the toaster. The flat was much bigger than she had anticipated. A large living room with two tall sash windows looking out onto the noisy street below. Red lights flashing every few seconds even though it was daylight. Long fancy see-through curtains drooped on the floor. Delia had mentioned on the way over that she had read a book on interior design and renovated it herself. That the flat had been emptied by the previous tenants who had peddled off everything that moved, including the carpet, which had been nailed to the floor. So everything in the flat was chosen by Delia? Fran was well impressed. The high-ceilinged living room was clean and tidy. The opposite to what Fran would have expected from Delia who had earlier referred herself as a messy cow. Everything was organised. A television sat in the corner on a low table. A green velvet sofa dominated the room. A colourful high-pile rug covering most of the floor space. Books everywhere. Some stacked neatly on the gold side table that looked far too noble and posh to belong to Delia. An expensive-looking table lamp with a crystal base sat on a marble-topped chess table.

A flag was tacked to the wall alongside a painting of a black bull. A red-and-yellow flag. Fran thought it might be Spanish, but she wasn't sure. She had given up Geography after her Inter Cert four years before. What the hell was Delia Blake doing with a foreign flag hanging on the wall?

Fran had to check herself. Here she was barely inside the door and she already making judgements. Had she not listened to a word Delia had said about making judgements? And why shouldn't Delia Blake own a fancy chess table and a posh lamp? And why couldn't she have the Spanish flag, or any other flag for that matter hanging on her living-room wall? Fran's mind wandered. If Delia could afford this grandeur, why did she show up at home dressed like a prostitute? Giving them all plenty to gossip about. *Stop it, Fran!* She was beginning to sound like her mother.

On the shelves along the walls. More books. Travel books, history books, interior design books. All sorts of books. Some in Spanish. No one in a million years would have guessed that they belonged to Delia.

Delia assured her having a bathroom in the flat was an unusual addition in such an old building in Soho. No need to go into the hall in the dead of night to take a pee. No need to pass the loose-cannon person next door who couldn't be trusted.

Delia appeared in the kitchen wearing a black polo neck over a knee-length skirt. Black stilettos. A string of amber beads around her neck.

"Jesus, Delia, but you look like a proper lady!"

"A lady, is it? And who else could I possibly look like only the lady

I am?" Delia did a twirl. "Right, I'm off, Franny. I've to drop this lot off to the cleaner's on the way. No washing clothes here – only smalls. Hang them on the plastic wire over the bath and they'll be dry in no time. The launderette's just down the street, a once-a-week job. That's the best thing about Soho, everything is either just down the street, or around the corner. Better rush – I start at eleven. Have a good snoop around there while I'm gone – you've my full permission. Here's the keys." She put the keys on the table. "Remember to lock the chain the minute I've left and don't dare open the door for anyone. Some very strange people around these days."

Picking up a slice of toast, Delia was gone.

Once Fran had picked up in the bathroom after Delia, she wiped down the bath and squeezed out the sponge, replacing the now soft bar of scented soap in the wooden bath tray. She hoped that Delia wasn't going to make a habit of leaving her stuff lying around for her to pick up. "Maid or no maid!" she said aloud. Delia's clothes had been left where they landed, her yellow boots lying on their sides behind the door.

The green toilet set reminded Fran of one she had admired in a hardware shop in Limerick. A rubber shower hose to match. Fran hung the towel used by Delia behind the door. Yawning as she left the bathroom, she headed towards the double bed which was covered with a puffy white continental quilt, a circular nightstand with a lamp sitting on its glass top at one side. She switched on the lamp.

Fran opened the wardrobe expecting to find at least some of the mess that Delia had referred to earlier. But everything seemed to be in its place and neatly folded. Her eyes opened wide with surprise at the line of stylish clothes that she would never have expected Delia to own. Dresses, coats, suits, all the best quality.

A row of stilettoes all neatly faced outward on a shoe shelf at the base of the wardrobe. All of them looked too small for Delia. Now that was very strange. Maybe they belonged to this Jenny one that Delia had mentioned earlier. But that didn't make sense either, because Delia told her that Jenny shared the walk-up, not this place on Wardour Street. After giving it some thought, Fran decided to keep her mouth shut. She was not in a positon to go challenging Delia who obviously had a lot more going on than she liked to admit. And if Delia chose to refer to herself as a messy cow, then so be it. If anything she was the opposite.

Fran sat on the bed. She felt sad for her friend after what she had told her. There were times when her mother had driven her to distraction arguing a point. But at least Fran had been heard. Her voice had been acknowledged. They had hugged and made up more times at home than she could remember. But she knew what she had to say had value. Fran had grown up feeling loved, smothered with kisses and hugs.

And there was Delia. Delia who when she tried to speak out in her own home was branded a liar. Fran understood now. Delia was crying out to be noticed. Because that was the one thing she had been deprived of when she needed to be heard. And no matter where she got it, good or bad, Delia craved attention.

Fully dressed, Fran fell asleep cuddling a pink satin cushion that smelt of Delia. She left the lamp on.

"Franny, wake up, come on, shove over!"

Fran thought she was dreaming when she opened her eyes and saw a stark naked Delia leaning in over her, pushing her. She thought she had just shut her eyes.

Delia grinned, inches from her face. "*Aaaw*, stay awake, Franny, and keep me warm. Come on, I'll slip in beside you and snuggle up – I'm feckin' freezing."

Fran moved to the far side of the bed. She was wide awake now.

Delia laughed. "Franny, come on! I'm only messing. You look like you've seen a ghost. Go on with you, off out to the couch if you want, or you can stay where you are. I left a blanket out there for you. The bed here is big enough for the two of us, but if you're staying on we'll sort something better out. Maybe borrow a pull-out for the corner over there. Come on, make up your mind, girl, I need to get a few hours' kip after the day I've had."

Fran was half asleep. She headed straight for the couch. The image of Delia's breasts hovering over her face would remain with her. She had never seen a fully naked woman in the flesh before, apart from herself when she was getting out of the tub. Well, she had seen her mother naked once, when she had walked into her bedroom unannounced. But she had never in all her life seen breasts like Delia's.

She picked up a book from the coffee table and flicked through the pages. Philosophy.

She put it down again and lay back, her eyes closing.

Hours later, Fran woke to find Delia shaking her. She was leaning over her, wearing the red bath towel she had picked up earlier, her dark hair dripping down on Fran.

"*Wakey wakey!* It's after one. Rise and shine, Franny!"

Fran didn't know what day she had, never mind the time. She couldn't believe she had slept so long. In her clothes. And on a couch.

"I'm back to work for four, so we've two hours to go. Let's have tea and toast. I'll go get ready, so be a pet – you know where the kettle is."

Fran got up and did what was asked of her.

When Delia appeared in the kitchen, Fran told her she looked amazing. She looked like the Delia that Fran remembered. Without the hairpiece and the heavy eye make-up she looked softer. Her damp hair had been cut in a bob, perfectly parted down the middle. Her fair skin was fresh without make-up. Freckles were dotted across her nose. She wore the same string of amber beads that she had worn the day before, but this time she wore drop-earrings to match, a grey A-line skirt to her knees, a black sleeveless top. Stiletto heels. Clothes that weren't made for someone two sizes smaller. Fran couldn't believe the transformation.

"Delia, if I may say so, you might have got things a bit mixed up arriving back in Ballygore in your working clothes."

They both roared laughing before Delia grew serious.

"I got fuck-all mixed up, Franny. I knew exactly what I was doing. I wanted to shake things up back in Ballygore. I'm nothing but a vulgar whore back there, so why not live up to my name?"

"You are everything you need to be, Delia. And more."

"I agree. Right. Let's have that tea and toast. We'll go walkabout then. You won't need a coat – the sun is shining out there."

"Oh – I'd better go have a wash myself and change my clothes before we go out."

"OK. But you'll need to hurry yourself. I want to give you a quick tour before we stop for coffee. The work flat is just around the corner on Berwick Street. Remember we passed the stalls yesterday, so that's where we're headed, one street over. It changes around here throughout the day and once the markets close shop, you'll see a different side. Just keep your wits about you. You'll soon get the hang of it, Franny, and as long as you know how to use your knee you'll be fine."

Dressed in her blue-and-yellow floral shift dress and navy-blue slingbacks to match her cardigan, Fran set off with Delia on their way to meet the girls.

Delia raised a finger at the door of her neighbour as they passed. "Fucking tramp is all that one in there is. If I'd know the kind of neighbour I was getting, I'd never have moved in, but I've a feeling she'll leave us alone for now."

"Well, I won't be meeting her. I haven't a notion of going outside the door on my own. For now anyway. What's her name so as I know?"

"Ada. Ada the Adder."

Fran decided not to respond.

"So come on, Franny, time you met some of the coffee girls. We meet for a catch-up most days around three, mostly at the Golden Egg on Old Compton, or the French House. Everything is nearby so you won't get lost and if you find yourself on Oxford Street then you need to turn back, if you see Leicester Square do the same thing. So this is Wardour Street. Runs parallel to Dean Street which is at the bottom of Old Compton Street. Then there's Frith Street where you get the ham on the bone, and Greek Steet is the one after that, where we get the bread at the French baker's. I know it's all too much for you to take in for now."

Fran was too busy inhaling the aromas around her.

"Oh the smell, Delia ... Delta."

"Follow your nose and it will take you where you want to go. So the butcher's is just across the street there. Remember, Old Compton Street is at the bottom of Dean Street, it runs along the bottom over to Charing Cross Road, which borders Soho, as does Oxford Street at other end. There's nothing you can't get here in Soho, as long as you know where to look for it. Nothing."

Fran looked around her, trying to take in what Delia was telling her.

"Oh, by the way, the cinema over there next door to the Golden Egg, is a blue movie house, very different to what you'll be used to at home, so it's a no go. Blue here isn't the same as blue at home. The off licence is there too. You'll get to know the place in no time."

"You weren't lying when you said everywhere in Soho is just around the corner."

"You got it, girl. Ronnie Scott's on Frith Street is great for the jazz. I'll take you to the 2i's Coffee Bar one of the days. Everyone knows where that is. Full of musicians and actors. Some laugh. And no matter where you go some of the coffee girls will turn up. Just remember to mind what you're saying. They're a great bunch but I wouldn't be telling them my private business. You'll meet someone you know no matter where you go here. We're headed for Meard Street, left out of the flat and another left, and you're there. Most places are off Wardour Street."

Fran couldn't keep up with all Delia was telling her. "I'm dying to see the walk-up. Imagine. Me, Fran Gaffney from Ballygore, arriving at a brothel in Soho. To work as a maid if you don't mind. A maid in a brothel, like. Why are you looking at me like that, Delta dear?"

Delia rolled her eyes and laughed.

Fran was feeling animated, knowing that as long as she had Delia by her side everything would work out and, if it didn't, she had plenty of money to buy herself a ticket home. She wasn't in a hurry, her job at home had gone, she had no friends to speak of, and if her mother had her way she'd be stuck in Ballygore for the rest of her life.

"I'm kind of chuffed you're here, Franny. I need you in my life to keep me on the straight and narrow. We'll meet the girls for a quick coffee and a bite to eat before I change for work. I leave a lot of my stuff at the walk-up. Don't ask me why."

"Your place. It's so – so – glamourous. And all the shoes. And the skirts and blouses. Who'd have thought that Delia Blake would end up in a place like this?"

"I see you've had a good poke around, Franny. Well, when you see the work flat later on, I hope you'll be saying the same thing."

Chapter 28

FRAN

The Coffee Girls

Fran followed Delia in the door of a noisy cafè on Meard Street. She pointed to a table in the corner where a group of girls sat. One of the girls spotted Delia and began pulling chairs across from a nearby table for them.

"Meet the coffee girls, Franny!"

A slim blonde girl stood up and offered her hand to Fran from across the table. Her thick blonde hair to her shoulders was perfectly curled up at the ends. She wore a red off-the-shoulder top, lipstick to match. Attractive.

"Welcome to the West End, love. I'm Jenny. I work with Delta. Love the short bleached hair. You here on holiday?"

Delia cut in. "Yeah, that's right. I brought her over for a while, Jenny, to show her the ropes."

The girls laughed. Fran didn't know where to look.

Delia beckoned to the waiter, asking for two coffees with milk.

The girl sitting next to Fran smiled at her. Her dark hair was styled in a short bob, and she wore a baby-blue fitted top over a white pencil skirt.

"Pleased to meet you and all that, Fanny, innit? I'm Barb."

Fran was touched by the friendly greeting – except that Barb had just called her Fanny. Fran's face reddened – she turned towards Delia, who was now deep in conversation. Jenny was handing her a bunch of keys.

Delia smiled at Fran. "Me and Delta just catching up, love, work talk – chat away to the girls there."

Just then a tall slim girl with long dark hair and the brightest blue eyes that Fran had ever seen, leant across the table to offer her long slim hand. Fran thought she looked more like a doll than a human.

"Fanny, I'm Lily, welcome to the West End." Lily's voice was high-pitched.

"Good to be here, Lily, just for a holiday. *Em* . . . just to say that my name is Fra–"

"Fanny – your name is Fanny," Delia cut across her. Winking at Fran, she turned her attention back to Jenny.

Fran's face burned as she nodded reluctantly in agreement. Fanny. There was no point in protesting.

Fanny had arrived in Soho.

Penny, a friendly-looking redhead with a fringe, leant across Jenny and waved at Fran.

"Nice to make your acquaintance, Fanny. I'm Penny. I work most days at the Sunset on Dean Street."

Fran picked up the Irish accent. She wanted to ask where she was from at home. Had she ever been to Ballygore? Probably not.

She wanted to know all about Penny, because she was Irish and Fran could understand every single word she said. But she decided to leave it for now.

A girl in a red dress sat near the door to Fran's right. Fran wasn't sure if she was one of the coffee girls or not. She was biting her nails and looking out the window. Looking behind her. Smoking. She appeared nervous and jittery and every now and then she would look straight back at Fran.

She hadn't offered a welcome, so Fran decided to pay no heed to her. Suddenly the girl jumped up.

"*Eh up, cock!*"

She was waving her hands furiously as she hurried out the door.

Barb leaned across the table to whisper in Franny's ear. "That poor doll, Roxy, don't give a toss about nothing, except where her next fix is coming from. She's spotted her dealer. Not long out of hospital after the sleep therapy, so don't take no notice, lovey." Barb patted Fran's hand.

Dealer? Fran repeated in her head. Had she heard right? What kind of a dealer? Did she mean a drug dealer? Hardly a cattle dealer. What had she let herself in for? She lowered her head and stared into her coffee cup.

Who would have believed that two days before she had been sitting in the boot factory in Ballygore, banging away on the keys of her typewriter, with Alice Coyne sitting across the office from her. She had been happy in her ignorance.

Here she was, in Soho in the West End of London, right in the middle of prostitute alley as her mother would have called it, drinking coffee with a crowd of prostitutes, one of whom had just run off to chase her dealer.

Delia was waving over at her, trying to get her attention.

"So we're agreed. Fanny, is it? Girls, don't even ask!" Delia had a smirk on her face. "Jaysus, Fanny, don't be looking at me like that. Fanny is a fine respectable name. Fanny Craddock?"

"Fanny? Come on, Delta! How many more times are you going to change my name? OK, OK. Fanny it is, if it keeps you happy."

"Lighten up, Fanny, I'm messing with you. Girls, this is Franny. Get it?"

The coffee girls drank coffee, smoked and entertained each other for twenty minutes, before going their separate ways to begin their shifts.

"We usually catch up at Le Macabre on a Tuesday, but I thought it might be a bit much for you. We can go there another time. It's horror-themed. Coffin lids for tables, black walls with skeletons and candlelight. Jukebox playing death marches and the like. You know the type of place?"

Fran thought she was joking.

"I'll take you to the Isabella on Frith Street tomorrow for lunch. Oh, and we'll have to go to the French baker's on Greek Street for bread. It's next door to L'Escargot. Franny, there's so much for you to see. I know you're going to love it here. Franny's Fanny."

"How many, *em* . . . customers do you see in a day, Delia?"

"*Delta!* Depends. Could be twenty, could be thirty, could be less. Could be more. And before you ask there's no group discount, I've had a few smart arses from home trying that one. Irish. So you'll be busy out, Franny. Very busy. Come on, time to get back to the walk-up to set up. Two minutes and we're there."

Fran wanted to run out the door.

Once they had left the narrow street, Fran and Delia stepped back onto Wardour Street, heading for Berwick Street. Fran could see the traffic on Shaftsbury Avenue in the distance.

They walked along Berwick Street. Fran was far too busy looking around her to notice that Delia had turned into a doorway next door to a shop selling Algerian coffee.

"Franny!"

A paper sign was nailed to the door, which read *Dark chest for sale 1st floor*. A second sign underneath read *Models come up. 2nd floor*. Fran held her breath and followed. The hallway smelled of stale urine. Squashed cigarette packets and buts lined the floor along with whatever grime the wind had carried in.

Delia pointed to the floor, saying there was a price to be paid for leaving the door wide open with fellas passing by, dying for a leak.

Fran followed Delia up the dark stairway. The dark paint on the lower half of the wall was peeling off, showing the concrete behind.

"There are two walk-ups here," Delia explained as they climbed the stairs, stopping when they got to the first floor. "Our place is up above on the top floor. That law they brought in fifty-nine did away with the girls working the streets, then when the trade came indoors, they decided to make the brothels illegal. But it's only considered a brothel if more than one girl is working in a flat. That's why the doors have separate bells and myself and Jenny work the shifts. We can't advertise our trade, so we pin the signs on the door below. So the customers come in the door and up the stairs and ring the red bell on the walk-up and if a girl is free they'll be ushered in by the maid. Simple. Which is where you come in, Franny. We have a small cubbyhole of a waiting area where the customers can wait, like. We like to look after our regulars first." She pointed towards the door on the first floor. "Down here they only have the one room so the customers wait their turn out on the street till the girl is free. Come on – up one more flight."

Fran's heartbeat began to quicken. No matter how many times Delia called it her working flat or her walk-up, no cover-up name could make it more than what it was. A bloody brothel. And here she was about to start working as Delta's maid.

"Delia, I think I've made an awful mistake . . . in fact, I know I have."

Delia walked on and ignored her. Fran had no choice but to follow. She wasn't about to be left standing on her own in a dingy stairwell in Soho.

They walked to the end of the landing to two black doors, one with a red-lit bell and a yellow paper sign pinned to the door. *"Model out – back in ten."*

"Da – da – da – da!" Delta sang. "Here's where it all happens, Franny. Your new place of employment. If you want it, of course. No qualifications needed, just a savvy head – you'll get the hang of it in no time."

Hugging Fran, she pressed the bell before unlocking the door. A loud grating sound flooded the space around them. Delia flicked the light-switch. It took a few seconds for Fran's eyes to acclimatise. The dim light didn't make much of a difference, but she could see enough.

It was very different to the flat on Wardour Street. Light or no light. The space was small and grotty. The smell of air-freshener caught in her throat.

"So here's the waiting room, babe, which I expect will be fully occupied for the evening." Fran looked to her right behind the door where three wooden stools sat close together in an alcove. Across from the waiting area was a small arch with a beaded curtain tied to one side.

Not a window in sight. Just chairs and dirty peeling walls and a beaded curtain separating the waiting room from the tiny kitchen.

Delia explained that there were no facilities offered to customers off the street, other than what they came for. Not even a cup of water. Well, maybe a cup of water if they're about to choke on the premises. Paper cups in the press. Bathroom down the landing was strictly for staff. The key was kept on a nail to the left of the arch as you entered the kitchenette.

"We make an exception for the regulars," she said, "so by all means offer a cup of tea. I will point them out once they arrive. They won't always accept, of course, but offer anyway."

Fran jumped with the sound of the heavy beaded curtain being dropped into position by Delia.

"Here's your office, kiddo."

The door and walls of the dilapidated kitchenette were painted a pasty red colour, with a crooked red lampshade hanging from the centre, the frill falling loose where it had become detached from the rim, a heavy maroon-coloured curtain covering the back wall.

"There's the fridge, small enough, big enough. Tea and coffee in the press overhead and everything else in the press below. Kettle and cups there too. Booze in the box over there. And everything else a few doors up and a few doors down." She turned to Fran. "Well, what you think?"

"I don't know what to think, Delia."

"Never let a customer pass through the beaded curtain, Franny. *Never ever.* Or into this room, unless I give the say-so. That way there's some control. If I'm suspicious at all, I'll give you a shout through the door."

Delia reached up and pulled back the heavy drapes, revealing a door which had been painted the same pasty red colour as the walls. Fran would never have expected to find a door behind the curtain. She said as much to Delia.

"For our use only. Keeps us safe if anything starts up outside on the landing. No-one uses this door apart from us, Franny, so the key has to be kept at all times on the rim overhead. The customers' door leads straight out onto the landing."

Fran was lost for words. She put her hand to her mouth to stop her from opening it. Delia reached up for the key and unlocked the door. She flicked the light switch. It was exactly what Fran had expected Delia's bedroom to look like. Two cream wardrobes sat at either end of the room which was certainly big enough to hold them. One had an open suitcase perched on top, an array of coloured clothes falling over the sides. Boots and shoes piled beside it in the corner.

The other stood neat and tidy, nothing out of place.

"Yours, Delia?" Fran pointed at the messy one.

"*Delta!*"

"How did you guess? Jenny owns the neat one. We work separately but together if that makes sense. Separate stuff and that."

"Of course," Fran answered.

Two black polystyrene heads, wearing false eyelashes, stared back at Fran from a dressing table at the far end of the room. Delia pulled back the curtains on the only window Fran had seen since she arrived at the walk-up. The neon lights outside flashed red every few seconds, creating a sultry atmosphere in the room. A plastic bin sat under the window ledge.

244

"That'll have to be emptied at the end of each shift. Counted and emptied. Keeps a track on how many customers we've had."

An iron-framed double bed sat in the centre of the room, covered in a tiger-print bedspread. Delia grabbed a pair of handcuffs from the nightstand before tossing them in under the bed.

"The whips and feathers are kept here in the box to the left, my beloved Franny, but that's Jenny side of things. If you move the box over to one side you'll see where the dosh tin is kept. We only ever keep a small float in it overnight."

Fran thought she was going to pass out when Delia told her that she'd have to take the dirty linen to the launderette. What had she landed herself into? The shock was surely evident on her face, but Delia didn't seem to register how she was feeling. She hoped she did, because she wanted to look her straight in the eye and tell her. She wanted Delia to know that her heart was pounding so loud and so fast that she could hardly take in a word she was saying. That she was scared out of her life and that it was all a big mistake and she should never have left Ballygore, that she was sorry that she had agreed to fill in for her maid, because she couldn't in a million years see herself doing what Delia was expecting her to do. She felt sick.

Be brave, Fran, she told herself. *Be brave.*

"The peephole, Franny. Franny, are you listening to me at all? You're a million miles away and we need to get on with it. The peephole is there on the door. Just in case. Jenny came up with the idea of charging punters who are partial to a peep, but we decided to hold off on that one. Anyway, Kitty up the street has a mirrored wall, so we send them over to her if they ask for it. What you see is what you get here. Straight up."

Fran tried to imagine what Delia meant. She couldn't imagine.

Because she was beyond horrified by what Delia was saying.

"Wake up, Franny! Any questions? "

"Oh, plenty! What should I wear?"

"Just smart middle-of-the-road stuff. Like you're wearing. But you're quite a looker, Franny, so don't be surprised."

"What are you talking about? Don't be surprised at what?"

"Surprised if you get propositioned, of course. You'll have to make it clear that you're the maid."

Suddenly Roy's face flashed before Fran. He had all but propositioned her. He might just as well have slipped her a ten-pound note to pay her for services rendered. Because the only difference between what she had done with Roy, and what Delia and Jenny and the rest of the coffee girls were doing with all those different men, was payment. Money. Like for like. Once the thought occurred to her, she calmed down.

Hadn't she longed to spent time with Delia? Hadn't she longed for excitement and now she had it. It was only going to be for a week or two, until Delia got sorted with a new maid.

Since she was a child all she had ever wanted was to be included and accepted – as herself and nobody else. No acting or pretending. No script to follow. No hiding behind herself or anyone else. Just Fran. Take it or leave it.

"No bother at all, Delia, just show me the ropes. Oh Jesus, I didn't mean that."

"No ropes, babe – you've seen the handcuffs already. Oh, I nearly forgot. Jenny brings her own maid with her. She has a rota going with a couple of students."

Fran felt better already. If the work was good enough for college students then who was she to turn her nose up at it?

"Well, it's . . . "

"It's what?"

"It's *aaam* . . . different . . . from your own place."

"Home is home, dear Franny. This place is strictly work. Nothing at all to do with me how the landlord keeps the place as long as the punters keep coming up the stairs. Now take a peek out the window there – it gives us a prime view of the street below, so we can keep an eye. The runners on the street below will give us a whistle if the Old Bill are sniffing around so keep your ears open. But the cops don't give a toss cos they're in on the game themselves. Here in the West End everyone knows everyone else and we're all on the payroll ... if you get me."

Delia carried on rooting under the bed.

"Now here's the box of tools. I'll show you where to go tomorrow to keep it topped up. Think of them as little packets of . . . Oh, never mind . . . I'll see to it myself that they're knotted. After the act. Trust me, as long as the johnnies are accounted for, life is a lot easier. They're not allowed bring their own, cos some of them like to play the smart arses and prick a hole in the rubber."

"How do you know?"

"How do I know? I know because a few of the girls found out the hard way. So there. It's your job to run to the chemist's on the corner a few doors from Greggs. I'll show you tomorrow. Ask for Pete – he looks after us – we keep that box filled to the brim and bursting. Oh and keep it out of sight, in case some tosser decides to grab a fistful on the way out. Right. We got everything covered so for this evening. Wait till you count your tips at the end of the evening."

Delia said she needed to get changed. She asked Fran to take the sign off the door.

"So you get here a few minutes before me once you get the hang of things."

Fran nodded. She had already decided that she would be on the mailboat home the very next week. Delia could rattle on, Fran had heard enough. She would give it a week.

"There's a box of marigolds under the sink out there. I bet you'll never guess where the johnnies are made. In the London Rubber factory here in East London where they make the rubber gloves. Biggest employer in Chingford so it is. Illegal, of course, in Holy Catholic Ireland."

Fran felt her stomach turn. Everything was happening so fast. Too fast. She hadn't realised she was to start that very evening. Yes, she had agreed to help out. Yes, she had agreed to keep the place ticking over for a few days. But a box of rubber condoms? How could she face into a chemist's and ask for them? And from a man. But she would. Because she had told Delia that she'd give it a try and she couldn't back out now. She'd stick it for the week and be on the train bound for Holyhead the week after that. She'd figure out what she'd do next once she was on the boat facing for home.

"Time for tea, Franny – come on, we'll have a quick cuppa before we start the shift."

Fran was beginning to panic. Delia told her to relax and keep in mind that she was in London now and not in Ballygore. Fran listened with her eyes wide open as Delia repeated that she was expecting at least twenty customers before closing up for the night. "Sit them there in the waiting area. Three chairs – three tricks. By the way, Franny a trick is a client. No hangers-on. Regulars first – ten to fifteen minutes should do them. Twenty for some. Oh, never mind, I'll explain as I go. You'll soon recognise the regulars. No punters allowed to loiter in the landing. Too risky."

A small stool sat behind the plastic beading for Fran to sit on.

When the last punter had left, the plastic beading was to be knotted and tied back behind the hook, opening up the space for Delia and Fran to sit and have a cuppa. A double gin and bitter lemon for Delia. Then one for the road.

Fran's heart was thumping when she answered the door to the first customer but she was determined to keep her word. Delia had promised to pay her five pounds a shift along with the tips left for her by the punters.

"The maid does really well, Franny. It's different for us girls – we have a set price, so the punters pick a service of the menu. The maid's tip is up to the punter. Jenny has a list up there on the wall if you want to take a look. By the time they get to leave the tip for the maid they're in great form and splash the cash. You'll have to trust me on that one."

Fran had seen the poster on the wall. On the face of it didn't offend her. Services on offer for a price. Underneath it said: **The management reserve the right to withdraw services at their own discretion.**

"OK, Delia, I'll have to take your word for it. I haven't a bull's notion of what much of it means . . . well, I kind of do . . . what I mean is, I'm nowhere near as horrified as I was."

"*Delta!*"

From the moment she let the first customer in Fran was run off her feet. Delia called her in between each customer to chat for a minute or two. Fran would bring her up to speed on how many were waiting and ask what she needed to ask.

It was after seven before Fran got a chance to sit down in the tiny kitchenette. Three regulars sat in the waiting area. Delia was running late.

Fran spent the evening in and out of Delia's room. Opening and closing doors. Showing the punters in and showing them out. Making tea. Making more tea. Delia collected the money herself which suited Fran. The men in the waiting room were mannerly, far from the creepy types she had been expecting. These men looked perfectly normal. They sat close together chatting, as if they were at the barber's. Delia had told Fran what to expect of the regulars.

Ivan sat upright in the middle chair, looking at his watch every now and then. Impatient. The bald old guy that came after him was Steve who, according to Delia, turned up like clockwork every Tuesday at six o'clock and was home again in time for tea. Fred the third regular, a middle-aged guy, had a tendency to bolt out the door and down the stairs. A nervous type. Delta had asked Fran to keep an eye on him.

Once the regulars were seen to, the rest of the punters could sit in the waiting area. Three at a time.

It was full for the evening.

At the end of the shift Fran felt exhausted.

Fran asked Delia what all the commotion had been with Ivan, her first customer of the evening.

"Oh, I forgot to say – Ivan needs to see me before the others. With all the roaring he does at me he'd frighten the divil away."

Delia told her that Ivan liked to sit on a chair at the end of the bed and talk at her. Just talk. Delia said it was all the one to her what he talked about, as long as she got paid. As long as she appeared to be interested in what he was saying. He stayed for fifteen minutes. Fran was to tap on the door when his time was up.

"Poor sod, Ivan. He was a big shot back in the day, you know. A director of some sort, he never quite said, but I know by the soft hands and the clobber on him. Real lawdy-daw. All he asks me to do is sit on the bed and listen to him – with me wearing whatever he has managed to nick from his old lady's drawer. Usually it's a camisole or a slip, nothing too creepy. The best of silk. Beautiful Lace. Expensive. She's not my size, I tell you – she's one big lady, if the size of her slip is anything to go by. And I'm bigger than most. So I lie back against the pillow and, every now and then, in between his little speech, he'll roar at me in his posh accent *'Shut up, you nagging bitch!'* even though I haven't opened my mouth at all. I lie there and pretend to look interested. And he waffles on about politics and history shit. Sometimes he brings a newspaper and reads it aloud to me. The *Financial Times*. And I nod every now and then to let him know that I'm tuned in. *'Put a sock in it, you annoying wretch of a woman!'* he'll say."

Fran burst out laughing. She couldn't help herself.

"I flash my eyelids at him, pretending to be all subservient. He asked me to pant like a dog at one stage, *"Pant, you insolent woman!"* but I sat up straight and told him where to go with that one. He swears at me most of the time, calls me a dirty bitch and roars at me to quit interrupting when he's talking. And I lying back all relaxed, watching the clock over his head. Sometimes he pays for a double session. Then I go change behind the screen, and hand him back his missus' slip, which he folds ever so precisely before putting it in the inside pocket of his overcoat. He hands me the money and thanks me like a proper gent and off he goes. Another happy customer."

"So what does he get out of it for himself? I thought they came for the sex."

"Apparently his old lady has been ignoring him for years. She likes to have control. So our Ivan comes to me and goes home knowing that she's gone off to her big job, wearing you know what the very next day. My best bet is that he slips it straight back into her drawer and she never suspects a thing. It's all about control, kiddo. Power."

"Jesus, I suppose the other two want you to wear their underpants." Fran giggled. She figured her sense of humour might just come in useful if she was to survive working for Delia.

"Well, if you want the truth, the one nearest the door is a dote. Fred's in his fifties. In and out. The other guy, Steve – must be in his seventies – takes a little cajoling and more often than not it's a no-show. Happily married for fifty years, he told me. In this line of work you have to take them seriously. If I were to give him his money back, I'd never see him again. I don't ask what he does after leaving here, but I know where he goes before he gets here."

"Well, from what I've seen this evening 'tisn't to the church he's going to say a prayer."

"He goes to the peep show. To help him along. Looks in through a slot at one of the girls stripping, gets himself all worked up and can't wait to get here to see me to work it off. Sometimes I let him jump the queue and sometimes, like this evening, I let him wait his turn."

"I'm learning. Can't say I'm impressed but I'm learning. Jesus, 'tis a far cry from Ballygore! To be honest, I was dreading all this, I nearly got sick with the thought of it all earlier. I never ever thought about this stuff before. Do many Irish lads come here?"

"I can spot them a mile away and they running in and out of doorways and up and down the street like kids in a sweetshop. They want it all. And they can have it if they fork out for it. They get drawn into one of the clip joints where they're promised all kinds of tricks with the girls. The drink is only coloured water in the dodgier joints and they pay through the nose for it. They're turfed out then once the dance girls work their magic on them. No touching allowed so they run up the street looking for an open door. They gallop up the stairs here ready for action. They're the easy ones."

"I think I've heard enough for now. It's a lot to take in. You've seen it all so, Delta. See, I'm learning to call you Delta. Did anyone from home ever recognise you?"

"No. And, if they did, who are they going to blab to at home? They'd have the parish priest down on top of them. Old Father Mac at home in Ballygore would be naming and shaming them from the pulpit on a Sunday morning. Remember, even the most honest people have a dark side."

True to her word, after her shift Delia handed Fran her tips. It had been a busy night and she had made twenty pounds. She couldn't believe her eyes and thought Delia was getting it up for her. Almost two weeks wages back in the boot-factory office and she had made it in a couple of hours. And Delta had promised her a fiver on top of the tips. At this rate she wouldn't be touching the money in the bank. She have more than enough by the end of the week to pay Delta back and enough to cover her stay. Maybe she'd hang around for a while after all. Making a mental note to send a postcard home at the end of the week, Fran went to empty the bin.

Chapter 29

FRAN

Delta's Maid

After spending a week working at the walk-up in Brewer Street, Fran decided to stay on for a while longer. She was in no hurry to go home and Soho wasn't so daunting after all. It was fun and she loved being part of it all, hanging out with Delia and the coffee girls. She was where she had always wanted to be. Part of the gang. She felt comfortable in Soho. She felt she belonged.

They went to jazz clubs on Delia's night off and danced in the basement of the 2i's Coffee Bar till three in the morning. They went for pizza to the Roma and ate burgers at the Wimpy Bar on the corner.

Fran sent a postcard home to say she wouldn't be home soon after all. She'd stay on for another few weeks. They weren't to worry because she was fine. A month later she wrote that she was loving London, that she had seen Buckingham Palace from a bus window, that she couldn't but see it, when 'twas right there in front of her.

She knew her mother would be fit to kill her when she read the postcard. Especially when she had told her not to expect her home for another couple of weeks.

Three weeks later Fran decided to ring the phone box across the street from her house in Ballygore, because she knew her mother would be going out of her mind and her father wouldn't be too happy with her either. Her mother wouldn't give it to anyone to say that her Fran had gone off with Delia Blake and hadn't the common courtesy to ring home.

When Brigid arrived at the phone box to take the call, she was fit to be tied and between the crying and the shouting and the silence the line went dead. Fran felt bad. But she wasn't going home and that was that, because she was having such a good time with Delia but she wouldn't be telling her mother that. So she put the Irish ten-pound note her father had given her in an envelope, and posted it home to her mother for her birthday.

She sent another postcard home two weeks later to say that she had picked up a job for a couple of weeks – that she had met a lovely bunch of girls from all over the place and they were sharing a flat in an nice green area. That she mightn't be home for Christmas as 'twas her busiest time at work. That she would send presents home before Christmas and to be on the lookout for them. She was going to tell a lie and say she had a job in a chemist's shop. But then she didn't. The less she said the better and as long as she sent the odd letter home with a few bob enclosed for her mother, she was doing her best to keep in touch.

Fran rang the phone box again the week before Christmas. She asked the woman who answered if she'd happen to have a pen and paper to take down a number, to give to Brigid Gaffney across the road. The woman said she had, because she was on her way to the Bingo Hall and had her two lucky pens in her handbag. So she asked who was speaking and, when Fran told her, she said her name was Molly Redmond and that she knew Fran well. Then she asked more questions, even though she had said she'd go across straight away to deliver the message. And when she got off the phone Fran cursed herself, because the phone call cost her a fortune, and her mother wouldn't be too impressed to know that Molly Redmond knew about her daughter's set-up over in London.

Fran and Delia spent Christmas at the flat on Wardour Street with Penny with the red fringe and the Irish accent, who couldn't go home, because she didn't have a home to go to anymore. Barb came around, because she was on her own and Jenny was working the night shift in the walk-up on Boxing Day, so she came over as well for a couple of hours. Roxy, they said, had gone back into hospital for another stint of sleep therapy to get her over the Christmas.

Fran and Delia bought a cooked stuffed chicken at the Italian deli and ran home in the wind and the rain, with the chicken wrapped up in tinfoil in a plastic bag to keep it warm. They bought red and green crepe paper and glue and Fran cut out the shapes like she had seen her mother making at home, to hang from the four corners of the room. She ran thread through the decorations and tacked them to the ceiling to make the place Christmassy. And it did. When the girls came over at three o'clock, Delia produced a bunch of tinsel and they wore it around their necks and they laughed and sang Christmas songs.

Fran divided what was left of the chicken, after she caught Delia chewing on one of the wings. She swore she hadn't taken a mouthful off the second wing. Penny was put on guard duty. Smash powdered potato served straight from the milk pan. Two tins of garden peas with a spoon sticking out of each, a half-pound of soft butter. And a bowl of crispy Paxo which had been mixed with the stuffing from the bird. All laid out on the coffee table which Jenny said could do with a good wipe.

Delia told her she knew where the fucking door was if the place wasn't up to her standards. "And, anyway, that's Franny's department to keep the gaff clean," and they all had a good laugh. They each put their plates on tea towels on their laps and nothing ever tasted as good.

Delta put the gold lamp on its side on the floor and they played cards on the chess table and Delia won every hand because she was cheating and hiding the cards up her jumper and under her skirt and producing them at the right moment and they all laughed and said nothing because the laughing was more important than the cheating and 'twasn't as if they were playing for money. And they drank sweet yellow stuff from a bottle that Penny had brought with her, and the more they drank, the better it tasted, until it was all gone and they found a bottle of red wine which they drank before opening a bottle of Mateus Rosé that Delia found in a small wooden crate at the back of the wardrobe.

They laughed and they sang and Fran was happier than she had ever been. She ran out to the hall with the intention of calling the phone box at home, but she ducked straight back in again when she thought she heard a noise coming from next door. And they all laughed when they saw the look on her face.

When Barb asked if there was any sign of Camilla, saying she must be due back any day now, Delta told her to shut the fuck up and mind her own business. Barb looked as if she were about to cry. Delia said to forget about Camilla 'twas Christmas after all and Fran asked who Camilla was, and Delia glared at Barb and said now look what you're after starting and off she went to open another bottle of Mateus Rosé and they had the best Christmas ever.

But Fran knew by the look on Barb's face that something wasn't right.

And they were all as sick as dogs the following day, but it didn't matter because they had been together and that's all that counted, and they minded each other and knew they were safe in each other's company.

Jenny went back to work the following day, because she was heading back to her homeplace for the first time in a while and didn't want to disappoint her regulars before she took off. Delia said she was thinking of taking a few days off herself and maybe she would – business might be slow enough seeing as 'twas Christmas. Family time. She said she herself was feeling a bit tardy after the bloody mixture they had consumed on Christmas Day. And it wouldn't matter all that much if she took a break. Delia puked into a bucket and said she needed to have a good think. Fran could tell that Delia had something on her mind. She seemed agitated when she asked Fran if she had seen the bitch from the flat next door at all. The Ada one.

Fran's mother rang the coinbox in the hall the day after that, and lucky enough Fran was there to answer it. Her mother said that her father couldn't get over the fact that she hadn't bothered to ring home on Christmas Day. That she herself had stood above in the phone box like a right eejit, to see would it ring. That the neighbours were all hanging around waiting for their calls from England. So she stood in the phone box pretending that she was waiting for her own call. And the smell nearly turned her stomach with all the newspaper on the ground. Damp with fellas urinating on the floor. "'Twould knock you out, Fran, so it would."

She said that her father had been very put out, that they hadn't reared her to be so ungrateful. Brigid said she had decided to go ahead and use the money that Fran had given her out of the claim to have the phone put in, that she couldn't be depending on the likes of Molly Redmond to be passing messages forwards and backwards. That herself and Dan had talked about it and agreed it was the right thing to do. And then she'd have no excuse to call them once they had given her the number. And Fran told her to go ahead, that'd be a great idea, but she'd every intention of coming home in a couple of weeks either way. And her mother said that she had heard it all before and where had that got her? No place. So Fran got defiant and said she'd be staying in London for another while so. They would keep in touch by phone. She lied and said she had tried the phone box several times in the meantime and the phone had been engaged.

She told her mother to be sure and let her know the number if the phone was connected in time for her birthday on the thirteenth of January. Her *real* birthday. To ring the coinbox in the hall and ask whoever answered to put the note in under the door of the flat. But she wasn't to talk to Ada because she'd never get the number. That seemed to pacify her mother because her tone changed and she asked had she any other news. *Beep . . . beep . . .* and her mother's money ran out and that suited Fran because she didn't have to be lying about things and making up stories to suit her mother. They were fine at home and that's all that mattered for now. Fran was having the time of her life in Soho with Delia, but in her heart she knew that it was drawing to a close.

Chapter 30

FRAN

Lies All Lies

By the time Fran found out about the flat in Wardour Street it all began to make sense. Turned out Delia's tendency to fabricate stuff on any given day had up-ended on her. Fran had known that Delia told tales and exaggerated stories for effect. It didn't change the way she felt about her. Delia was Delia.

The coffee girls had passed comments here and there. Sometimes in jest and more times not, Fran wasn't entirely sure. But she made sure never to join in when it started. Not always obvious. But there.

It was Jenny who had told her the truth. Saying she felt sorry that Delta was making such a wally out of her. The girls had drawn straws and she had picked the short one.

Fran was careful not to overreact as she listened. She would never turn her back on Delia. And certainly not in front of the girls.

Their flat on Wardour Street had not been rented by Delia. It had not been let and sublet and underlet like she had tried to make out. The rent had been paid by a Spanish girl, Camilla, who had lived there for the past eight years.

According to Jenny, Delia had been kicked out of her previous flat when she was caught by the landlord working from home. Every stitch she owned had been dumped out the window onto the street below. So Delia moved her stuff into the walk-up on Brewer Street, until she found a place. And she did. Camilla's place.

Camilla had moved back home to Valencia to recuperate after being attacked by a nutter with a Stanley knife in a fancy hotel room in Knightsbridge. She had been tied up and sliced across her face. Left for dead until one of the cleaners found her.

Camilla, a dark-skinned beauty not unlike Delia in stature, had come to London to study ten years before, working every hour in between to support herself. She had given up on her studies to become a full time working-girl like themselves – except that Camilla considered herself to be a step above. She had become a top-shelf escort. Camilla planned on returning to Spain in the New Year having saved enough money to buy herself a place there.

She had paid the final three months' rent in advance knowing that the lease was up. The flat on Wardour Street was changing hands. Camilla had made arrangements to ship the contents of the flat to Spain, once the paperwork came through. Everything she owned.

Delia hadn't paid a penny rent in the four months they had been there. She had taken advantage of Camilla's misfortune for her own ends. And brought Fran in with her to soften the blow.

Delia had gone to visit Camilla in the hospital with two of the coffee girls when they heard what had happened. Camilla, who according to Jenny had always maintained a haughty distance, was unrecognisable in the bed, battered and bruised and covered in great big stitches. Her thick black hair, which had always been immaculate, was pinned back off her face, showing bald patches over both ears where it had been ripped from her head. One of her wrists was broken, along with two of her ribs. But the main damage was done to her face. Her father was coming from Spain the following week to take her home once she was able to travel. He might insist, she said, on checking the flat before they left for Spain. And she didn't want that.

Camilla had no idea how badly disfigured she was because she hadn't seen her face. But the girls knew. Camilla wouldn't be back to work any time soon. If ever. And certainly not to her former career on the top shelf. The jagged stitching across her forehead looked angry. Black stitches from one cheek to the other, across her nose and over one eye. Swollen fleshy gaps between the stitches. Camila told them that one of her eyes had popped out of its socket and they had to stitch it back in. Her face was purple and swollen where she had been punched. Caked blood on her face. On her scalp. Her good eye was bulging, her cornea a deep red colour.

Jenny said they were all a bit fragile, having seen her. They had seen plenty of shiners and broken ribs and cuts and bruises. But never this. They couldn't bear to look at her in the bed and left soon after. So much for being a high-class escort.

Delia had insisted on staying on a bit longer, which they thought was out of character. She was squeamish at the best of times. Then Barb reminded them of Delia's ordeal with Red Eddie – they decided she was hanging around Camilla to offer support. Solidarity. Delia was acting like a proper sweetheart.

Later, when Delia told the coffee girls that she would be looking after the place, they saw no reason to doubt her. The girls believed that three months would not be near enough to have Camilla even half right, unless she wore a bag over her head. Camilla must have damaged her brain if she thought she'd work in the business again. Her face was destroyed.

It was much later they found out that Delia had persuaded Camilla to hand over the keys of the flat, promising to remove all work-related merchandise. Someone had to do it. She presented an effective scenario of Camilla's father's face should he come across the tools of her trade back at the flat. Her family in Spain understood that she had been attacked on her way home from her job at the college library.

Camilla agreed that the weeks ahead were uncertain for her. She certainly wouldn't be subletting the flat. Everything she had worked so hard for was there.

Delia promised to hand the keys over to Ada in the flat next door once she had checked the place over. Camilla wasn't to worry about a thing. Respectable Ada would hold on to the keys until she heard from Camilla.

Delia moved herself into the flat the same day that Camilla was leaving for Spain. She left for Ireland a couple of days later, having frightened the life out of Ada next door. Delia threatened to put Ada in hospital when she rang the bell to enquire about the keys. She said that they could make up the bed for her that Camilla had been in. She asked her if she liked hospital food – that she'd be sucking her dinner through a straw if she opened her gob. Ada got the message. She was so terrified she avoided having anything to do with the flat. Or Camilla.

Jenny told Fran that she had heard it in one of the clubs in November that Camilla's recovery was proving to be a lot tougher than she had first imagined. She had seen her face on her way to the airport and had collapsed into her father's arms. Seven weeks had passed before she was anyway right to think about her flat in London. She was confident that Ada was keeping an eye. Camilla began calling the phone box in the landing, expecting to speak to Ada. Nothing. She called several more times. Nothing. She sent a telegram. Ada was scared out of her wits – she wanted nothing to do with it as long as Delia was in the same building.

Then Christmas came and went.

Delia played it down when the coffee girls decided to confront her, saying they were hearing all sorts. And what about the change in her style? She got defensive, as was her way, telling them they had some cheek to go accusing her. Her story changed depending on who was asking. She said that she had an arrangement with Camilla, who must have been doped out of her bloody skull on the day. And what was the harm in borrowing a few bits of clobber? At least she hadn't moved all of her own stuff in, cramming up the joint. So technically it wasn't as if she moved in, was it? She had stacked her stuff in the walk-up along with some of Camilla's work gear. She had made use of the three months' free rent. What was so wrong with that? Franny was keeping the place shipshape. Cleaning and all. Nothing for nothing in this life. When they accused her of bullying Ada, Delia said that Ada was in on it. That she had known all along that Delia was minding the flat until Camilla arrived back. The girls discussed it between themselves before deciding that Delta couldn't get her story straight, because she lived her life without a plan and made it up as she went along.

Fran knew that Delia was struggling with the truth. She had been correct about the cleaning though. The flat was as clean as the day Fran had walked into it. Spotless. Fran the maid.

Ada next door worked as a senior typist in the council. She had made a few attempts to waylay Fran in the hallway when Delia was not about. She came to the door while Delia was out, twitching nervously, saying that she was getting telegrams from Camilla asking why she wasn't answering her calls. Ada admitted that she was far too scared to respond to Camilla, that she had been her neighbour for the past five years but 'twasn't as if she owed her anything. She grabbed hold of Fran's arm and said that Fran looked like a decent sort – maybe she would be so kind as to have a word with Delta, before Camilla turned up and all hell broke loose.

Fran pulled her arm back and closed the door in Ada's face, convinced she was the lunatic that Delia maintained she was. She told Delia when she returned, believing it to be the right thing to do. She avoided Ada after that, until she heard the banging through the wall and heard Delia's voice threatening Ada, who was crying, saying that she wanted nothing more to do with any of it. Delia walked back in the door of the flat rubbing her hands together, saying that it was all sorted next door, and to let her know if the mad cow came near her again. Then Fran remembered Barb asking had Delia heard from Camilla at Christmastime.

New Year's Day was the last time that Fran saw Delia. She had walked off, saying she'd be back in a while. And that was the last Fran saw of her.

When Delia hadn't shown up by the following day, Penny said she feared that she was up to her old tricks again. True to form. The coffee girls said they couldn't believe that Delta had hung around for a full four months. But she had. And now she was gone again.

Penny said that she couldn't tell the truth in a fit, and if Fran was in her right mind she'd head straight back to Ireland while she had the chance.

Fran was worried. She decided to hang around to see would Delia arrive back. If not she would pack her bag and make her way back to Ireland. She decided to give Delia no more than three days. Her heart cried for Delia.

Camilla turned up at the flat a day later, barging in the door with a tough-looking henchman, demanding her keys back, saying that she'd break Fran's face if she didn't step back and do as she asked. Fran thought she was going to die. Camilla pushed her into the living room, shouting at her to sit down. She wasn't to move. It happened so fast Fran scarcely had time to be terrified. She did as she was told. The henchman stood over her, glaring at her, while Camilla rushed around, lifting lamps. Checking the gilt table. Checking her artwork on the walls. Then she headed for the bedroom. Fran didn't need to understand a word of Spanish to know that Camilla was cursing. She heard the wardrobe door being banged shut before Camilla reappeared in the living room.

She sat beside Fran on the sofa, removing her scarf and revealing the extent of her injuries. Her face was badly scarred.

Half afraid she would end up scarred herself, Fran did her best to remain calm. Camilla's nostrils were bigger than Fran had ever seen on a female. She could see the dark hairs inside.

Fran said she had to go to the bank when Camilla eventually demanded six hundred pounds from her. Rent and retribution. Camilla would wait for her. The henchman would accompany Fran.

As soon as they returned, Camilla snapped the money from Fran. Then she demanded damages on top of the six hundred pounds. Her clothes were ruined. She said she wasn't about to let a thieving slut like Delta take everything that she had worked so hard for. Camilla pointed towards a chip at the base of her lamp. The feet of her gold leaf table were ruined, she said. And, seeing as Fran had taken up residence there also, she had better pay up, given that Delta was nowhere to be found. Fran felt relieved for Delia whom she now believed was laying low.

But when Fran went looking in the bedroom for the cash she had put away, almost two hundred pounds, it was missing. Gone. She went to the bank for a second time and withdrew another two hundred. She paid Camilla the money. She had until the end of the day to remove herself.

When she met up with the coffee girls, they advised her to run like the wind and have nothing at all to do with Delta if she appeared back. It was up to her. Barb said she was more than welcome to stay a few days at her place until she got her stuff together.

It was time to go home. Time to return to Ballygore, having spent the best time of her life in Soho with Delta and the coffee girls. Even if she had been duped by Delia, Fran knew that she would get over it in time. Delia had pulled a fast one and taken off. But then again that was Delia. Beholden to no-one. Fran had earned her keep and felt comfortable in Soho. She'd had the time of her life. Delia would show up when she was ready.

Chapter 31

SADIE PRATT

January 1946

Sadie Pratt stood at the top of the stairs, holding Baby Clarke.

She could hear voices coming from the room a few feet away where she was headed. She had been warned by Matron not to appear anywhere near the private rooms. She was to leave Baby Clarke in the cot outside Room 4 and return to the basement. Mrs. Clarke was feeling much better. Matron said she would take the baby in herself. The door was slightly open. Sadie recognised Matron's high-pitched voice. She was sharing a joke with Eunice Clarke. They were laughing. Must be a very funny joke, thought Sadie. Listening. She stopped dead in her tracks, the baby asleep in her arms. Sadie's ear picked up on her name.

Her heart sank. They were talking about her.

"Matron, I hope you don't take this up the wrong way but I'm surprised that you allow the Pratt girl near the patients. She's filthy. And you're telling me that she has it in her head to train as a nurse?"

There was no mistaking the laughter from the room. They were laughing at her expense. Matron's voice.

"I take no notice at all of poor Sadie, 'tis all in the head with her. The only reference she'll be getting from me will be for a cleaning position and even at that I'd be hard pushed."

More laughing.

"Is it any wonder I fainted the other day when she brought the baby up to me. I was certain the baby had a full nappy. And the next thing I knew, I woke up to find myself being prodded and poked by you all."

"Eunice, you're all well again, everything's been checked and in order. I can't apologise enough for Sadie, she shouldn't have come near the room. She will remain downstairs from now on – nowhere near the wards. I've had the nursery staff off all week with a bug. I'll bring the baby up myself from now on. And I'll have a word with Miss Pratt, don't you worry."

They were sneering at her. Calling her filth. Whatever about snooty Mrs. Clarke, Sadie was devastated to hear what Matron had to say about her.

"And I hope you're not leaving her anywhere near the kitchen. I'd rather starve than eat anything she has touched. I just have to think of her and I retch."

"Eunice come on now, all jokes aside, that's a bit over the top. I've pulled her up several times and she improves each time, and then she slips back. But where would I find a replacement who'll work as hard as she does? She works like a Trojan I'll give her that – but I'll have a word with her. Again. We wouldn't want our mothers to be suffering unduly, now would we?"

Sadie had already turned around, she was headed for the stairs.

Baby in her arms. She was far too upset to think. She rushed back down towards the nursery – Matron would no doubt come looking for her as soon as she had seen to the other mothers on the top floor. She was in trouble again. She felt sick.

Matron had used her like a workhorse. She hadn't a notion of supporting her with her nursing career. Sadie was devastated. She had worked so hard.

Back in the nursery, she stood at the bottom of the empty cot with Baby Clarke in her arms. There were eight babies in the nursery, each wearing a paper nametag on their ankle. Matron maintained that the ankle-tags were better than the bracelets. They didn't irritate the babies' faces. Blue for the boys at the left hand side of the room – pink for the girls to the right.

She read the pink card on the wall behind the empty cot.

Baby Clarke. Dob 13/01/46 Time 11pm. Mother's name Eunice. Father Malcolm. Wght. 7lb 12 oz

The infant in the next cot was sound asleep. Swaddled. The pink card behind the cot read: **Baby Murphy – Illegitimate (Doctor Gordon's – to be boarded out). Wght 8lb 4oz Dob 13/01/46 Time 2.00am**

Eunice Clarke, had been downright rude to Sadie when she had brought the infant up to her on Monday to be fed. Sniffing at her. And now here she was, blaming her for passing out in the bed, when Matron knew damn well it had been all the blood she had lost after the delivery that had weakened her. Sadie knew because she had to collect the soiled sheets from outside the delivery room first thing on the Monday morning. Matron hadn't bothered to check on Mrs. Clarke before the baby was brought up to be nursed and now she was glossing over it. Blaming Sadie.

The Murphy baby was being placed in a good home once the paperwork was completed. She would be eventually adopted, God knows where, and 'twasn't as if her birthmother was in any position to rear her. Sadie knew the mother to see her around the town. She wasn't a local, but she knew her to see. She'd seen her leaving Matron's office with Dan Gaffney the day before and he having his arms around her and she crying into his shoulder.

Without giving it another thought, Sadie placed the baby down on the feeding chair and pulled back the blanket revealing the anklet on the purplish foot of Baby Clarke.

She removed it and placed it in the cot beside Baby Murphy.

Sadie unfolded Baby Murphy's blanket, removing her anklet which she quickly placed in the empty Clarke cot. It took seconds for her to switch the anklets. Time for feeding. Within a few minutes, Matron appeared at the door.

She handed Sadie a curved feeding bottle, before going straight to the cot marked *Clarke*. Matron lifted the infant up.

"Right, Baby Clarke, off we go to your mammy for a feed."

"Feed Baby Murphy there, Sadie, and for God's sake don't put your nose outside that door until I arrive back down. Nurse Dawson will be back in the morning along with Chrissie. You were given strict instructions not to go anywhere near the private rooms and in you went as bold as brass to Mrs. Clarke on Monday. You were told to leave the babies for feeding in the cots on the landing until I got there myself."

"Yes, Matron," Sadie stammered. "I thought I was helping you out, so I brought her straight in to her mammy. Matron, if I may say so it was yourself who asked me to take the babies up to the top floor. I did what you asked me to do and now I'm in trouble again, just because Mrs. Clarke didn't like the look of me. Chrissie would always ask for my help with the babies when you're not around, Matron."

"You are not to take orders from anyone except myself, Sadie, and in my absence I will leave strict instructions for you from now on. Is that clear? I will be having a word with Nurse Dawson and Chrissie, don't you worry."

Sadie could see that Matron's patience was running low. No point in antagonising her any further. "Yes, Matron."

Matron sighed heavily as she continued out the door with the baby.

"Best if you meet me in my office for a chat at two – once Mr. Clarke arrives. And smarten yourself up, you look like you've been dragged through a bush."

"Yes, Matron." Sadie lifted the baby girl from the cot. She sat down on the feeding chair and began feeding her. Once Matron was out of sight, Sadie sniggered. The infant in her arms fed hungrily from the bottle.

Sadie never got the opportunity to switch the babies back, even if it had been her intention. She had been ordered back to the basement by Matron having been told that she wasn't to set foot anywhere near the nursery, unless Matron had given her strict instructions to do so.

The floor in the basement needed scrubbing. Sadie chuckled to herself as she made her way down the back stairs to the broom closet. She hadn't thought it through. She hadn't thought any further than wanting to teach the Clarke woman a lesson.

It would be all the same to Nurse Dawson when she arrived back. She wouldn't have seen either infant. Nothing to worry about there. And neither would Chrissie. They had been out sick since Sunday. That ignorant bitch of a woman upstairs would hardly notice the difference. She would have put her snobby titty straight into the mouth of an illegitimate infant. And good enough for her!

The cheek of that Clarke woman to be talking about her that way. Just because her husband owned the boot factory, she thought she could lord it over everyone else. Sadie had heard them saying in the kitchen later that Malcolm Clarke had been so enamoured with his baby daughter that he had left a five-pound note with Matron.

In the weeks that followed Sadie had enough to be doing to keep her job to be giving any more thought to what she had done. When Matron asked to see her for the umpteenth time she knew what was about to take place. Too many final warnings.

"Sadie, look, I know you work very hard here and you've never objected to anything I've asked you to do. But you're just not cut out for mixing with the patients. They're uncomfortable around you. Surely you know this. And I have to listen to the complaints. Your hygiene remains a huge issue and how often before have we had this conversation? I know it was myself that heaped the extra work on you, but Nurse and Chrissie are both back now so we're back to normal. Do you understand what I'm saying to you? This is your very last final warning, Sadie. No more."

No matter how hard she worked or how willing she was to learn, Matron would never write a decent reference for her now.

Sadie went ahead and wrote her own reference in the end – she copied Matron's signature at the bottom of the page in pure frustration. It was to be the end of her time at St. Mary's. Matron sacked her and told her she was lucky she didn't go to the gardaí. She'd laughed as she showed Sadie the letter she had posted to the training hospital in London.

Matron was shaking with laughter. "Sadie, how could you ever have thought that this letter would be taken seriously? It's full of simple mistakes. And is that a tea stain on it?"

Sadie knew what was coming.

"The Registrar over there sent it back to me. You've been given plenty warnings at this stage and I'm sorry to say that we can no longer employ you. Trust has been broken, Sadie. Your wages will be sent out to you."

Chapter 32

DELIA BLAKE

On the Run

When Delia opened her eyes on the park bench it took a few seconds for her to realise where she was. Brushing a bluebottle away, she squinted through the foliage above her head. The low winter sun blinded her eyes. She threw back the wet plastic sheet, allowing the pockets of rain to spill on the ground. Covering her eyes with her hands, she stretched out on the bench. The weather had improved, after the snow of previous weeks. Weeks that she didn't want to dwell on. Images of herself and Franny as they trudged through the snow in December, kicking the slush in front of them, laughing and cursing as they made their way back to the flat on Wardour Street. Back to Camilla's.

The coffee girls had found out about the flat – they were giving her a hard time. The game was up and they had told Franny. The pressure had been too great and Delia knew that it was only a matter of days before everything could change. For once in her life she had been contented. Happy to have Franny by her side. She feared that Franny would up and leave with all the upheaval. Jenny had left for Sheffield to take care of her father, she wasn't due back until the following week. Delia decided to stay at the walk-up for a night or two. To clear her head. She had no immediate plan. She needed to find a new place for herself and Franny. Quick. A decent place. She wouldn't have been able to think straight back at the flat with Franny and the girls in her ear.

Delia had known that the three months were coming to an end – she had known that she couldn't hold out for much longer. But herself and Franny were having such a blast that she put off the inevitable.

She had known that the rent was up on the flat, even if Camilla had never turned up. But she had and it was over. Franny and herself had spent four months together. Christmas at the flat had been the best she had ever remembered. Franny would return to Ballygore, no longer the naive, eager-to-please girl Delia had brought over from Ireland the September before. Wherever Franny ended up, she had seen the ways of the world. Surely that must account for something.

Delia held on to the bench to steady herself when she sat up. Running her fingers lightly over the initials she had etched with her penknife the night before. D x F.

She needed to move on. She had promised to meet the coffee girls on the corner of Berwick Street, when they had come across her in the street two days before. To get them off her case. To fob them off. She had been down this road before. Another meeting to sort her out. Another meeting to tell her she was fooling no-one except herself. Another meeting to tell her they would help her get back on her feet.

She pulled up the cuff of her jacket and looked at her wrist and remembered. She had exchanged Camilla's watch for a can of cider. Didn't matter. And whatever time it was, it was probably too late to meet the girls. Delia knew that she was in no condition to be showing up anywhere.

She hadn't noticed the park attendant approaching. Her head when she lifted it was heavy. Pain shot through her temples.

"No time for self-pity, Del," she said aloud, straightening herself. Not now.

"Miss, you can't stay here – look at the sign. No loitering. Pick up your things and move on."

"Who's loitering? I'm sitting here enjoying the crisp morning air – if it's all the same to you. Is that against the law these days?"

"Miss, I saw you here this last few mornings and let you be, seeing as the park was quiet. People are moving about now being the weekend, so come on, pick up your bag and move along. The Old Bill walk through here all the time."

"I don't suppose you have a ciggy?"

"I quit. Move on, miss."

Delia smoothed herself down as best she could. She had enough clothes on her to keep out the cold. Every stitch she owned. Layers. She kissed her fingers and touched the etching.

Leaving the park she headed for the nearest public toilets, careful to keep her head down. The last thing she wanted was to be recognised.

She stood on Carnaby Street watching the live models undress in the window of the Lady Jane, the first fashion boutique in Soho. It was here that Jenny and Audrey had brought her the day she started working for Red Eddie. Delia couldn't but notice her reflection. She might just escape being recognised after all. She scarcely recognised herself. The orange woollen hat she had nicked from a stall on Berwick Street covered her head. Her hair inside was flat on her head. Her face was round and puffy, her eyes swollen. The baggy coat she wore was from the Lost and Found at the bus station. The jacket underneath she had picked up in a squat. At least everything inside of the coats belonged to her. The same clothes that she had walked out of the walk-up in the month before. She had used the inside of her polo-neck to clean her teeth.

She looked down the street, there were people everywhere. Sitting down on the pavement against the wall was her best chance. She had been here before. Taking off the outer coat she sat on it. The jacket inside would have to do until her body temperature told her otherwise. Holding her hand out, she kept her head bent.

She watched people's feet as they passed. She looked at their shoes. A tactic she had used in the past to keep her mind occupied as she waited for the coins to drop. She didn't have to meet their eyes. Men and women. Red shoes, green shoes, brown shoes. Stylish shoes. Slingbacks. Scuffed boots. She thought about Franny and her obsession with shoes. Delia wasn't fussed about what she wore on her feet these days, as long as they covered her feet.

The black stilettoes that had stopped in front of her were nice. Beside them a pair of green patent ones. Then a pair of white slingbacks. Looking up along the length of the legs in front of her, she knew before she got to the faces who they belonged to. She tried to get up. To run. The owner of the black shoes bent down in front of her. Blocking her escape. Too late, she hadn't been quick enough. Eye contact had been made. Penny, Barb and Audrey from the Regency, were looking down at her. The coffee girls had caught up with her. Franny wasn't with them.

"We knew you wouldn't meet us like you said. We're here now

so go on then – try doing a runner," said Audrey.

Delia looked straight up at Penny. "Sorry, Penny . . . really sorry. It's just that . . . I lost my watch and you know what I'm like for time. I wasn't trying to avoid you."

It was Barb who answered. "Yeah, you was, Delta. You silly bugger, you done us wrong. We guessed you wouldn't show, so here we are. We have news for you. Tell her, Penny. Tell her what Franny only gone and done for her."

"So what did Franny only gone and do for me then, Penny? Spit it out." Delia was playing for time.

"Not here, Delta."

"Come on up. *Up!*"

Audrey and Penny grabbed her by both arms before pulling her to her feet. Delia picked up the coat, attempting to put it on while Barb grabbed her arm.

Barb's face turned pale. "You're proper mingin', Delta."

"You were always a high and mighty bitch, Barb. So what? Delta is mingin'. Now fuck off the three of you and leave me alone."

She tried to break away. But they held her.

Penny spoke. "That won't be happening, Delta. Come on, we'll go back to my place where we can talk. You can stay at mine for a couple of days. We've already had Fanny staying between us – she's gone back home to Ireland. Come on!"

Penny and Audrey linked Delia along the street. Barb tottered behind.

"OK . . . OK . . . I'm sure you don't want me dirtying up your place, but I could do with a wash if the look on *her* face is anything to go by." She nodded at Barb. "But I'm not hanging about. I'm off again once I've cleaned myself up.

"That's up to you, Delta – where will you go?"

"I've a job offer in a hotel with a flat going with it up north."

The girls knew Delta's form. There was no job and no flat and, even if there was, no one would hire her with the state she was in. It would take more than a wash and a clean bed to sort this out.

Audrey winked at Penny. "Of course, Delta, that's great news. But you're right – first you need to clean yourself up. As Barb just said, you do stink."

Delia looked straight back at Barb. "Do I, Barb? Do I really stink? Are you judging me because I don't smell good enough? Maybe I better stay where I am? I wouldn't like to be messing up Penny's flat."

Penny cut straight in. "Oh, will you quit the shit, girl? Now walk with us, or we'll drag you there."

People were passing, looking back to see what the commotion was about.

"Oh for God sake, give me a minute! And what the fuck are *they* looking at?"

Once back at the flat Penny went to run a bath. Barb sat down on the settee beside Delia who let it be known she was in no mood to be explaining herself. She got up and paced around the flat, watching the door.

Penny called to say the bath was ready and she had laid out fresh clothes on her bed. Barb had to leave – she made Delia promise that she wouldn't be gone when she came back later.

"Look me in the mincers, Delta, and tell me you won't take off."

Delia swore on her life. Audrey had to leave, to get ready for work. The girls had agreed to take it in turns to look in on her between shifts.

280

When Penny and Delia were alone, Penny told her that Franny had paid off the debt owed to Camilla.

Delia could not believe what she was hearing.

"What? What? You mean they got to Franny? Penny, did they hurt her? Rough her up? Oh, Jesus!"

"No, Delta, she's fine."

"Oh Jesus . . . she paid them money? How much did she give them?"

"Never mind how much. Well, OK . . . She gave them a couple of hundred. Along with the rest, I'd say. She never said."

"You stupid, stupid bitch, Delia Blake!" Delia lowed her head.

Taking a few minutes to compose herself, she explained to Penny what had happened.

"They must have been watching the flat and followed me back to the walk-up the night I left Wardour Street. I just needed time to get my head straight. Jenny was out of the way, so I decided to crash at the walk-up for a couple of nights. I knew that Camilla would turn up one of the days. But I wasn't expecting the fucking tornado who showed up with her the following morning. A big burly bloke who burst through the door and knocked me about, leaving me in no doubt as to what was coming. They wrecked the joint before they left and said if I showed my ass in Soho anytime soon my face would look like a jigsaw puzzle. They poured a cannister of petrol all over the place and into the wardrobes. All over Jenny's clobber. I gave them every penny I had on me. Almost two grand. Every penny I had so they'd leave us alone. So much for fucking high and mighty lady escort, Camilla. Every penny I had in the fucking world, because they told me they were coming for Franny if I didn't give them what they wanted. And how could I face Jenny when she came back, with the state of the walk-up? So I ran."

"Never mind, Delta, it's all over now. Jenny got back. She knows the score. She got kicked out of the walk-up, so she's working with Audrey at the Regency until she gets a place sorted. Jenny's a trouper, she'll be fine, so no worries there. And Franny coped much better than any of us would have thought. She proper stood up for you. Told us that the cash they got was what she had earned at the walk-up. And a bit more alongside. Easy come and easy go, is all she said."

"Oh, Franny . . . and I thinking she was the gullible one."

The morning that Camilla had turned up at the walk-up accompanied by a thug from the East End, Delia knew immediately that they meant business. Camilla looked a lot tougher than the vulnerable girl who had handed her keys over to Delia from her hospital bed.

Camilla told Delia that her flat on Wardour Street had been watched ahead of her arrival. Camilla had insisted they hold back – she said that she wanted to be there herself to witness the look on Delta's face when she ripped her apart and took everything she had ever owned from her. Shut her down. No one fucked with Camilla Torres and got away with it. She had threatened to stick Franny's head in the oven if Delia didn't comply with her requests. Delia handed everything she had over to her. Afterwards she removed herself from the scene, not wanting to implicate Franny, Jenny and the rest of the coffee girls. And off she ran.

Chapter 33

FRAN

Homeward Bound

The day before she was due to leave for home, Fran joined the coffee girls for one last time. She told them she was sorry she didn't get to say goodbye to Delia – they would catch up in Ireland at some stage. Once Fran had steered the conversation away from Delia, she told the girls she would miss their company. They assured her that there would always be a welcome for her back in Soho. And a job if she were open to it. And when they heard from Delta, they would be sure to tell her to get in touch.

Fran had felt the warmth offered by these women, who for whatever reason had ended up in Soho working in the sex trade. Maybe like Delia they were running away, chased from their own lives.

Fran had learned more about survival in the past four months than she had learned in all her years of living at home. She learned how not to take people at face value.

It was Delia who had given her the greatest gift. Unknowingly. Through Delia, Fran learned about empathy. She learned how to accept. Not to be too quick to judge. Having spent her life in Ballygore adored by her family, she had been blindly searching for something that was there all along. Not everyone was so blessed.

Fran would be forever grateful to Delia who had taken her on a journey, showing her a side of life that she and others like her would have scorned. Dirty. A life lived by girls of loose morals. The Fran coming home was a very different version of the naive girl that had left Ballygore the September before.

She had learned more about life. A life that people didn't know much about. Or want to know about. A world of shadows. An underworld cloaked by secrets. But Fran knew different. She had been warmly accepted into the Soho community. She had experienced a sense of true camaraderie and trust. Living in Soho had been an eye opener.

Fran boarded the train from London Euston, bound for Holyhead. She was relieved to be in out of the rain. She excused herself to the man in the aisle seat, nodding her head towards the seat on the inside. Settling herself, she leaned her head against the window, damp with condensation. She closed her eyes. Fran had much to think about.

She was returning home to Ballygore without a notion in the world of what she would do once she got there. She would forever more consider Delia to be her best friend but, with all that had happened, she knew it was time for her to return to Ireland.

Her mother had been distant on the phone when she'd called to say she would be arriving home. Fran had offered little in terms of an explanation.

Brigid had all but dismissed her. Talking over her, telling her in a matter of fact way that the bed would be ready for her, as it had been since the day she had taken off with that tramp. The Blake one. A tramp without a scrap of self-respect.

She had added that the front door key hadn't budged. It was still hanging on its chain. Fran could put her hand through the letterbox and pull it out – in case there was no-one at home to receive her when she landed. End of conversation. Brigid hung up on Fran, leaving her standing in the phone box on Dean Street. The old Fran would have felt remorseful. Guilty. Fran pulled a face at the handset, shrugged her shoulders and sniggered.

Her mother had spoken to her as if she were a lodger. Fran wanted to ask after her father, who no doubt would be grinning from ear to hear on hearing that his wanderlust daughter was on her way home.

Fran knew that he'd be doing his utmost to talk her mother around. Persuading her to let it go. The fact that she had left for London for a fortnight's holiday and was arriving home four months later would have been the topic of conversation in the Gaffney household most nights of the week. No doubt.

She could picture her parents sitting on their armchairs at either side of the fire. Her father's head, she guessed, would be stuck in the *Evening Herald*, reading out odd bits and pieces to her mother, who would stop him every now and then to have her say. His Galway Brigid.

The seven-hour train journey to Holyhead passed relatively quickly. Fran dozed on and off, watching the houses and factories fly past. After that it was flat land all the way. She didn't feel the need to

285

offer conversation to the man in the suit sitting beside her. Now that she had time to think she felt drained by the events of the past few weeks and wanted more than anything to sleep. She crossed her fingers and thought about Delia and wished her well.

Camilla had scared her but then Delia had walked into her home and taken over and she unwittingly had been an accomplice. The money she had paid to Camilla was a small price to pay for her safety. Her maid money. The two hundred missing from the bedroom she had intended to give to Delia for rent. The rest she would put down to living expenses.

Fran had booked herself a first class ticket on the mail boat leaving from Holyhead in North Wales bound for Dun Laoghaire. The noise in the docks brought her back to the day she had made the trip across the Irish Sea.

Walking up the gangplank, Fran whispered a silent prayer for her friend. She thought about offering a few bob to one of the black-robed priests behind her, to say a Mass. She decided against it. Delia would want nothing to do with the Catholic Church.

This time around there would be no rushing ahead, pushing past people to board the *Hibernia*. No giggling or laughing. There would be no stream of questions on this trip that needed answering right away. No anxiety about where Fran was headed. No Delia to shove her forward to jump the queue in a hurry to grab a seat that was on hold for someone else. And no Delia to drag her by the arm once they reached Dun Laoghaire, through the port, and onto the train headed for home.

Finding a seat on the mailboat hadn't been difficult. A woman on her own. Gentlemen.

She put her suitcase resting on its side before laying her head on it as she saw other people doing. She would rest her eyes. Having had little sleep with the events that happened over the past few weeks, her head was fuzzy. Her ears were ringing. The air was heavy, a mixture of cigarette smoke, fuel and disinfectant. She would have plenty of time to rest properly once she landed back in Ballygore. Back to her own bed.

She jumped when she felt a hand squeeze her arm. She shrugged it off.

"*Get your arm off me!*" She reached for her handbag.

The warmest pair of amber eyes were looking sideways at her. The man sitting in the tub chair beside her was grinning.

"Oh sorry, miss, if I gave you a fright. Didn't want to wake you, just that you were sound asleep and you'll trip someone up if you remain in that position, with your feet splayed out in front of you like that."

Fran eyed the stranger suspiciously as a trickle of warm dribble ran down her chin. She brought her feet back in and wiped the side of her mouth. She had fallen into a deep sleep. Sitting up straight, she cleared her throat, flattened her hair at the back and pulled her coat across her legs.

The man handed her a white hanky which she refused.

"I feel bad now for disturbing your slumber," he said with a grin. "Can I get you a mineral? A tea or something stronger maybe?" He stood up.

"OK, OK … thank you, a tea would be fine, thanks," she answered while taking him in. He must be over six foot, she thought, as he walked towards the counter. She liked what she had seen so far. Long fingers. Clean manicured nails. She liked nice hands.

"The girl will bring the tea over in a bit."

He spoke nicely. She could listen to him all day. She wondered what part of Ireland he was from.

"How long more do we have?" she asked, looking at her watch.

"Well, you've been asleep for an hour or so, and we have a few hours to go yet. I'm Noel by the way. Noel Darmody."

"Frances Gaffney . . . Fran."

The two shook hands.

They sat side by side for the remainder of the journey, talking as if they'd known each other for years, once they had recovered from the initial awkwardness. He said he could never get a wink of sleep on a boat. She told him the hour had done her the power of good. Noel explained that he was on his way back from Cardiff where he had been managing a creamery for the past year. He was on the way home to Carlow where he was starting a new job the following week, managing a creamery there. He would be travelling with her on the same CIE train from Dun Laoghaire down as far as Portlaoise. He was being picked up there. Fran would travel on to Ballygore.

Back at Ballygore railway station, Fran beckoned a waiting hackney driver to take her suitcase. She landed at the front door ten minutes later.

Overcome with emotion, she hugged her father tightly.

He whispered in her ear. "Welcome home, love. Your mother is up all morning scrubbing. Pay no heed. She bought one of them fancy quilts for your bed above. She had it as a surprise for Christmas for you and, when you didn't appear, she had me put it in the attic. Well, she must have gone up herself and retrieved it, cos 'tis all set up for you, love. No more blankets for our Fran. 'Tis like I don't know what above. *Whisht* ... speak of the divil!"

Brigid appeared in the hallway, nodding her head towards Fran. Hiding a smile.

"Well, missy, come on till I see you. So you've finally decided to grace us with your presence, have you? Well, I want you to do one thing before you do anything else. Go straight down to that factory in the morning and apologise to Alice. If you've any hope of getting your old job back, that's the way to do it."

"Good to see you too, Mother, but I haven't a notion of going back to the factory, but I'll do as you ask about Alice, first thing in the morning. But right now if it's all the same, I need my bed."

"'Tis all ready for you. Tea is at six."

Her mother would come around in time. It was just her way.

"No hug for your mother, then?"

"Mammy, give over!" Fran walked towards her mother – she could see the smirk on her face.

"Welcome home, loveen."

Mother and daughter held each other in a warm embrace.

"Right, I'm off to my bed."

All Fran wanted to do was sleep. She would face the litany of questions later. She would have to offer some explanation. But right now all she wanted was to be left alone. To relax and think of Noel Darmody, with the amber eyes and the strong hands. They had talked like they had known each other for ever. She wondered had she just met the one. She felt she had.

She wished she could get hold of Delia to tell her that she had met a fella on the train. A fella who was going to ring her at seven o'clock that very evening. She'd given him the new phone number. She hadn't mentioned to Noel that the only reason her mother had the phone in was so Fran could ring her from a prostitute's flat in Soho.

Noel said he'd call her from the coinbox in the local pub. She was beyond excited.

The phone rang at exactly seven o'clock. Fran picked it up on the third ring – she didn't want to seem overanxious.

Her mother appeared in the hall. Smiling. She began dusting the hall table, lifting the phone book, dusting underneath it while Fran was on the call. Brigid was back to herself.

The following morning after breakfast, Fran did as her mother asked and went straight down to the factory to apologise to Alice for stepping all over her jacket. For her rudeness. She would never hear the end of it otherwise. She would have to face her Uncle Will at some point during the day.

Wearing her fitted brown coat, knee-length boots to match, a tiger-print scarf that Delia had bought her for Christmas, Fran approached the factory gates. Eunice Clarke was getting into the passenger seat of Lucy's car as Fran walked towards the factory door. Lucy was driving. Fran lowered her head slightly to wave across at Lucy who waved back. Then Eunice wound the window down. She stared straight at Fran who waved them on.

"I was just waving at Lucy, Mrs. Clarke."

The woman didn't speak. She wound the window back up and the car took off out the gate.

Fran thought it was odd. Maybe she mistook her for someone else. She knew Eunice Clarke to see. Maybe the woman was admiring her coat.

Alice peered up at Fran from over her typewriter, her pencilled eyebrows arched as high as ever. She accepted Fran's apology, saying that she had heard why she had left the factory in such a hurry that day. That no man was worth that. She advised Fran to put it behind her. She said she appreciated that Fran had taken the trouble to come down to meet her and she only after arriving back off the boat.

"I suppose you'll be looking for your old job back then, Fran? I'll have to see."

She told Fran that she looked different, that she had an edge about her that she hadn't noticed before.

Fran thanked her for being so understanding. She told her she wouldn't be looking for her job back at all. Because she wouldn't be staying around. It was satisfying for Fran to be so direct. And she meant every word of it. She asked Alice to keep it to herself, in confidence.

Alice half-smiled back, pleased to be privy to a secret.

"I won't open my mouth."

Fran knew that she wouldn't, because Alice wasn't the type to be talking. She chuckled to herself, realising that she didn't care.

Within four weeks Fran had introduced Noel to her parents. He had driven from Carlow to meet them. Brigid was well impressed from the moment she set eyes on him. A fine car he had, a cream Hillman Hunter with leather seats, and it parked just outside their own front door. Brigid was on her best behaviour.

Fran was more interested to hear what her father had to say the following day.

"I liked him, love. He talked about his parents and that's a good sign. The look in his eyes when he mentioned his family – I could tell he's not too unlike myself, he's a family man. But it was the way he held your gaze while you were talking that clinched it for me. I can tell he's a good 'un. Mind you, I never looked at another woman since the day I met your mother in the shop, but I'm around long enough to get the measure of a person. Only time will tell, of course, but I've a good feeling about this, love."

"So have I, Daddy, so have I."

Over the coming months, Fran and Noel saw each other whenever they could. They were going steady. Inseparable. Noel was managing the creamery, thirty miles away from Ballygore but he had every weekend off. Fran hadn't quite decided what she would do regarding work. She talked it over with Noel who told her to take her time. She agreed.

When Noel asked her to get engaged she said yes straight away. He said he'd ask her father for her hand as was the tradition. They talked about a springtime wedding, her favourite time of year. Hope.

Once they got married, they would move into the creamery house to begin their married lives. Noel said he wanted children and lots of them. Fran agreed. Plenty of room and that was for sure. Brigid was beside herself. Happy for Fran that she had met such a lovely man. Great job. Happy that Fran wasn't moving too far away. Brigid told the neighbours and anyone else she encountered about Fran's man. Making a point of dropping his credentials during the conversation.

Fran was happy. Delia had been right all along, The memory of the last time they had spoken came flooding back. "Someday, Fran, when you least expect it, you will meet the man that has been waiting just for you. Your soulmate. And when it happens, recognise it and don't let him go. I never met my soulmate – I'm just not a keeper."

Delia had taken off the very next day, doing what Delia had always done. Run. Fran hadn't seen or heard from her since. But she knew Delia would show up again. Someday Delia would breeze back into her life. It might be months or years, but Delia would turn up back in Ireland and, when she did, Fran would welcome her back into her life with open arms. In time she would tell Noel about her friendship with Delia. No need to be telling him about the time they had spent working together in Soho. If there was one lesson she had learned from Delia, it was: never give it all away. Keep something for yourself.

Chapter 34

RAMONA

Ramona was back in touch with Eunice, having left the city of Kiryat Shmona in Northern Israel. She was on her way back to Ireland, travelling through Lebanon. Back to Dublin. She would decide from there whether or not a future in Ireland was for her.

Lucy said that Ramona was simply living the life she wanted to live. It made sense. There was no ill-feeling towards Eunice. And Dermot was a bit eccentric and that was fine too because no two people were alike.

Eunice felt grateful to have her daughter back in her life. Time to let the past rest and rally forward. But the time had come for her to take a stand.

Eunice reminisced with a clear head. Ramona was her daughter, Malcolm's daughter, and nothing would change that. All those years wasted and she drowning in remorse.

The child who would run straight past her mother into

Malcolm's arms the minute she landed in the door from boarding school. The child who had spent more time confiding in the housekeeper than she ever had in Eunice. The teenager who had called home asking to speak to her father when she wanted more. Always more. Until she took on an air of defiance. Going out without saying where she was going. Arriving back when it suited her. Answering back.

Malcolm had been enraged at Ramona's insolence. He began shouting at her, threatening her, saying that if she continued the way she was going, she would no longer be welcome in his home.

He dared her to best him. She did, and stayed away for the night, testing her father's patience. He had driven the town searching for her and when he found her he dragged her into the car and brought her home and she kicking him. Lashing out. He locked the doors and windows and warned her against leaving the house without his permission. And when he got up the following morning she was gone, except this time he didn't go looking for her because he knew where she was. Will Murphy had seen her on his way in to work and had reported back to him. She arrived home two days later. Brazen.

Weeks had passed when Ramona began to stay away for weekends, telling her father to get over himself – that she was old enough to do as she liked – that she didn't need him or his money. Malcolm's relationship with her became more strained, she became more defiant than ever. He had high hopes for his daughter. Expected her to follow the Clarke tradition. She had the Clarke brain.

When she agreed to apply for Trinity College that January, Malcolm was relieved beyond words. He truly believed that she had come to her senses. He bragged at the golf club that he had reined his daughter back in. She was off to study business in Dublin.

Ramona had other ideas. She had been spending the summer visiting friends in the North – calling home two weeks before the start of the third-level academic year. Eunice had been having lunch in the kitchen with Malcolm when the phone call came. Collect.

Ramona said she couldn't face her father to tell him. She wasn't coming home. She would hang up if Eunice called him to the phone. She was going to work abroad for a year. Maybe more. She told Eunice to tell him, which she did, covering the mouthpiece. Raising her voice towards the kitchen where he sat. Ramona had deferred her course in Trinity College – she was taking off that very day. With friends.

"Check the top drawer," Eunice whispered as Malcolm passed her by at the hall table headed for the stairs, hand-signalling back to Eunice to keep her on the phone.

He found enough evidence in her room to know that she had upped and left. Her passport was missing along with her bank book. Malcolm never recovered from the shock.

Ramona had bolted from the Clarke grip, screaming at her mother over the phone that she didn't need her father's money. She said she was sick of being controlled by him – that she felt like a monkey in a circus ring. Malcolm was beyond angry when he came downstairs. He snatched the phone from her hand, shouting at Ramona, telling her that she was dead to him.

"*Dead, do you hear!*"

Dead to the Clarke family – if she didn't get home right away to sort things out.

Ramona banged the phone down.

Ramona's name wasn't to be mentioned in the house thereafter. Eunice took comfort the only way she knew how. Malcolm was beyond enraged that his princess had abandoned him. He cut off her allowances, expecting her to come running home. No one crossed Malcolm Clarke and got away with it. And when his action made no difference, he immersed himself in work.

Ramona's letters home were sporadic over the months following. Addressed to Eunice. Malcolm refused to read them. Eunice couldn't reply even if she wanted to. Ramona was moving around Europe.

When the letter came from Israel, Gretta placed it on the hall table. Ramona was living in a kibbutz. She sent a photo of herself in a yellow flowered dress, wearing a wide-brimmed straw hat, a tall man with a scraggy beard wearing Jesus sandals by her side.

Eunice felt sorry for Malcolm at the time. He idolised his only girl. And when he began to slow down, she could see that he was broken. She wanted to put her arms around him and plant a kiss on his head, to hold him and tell him that he had her. But she couldn't, because too much time had passed, and the intimacies of their marriage had evaporated.

Chapter 35

EUNICE

The Future

1970

Eunice tapped lightly on the glass pane with her fingertips, waving goodbye to her adored grandsons who had just left. She would see them tomorrow. She looked forward to their visits each day, watching out for the knock on the door which divided her new living quarters from the main house. Their voices calling out to her.

"Grandma, Grandma! Quickly, open this door! It's only us . . . me and him!"

Two of the sweetest boys who adored her. Boys who would never experience the trauma that she had experienced in her own childhood. Normal children living a normal life.

It had been five years since Malcolm passed. Five years since she had touched a drop of alcohol.

Eunice missed him. It hadn't been easy to look back. To take ownership. To see herself for what she was. A needy self-indulgent woman. It would take a lot more years for her to forgive herself.

But, in the meantime, she had every intention of doing what she could to repair the damage she had caused. With Lucy's help.

Since her daughter-in-law had come to live in Ballygore, life had changed for the better. Lucy's easy-going nature, her pleasant personality, helped her heal. Hearing Lucy speak of Malcolm with respect moved her. Lucy had, in her own way, coaxed the family together. Eunice began to let her guard down.

Lucy had been due her second baby when they'd moved in. She had only recently confided in Eunice that she had been all for the move down to Ballygore, because she knew in her heart that it had been Arthur's dream to run the factory since the day she had met him. She admitted her apprehension about whether two strong-minded women could live under the one roof. But they had. And a month passed before Eunice realised that she hadn't had a drink since the day she had found Malcolm dead in the hall. And she too far gone to call for help.

Once her in-built sadness lifted, Eunice realised that she had a lot to be grateful for. She grew to love Lucy, a stranger to Ballygore as she herself had once been. But without the baggage of someone else's wounds. The wounds of parents. Lucy listened as Eunice opened up about her childhood. There were no harsh judgements. Eunice had tormented herself enough – the time had come for her to appreciate those she loved. And top of that list was Ramona.

In many ways Eunice had wronged Malcolm. He had certainly been no angel. No doubt about that. But holding him responsible for her happiness had been a mistake.

In time Eunice would take comfort in knowing that her children had been in boarding school during the worst of her drinking days. They had not been around to witness their mother drink herself into a state. They had not been around to witness her crawling in a drunken stupor on the floor, unable to get herself up. But Malcolm had witnessed this. Gretta too. Golden Gretta who remained a constant in the Clarke family, doting on the children.

Watching Lucy mother her grandchildren softened Eunice.

When Eunice suggested that they build a self-contained flat for her at the back of the house, Lucy had been hesitant at first, saying she had no wish to take over the main house. Maybe they should wait a while. Eunice waited, but she no longer wanted to live in the big house. She wanted a warm compact living space, new carpeted floors under her feet. Minus the Persian rug. She would have a double bed all to herself, a ceiling at a reasonable height over her head. And maybe even a small dog.

It was a year later when Lucy announced in the kitchen that she had an idea she wanted to tell Eunice about, if she would follow her down the hall. She said she had talked it over with Arthur. She led Eunice to the heavy back door which she opened.

"Those huge Leylandii trees, behind the wall there, are taking all the light, Eunice. The wall is over six foot, high enough for privacy. Nothing behind but open fields. It's a good time for cutting, the birds will have left the nests by now. So what do you say we cut back the trees to the height of the wall? Maybe the time has come to look at plans for that extension of yours. We might plant a garden. Together."

Eunice smiled. "What a great girl you are, Lucy."

When the men came with their chainsaws to cut back the trees, Eunice looked after the boys while Lucy surveyed the work. Three hours later the last of the tractor trailers had left the yard, overflowing with dark green foliage.

With the trees gone, Eunice could see the mountains in the distance through a blue haze. Her mountain. Her eyes filled with tears.

Eunice began to leave food out for the birds. Arthur organised a load of topsoil for the back yard – they planted spring flowering bulbs in the winter. They watched the crocuses sprout above the soil and bloom in early March. They replaced the two stone lions at either side of the front door with planters, which they planted with lavenders. They had a low stone wall built around the house, with a wooden gate facing out to the right of the house, away from the factory. Arthur planted a fast-growing laurel hedge. Privacy.

The three women took their morning tea outside, on a fine day, while the children played on the lawn. And slowly and without warning Eunice found peace.

Eunice supervised the builders as they constructed the new extension to the back of the house. Centrally heated. Lucy insisted that two bedrooms would be best. For visitors. Ramona could stay when she visited. Or Gretta, now that her mother had gone to the care home. A large window in the cosy living area where Eunice could sit to read and admire her mountain. A small fitted kitchen. In white.

Eunice insisted that Lucy redecorate the main house as she wanted. Dump whatever she wanted to dump. No regrets. Eunice felt contented. Malcolm was gone and she missed him.

But on her own Eunice was stronger.

The memory of a corkscrew curl on a baby's head in St. Mary's hospital would remain where it belonged. Eunice would take her secret to the grave with her. Ramona was her daughter. Malcolm's daughter. A sister to Arthur and Dermot. A sister-in-law to Lucy.

An aunt to the boys. A Clarke. Too many years. A life full of regret. With a clear heart Eunice looked forward to the future.

Her heart had skipped a beat that day in the car with Lucy, just as it had done on other occasions. There she was, looking into the car. And in the factory yard.

Eunice wound up the window.

THE END

Printed in Great Britain
by Amazon

25717084R00179